The Dreaming

Wind Talker

Kim Murphy

*To Nora,
Best wishes,
Kim Murphy*

Published by Coachlight Press

Published by Coachlight Press October 2014

Coachlight Press, LLC
1704 Craigs Store Road
Afton, Virginia 22920
http://www.coachlightpress.com

Printed in the United States of America
Cover design by Roberta J. Marley

Library of Congress Control Number: 2014951128
ISBN 978-1-936785-17-9

to the memory of Uncle Dick
and Saber

1

Lee

THE PARTIALLY BURIED HUMAN SKELETON sent chills running up and down my spine. I had been a police detective for over a decade and viewed bodies in every state of decomposition. No flesh clung to the bones. No putrid stench lingered in the air. Why did this one bother me? The skull was partly intact, and enough teeth remained to send me a ghoulish grin.

My stomach churned, and I was relieved when my partner waved at me. Thankful to be away from the burial site, I moved in Ed's direction a few hundred yards from the grave and breathed in fresh air.

"Lee," Ed said, "the anthropologist will be here in a few minutes. Since you've worked with her before, I'd like for you to go over the details when she gets here."

"Sure."

"You all right? You look like you're not feeling well."

"Must be coming down with something."

"Take it easy until the anthropologist arrives." Ed returned to the grave.

Whatever had affected me vanished now that I was away from the skeleton. I spoke with a couple of the uniformed officers, waiting patiently, when a mud-spattered pickup truck pulled alongside us.

A petite woman, no taller than my wife Phoebe, got out and gave me a stern look. "Detective Crowley, I hope you haven't called me out on a beautiful Friday evening for a dog or a deer."

"Give a guy a break," I said with embarrassment, recalling all too well the previous case we had worked on together. "It's not like the skeleton was intact. How could I have known it wasn't a child's?"

"It practically woofed at you." She cracked a grin. "It's good seeing you again, Lee."

"Good seeing you, too." We exchanged a good laugh before I explained the present situation. "This one is human, Jan. The property owners broke ground to build a new addition on their home when the skeleton was uncovered. We need to know whether it's something for our department or Historic Resources."

She pulled out a bulky black gear bag from the bed of the pickup. When I offered to carry it for her, she declined. "I'm not an invalid," she said, throwing the bag over her shoulder.

I gestured the way to the grave site. "You sound like my wife."

"She sounds like a wonderful woman."

Thinking of Phoebe, I smiled. "She is, and you'd never believe me if I told you how far she's traveled just so the two of us could be together."

"It must have been true love. Let's see what you have for me."

We got closer to the burial site and met with Ed. That odd sensation overcame me again. I shivered.

Jan donned her gloves and bent down. She inspected the protruding pelvis. "Your victim is an adult male."

Normally I was amazed at how little she needed in order to identify the sex of a skeleton, but nausea returned to my stomach.

She studied the skull. "I can't be certain without extensive measurements, but the fact that he was buried facing east and has shovel-shaped incisors, I'd be willing to bet he's Native American."

Bile rose in my throat. Unable to control the sick feeling any longer, I turned away from the scene and vomited.

Someone patted me on the back. "Must be the fact that he could be kin," came Ed's sympathetic voice.

Not only did I appear foolish, but I looked like a rookie too. I hadn't had that kind of reaction since my early years when I had worked patrol duty. The fact that it was nothing more than a skeleton made my embarrassment worse. When I was certain I wasn't going to throw up again, I wiped my mouth with my handkerchief.

"If he's kin, he's a very distant relative," Jan said, still examining the skeleton. "Without further testing, there's no way to determine how long he's been buried here, but I'm guessing it's been for at least a couple hundred years."

Or longer? He could have been related, for I was Paspahegh, the last of my tribe.

Nearly two months passed before I saw Jan Kelsey again. She called me one afternoon and said she had some findings to show me from the skeleton that had been unearthed. While the case wasn't one for our department, I had followed up to make certain the Virginia Council on Indians had been contacted. The owners of the property had pursued a court order to have the skeleton removed to continue with their building project, and I had wanted to make certain that he received a respectful reburial.

I hadn't visited campus for a couple years when my former professor had solved the puzzle that Phoebe spoke Virginia Algonquian. I had a rudimentary knowledge of the language myself, and with Phoebe's help, my comprehension gradually increased. This meeting was a little different though, and I was uncertain what to expect.

Woods surrounded the red-brick buildings. I was walking along the dogwood-lined sidewalk, when several crows cawed furiously. With a loud racket, the birds dive-bombed a hawk flying overhead. Was it a sign from the spirits? I was too new to such things to sense any significance, but I had the feeling it could not be a good sign.

The confrontation in the sky held my attention until the hawk retreated, with the crows following in hot pursuit. Convinced there must be some hidden meaning, I entered the hall that housed the anthropology department and went up a flight of stairs to locate Jan's office.

She greeted me with a tight-lipped smile.

"What's wrong, Jan?"

"I think it would be easier to show you." She grabbed a manila folder and led the way down the hall to the lab. "A couple of the tribes have claimed the skeleton to oversee his reburial. They were gracious enough to let us study him beforehand as long as we did so with reverence, but I'm sure you're aware of the protocol."

Amazed that people presumed I knew proper conduct simply because I was an Indian, I let the comment slide. Normally I would have had some sort of comeback, but I was curious about what she had discovered.

Jan opened the manila folder and spread several papers across the table. "Pelvic and skull measurements verified that our skeleton was a Native American male. Resorting to a number or calling him John Doe seemed inappropriate. We called him Crow Spirit."

The same sick feeling I'd had while standing over the grave hit me in the gut again.

"Lee, are you all right?"

"It's nothing." I waved my hand. "My Algonquian name translates to Crow in the Woods."

She stared at me. Though I hadn't been raised in the Paspahegh way, where direct eye contact was considered rude, it made me uneasy all the same. *What the hell was wrong with me?* In my line of work I frequently used such techniques to intimidate others, but Jan's gaze indicated disbelief.

"Interesting," she said, swallowing before she continued. "We weren't allowed to do a carbon dating to confirm when Crow Spirit had been buried because a sample would need to have been collected, which is destroyed in the dating process."

Jan didn't elaborate, but I was aware that most tribes equated such destruction to a loss of spirit. What did I believe? Caught between cultures, I remained unsure.

"You had a question?" she asked.

I shook my head.

"In my professional opinion, Crow Spirit had been buried for over two hundred years. No fabric remained to give us a clue as to what he wore, so there's no way to verify whether he had been buried pre-European contact or after. No weapons were found, which is highly unusual. Men were often buried with them because they believed they would be needed in the afterlife."

"I'm aware of that."

"Sorry, I'm lecturing, but I wanted to give you a full report."

"I'm still confused why you called me."

She motioned for me to be patient. "I'm getting to that. Crow Spirit's cranial sutures were completely fused. There was some joint decay in the rest of his body, meaning that he had some arthritis. I'd estimate he was around forty or fifty, but not elderly. He had no cavities, which is a little unusual. Contrary to what many believe, the Eastern Woodland indigenous populations had their fair share of dental cavities even before the Europeans arrived, due to their starchy diet.

"The long bones, namely the femur and tibia, are measured to determine height. He was over six feet tall. While that's not out of the realm for this group of people, a man's average height was around five feet eight. John Smith had a habit of painting the Powhatan people as giants, but actual skeletal measurements reveal otherwise. He had a fracture of the left femur, completely healed, which means the injury took place long before his death. What puzzles me is how they managed to set the bone. I really wish I could have studied the femur further, but it was skillfully set for the time period. I couldn't determine a cause of death. There were no noticeable traumatic injuries, but I didn't really have the time I needed to make an in-depth analysis."

"If you're asking me to go to the Council, I have no authority–"

"No, that's not why I called you here."

"Then why? This is all very interesting, but I don't see what it has to do with me."

"If you don't mind my asking, what tribe do you belong to?"

No one would believe that I was Paspahegh; the tribe had been annihilated in the seventeenth century. "I was raised by a white couple. I never really knew my birth parents." The statement was true and allowed me to evade the question.

"I see." Another nervous swallow. "I think your partner may have been right. We may have uncovered one of your ancestors."

"My . . . ?" No wonder I had felt uneasy from the beginning. "Why do you think he's *my* ancestor?"

"One of my students does facial reconstructions. I had read an article in *Archaeology* several years back about a similar collaboration, and assure you we got permission before proceeding with such an undertaking. We treated the skull with complete respect. First my student made a plaster cast, then used markers to identify the depths of tissue. Sorry, I'm lecturing again. Let me show you."

She led me to the opposite end of the lab where a clay facial reconstruction sat on a table. Jan's student had used a black wig fashioned in the old style where warriors had shaved the right side of their heads to keep their hair from getting caught in their bowstrings. The prominent cheekbones and shape of the nose and mouth had an uncanny resemblance to me. It was almost like looking in a mirror.

"Well?" she asked.

Hadn't she stated that Crow Spirit's broken leg looked like it had been set skillfully for the time period? I licked my lips. "You said that he had broken his left femur?"

"I did."

Nearly two years before, I had broken my left leg from a gunshot wound. I clenched my fist to keep from crying out. Crow Spirit wasn't an ancestor of mine. He was me.

2

Phoebe

PHOEBE HAD GOTTEN THE BABY TO SLEEP round ten. Cranky and running a fever, Heather was teething. Though Lee's job often kept him late, he usually called. Barely able to keep her eyes open, she readied for bed. Too tired to fight sleep any longer, she slipped under the covers and drifted. The bed creaked, and the warmth of someone moved next to her. "Lee?" she murmured, still half asleep.

His lips met hers. "Phoebe . . ."

He trembled, but his hands touched and explored her body. Many times his job distressed him. Sensing his need and intensity, she wouldn't question him until he was ready to talk about it. 'Til then, she gave in the way she could. He raised her nightgown and clung to her, almost desperately.

Their fingers intertwined, and he was inside her. Vexed about what had happened, she comforted him. Had he investigated a heinous murder? Or the death of a child? Even afore Heather's birth, any child's death nearly sent him over the edge. She ran her hands from the firm muscles of his shoulders down along his bare back. Moving in synchrony, she breathed his name aloud. Like riding an ocean wave, she drifted against him—faster and higher.

The surf crashed ashore, and he held and kissed her as if ne'er wanting to let her go. "Thank you," he whispered afore moving to her side.

She held him, and he trembled once more. Patiently she waited, hoping he would speak about what ailed him, but he remained silent. Phoebe ran her fingertips through his hair. She imagined seeing him in the light of day. His hair was black, much shorter than his ancestors, and he had dark brown eyes and brown skin. They had known each other since childhood, but then they had been separated—by time itself—only to be reunited years later.

"I think I've seen my death."

His words had been so matter of fact that she shivered.

"Phoebe, I'm not afraid. I've seen too much death to be afraid."

His voice had been distant, almost monotone. Needing to see his face, she reached aside the bed and switched on a light. His brow was vexed and his eyes thoughtful. "Tell me what has happened."

"I can't."

Dead. At the mere thought of losing him, her heart pounded. "Lee—"

"What good would it do to tell you about something that I don't understand myself?"

She gripped his hand. "Mayhap we can figure it out together. Lee, we have been through too much for you to remain silent now."

His gaze grew fixed, and he let out a slow breath. "I'm sorry, Phoebe. I shouldn't have frightened you the way I did." He kissed her on the lips and settled back. "A human skeleton was uncovered a couple of months back. It turned out to be Native, and I thought it was a sign."

"The dreaming might lend you some answers," she suggested.

"The dreaming." His voice was barely above a whisper. "What if it tells me that I have witnessed my own death?"

The thought that she could lose him tore at her heart, but mayhap the sign was not the one he feared. Instead, hope could have been behind the meaning. "Then we shall deal with it—together." She grasped his hand.

"All right," he finally agreed.

"I shall prepare." As Phoebe rose, she wrapped a robe about herself. In the kitchen, she collected a candle and matches from the drawer and took them into the living room. She lit the candle on a coffee table.

Attired in gym pants and a T-shirt, Lee joined her. He sat aside her. "I'd like for you to lead the way."

"Aye." They joined hands, and she focused on the candle's flame. Like her momma, who hailed from Dorset in the seventeenth century, she was experienced in the ways of the dreaming. When they had gone to live with the Paspahegh, Momma admitted she was a *cunning* woman who traveled through realms. 'Twas something she could have never spoken aloud in James Towne. Such a confession would have exposed her as a witch, but the Paspahegh believed such visions were a form of passage betwixt worlds.

Phoebe's initial dreaming journey had been during her first moon time, and now, she moved quickly through the realms. She found herself engulfed by mist. A long-legged white hound appeared afore her. She latched onto Lee's hand and the spirit hound's collar. Together, they traveled through the fog. As they walked, Phoebe felt a contraction in her abdomen. She paced the floor as Lee coached her through the pain. This was a different century than the one she had grown up in. She had dispelled her superstition that men in the birthing room were bad luck and was grateful for his presence. Even so, she had circled the room and said a prayer in each corner to ward off vengeful spirits.

She lay on her side, and the midwife massaged her legs. The contractions became more frequent, and she returned to her feet. Water rushed betwixt her legs. The baby would soon arrive. The contractions came closer together, and the pain intensified. She refused to shame herself by crying out and grasped Lee's hand.

"You're doing great, Phoebe."

" 'Tis time to push." In Paspahegh fashion, she knelt.

The midwife spread a layer of absorbent pads on the floor.

She clenched Lee's hand. More pain. Her eyes brimmed with tears, but she resisted the temptation to complain. Her babe would soon be here. Blood ran down her legs, turning the white pads red. The pain gave way to waves of fire.

Lee urged her on.

She felt the babe's head betwixt her legs.

Lee held out his hands, and she gave another push. He caught Heather in his arms. His face beamed with pride. His presence had been right.

Phoebe blinked and the pain vanished. This was the world of the dreaming. She had relived their joy upon the birth of their daughter. Through the mist, they continued their journey. The room was ablaze with candles. Lutes played. Across from Lee, Phoebe stood in a flowing burgundy floral dress with black sleeves. She gazed into his dark eyes. They joined hands.

"Like the seasons," he said, "this ring forms a circle. It has no beginning and no end. Neither does my love for you. I devote myself to you for eternity." To avoid the webbing betwixt her ring and middle finger, he slipped the gold band on her index finger.

Her friend Meg handed Phoebe his ring. "The circle of time has brought us together, binding our love and lives. I join my mind and spirit to yours; in this world and into the afterworld. I devote myself to you for eternity." She slid the ring on Lee's finger.

They sealed their pledge with a kiss, and Phoebe realized that her life was now in the twenty-first century.

With a gasp, Phoebe stared at the flickering candlelight. Over the course of more than three years, the twenty-first century had become *her* time. Still feeling very much like a stranger caught in an even stranger world, she had doubted that she would ever fully accept life in this time period, but now the seventeenth century was almost like a dream. If it hadn't been for Lee, she would have most likely gone mad, and he had been in the present century for thirty-five of his thirty-seven years. He recalled little of that time.

"I don't get it," Lee said. "What does reliving Heather's birth and our wedding got to do with a buried skeleton?"

" 'Tis the circle of time. You have yet to make peace with the past." She removed the leather cord with an arrowhead from round her neck and placed it in his hand. "This is as much a part of you as Heather and me."

His fingers curled round the arrowhead. "My tribe."

"Your father. You have ne'er asked his name."

Lee's eyes narrowed. "My father was a cop like me."

"Mayhap the man who raised you was a cop, but your father was a warrior."

Anger at the horrific loss of his family changed to anguish. He was not ready to delve into the past. They would participate in the dreaming again, and he would learn more. For now, she wouldn't push him. He needed to uncover the truth in his own time.

The following eve, Phoebe agreed to meet Lee along with Ed and his wife Marian at a local bar and grill. At half-past five, Meg dropped by the house to watch Heather, and Phoebe drove her Fiesta to the restaurant. Unlike the smoke-filled tavern where she had originally met Ed, this establishment had padded chairs and linen napkins. She met Lee inside the door.

Even though he remained in his business suit, he wore the arrowhead round his neck and a copper band about his wrist. Unable to read his expression, she worried that he remained distressed by the dreaming on the previous night. An eve out would certainly help alleviate some of the stress.

Lee guided her to the other room, where Ed and Marian awaited.

"Phoebe!" Ed stood with a kind, smiling face.

She greeted him and his wife afore they all seated themselves round the table. After ordering the meal, they made polite conversation, except for Lee. Phoebe's concern grew, but Marian asked her about Heather. "Aye, I pierced Heather's ears the same time I did Lee's."

Ed sipped his ale and snorted. "Going Indian on us, Lee? What's next? War paint and a feathered headdress?"

Lee's gaze grew fixed. "In case you hadn't noticed, I *am* Indian."

Ed sobered. "Take it easy, partner. You've never been touchy about the subject in the past."

"I haven't been *touchy* because you of all people have never resorted to stereotypes before. Or maybe it's time for a few scalping jokes. Noble savage, perhaps? If that's not enough, we could—"

"Lee—"

"—pretend how all of us died out more than a century ago to make way for the progress of civilization. Never mind the fact—"

"Lee. You're right, and you have my humble apology." Ed glanced from Lee to Phoebe with a concerned expression.

"Sorry," Lee said. "I didn't mean . . . I don't know what came over me. You've always been the first to step into the crossfire when the racial slurs start to fly."

"That's why I shouldn't have joked about it. I've seen what you go through every day."

But Lee didn't usually react in anger when people made unthinking statements. Normally he responded with sarcasm. Phoebe's vexation heightened.

Marian broke the uncomfortable silence by inquiring about Heather again, but the remainder of the eve consisted of pinched smiles and small talk.

Relieved when dinner ended, Phoebe returned to the house in her own car with Lee following close behind. Meg wished them good eve and shuffled her own five-year-old daughter out to her car. In the past Meg often remained overnight, rather than wake Tiffany. "You're welcome to stay, Meg."

"I know, but I think it's best that I get home tonight."

She suspected that Meg detected Lee's angst. After a quick good-bye, Phoebe found him in Heather's room checking on their daughter. He touched her sleeping face, then, without saying a word, went into the kitchen.

Phoebe followed him. "Lee, speak to me."

He pulled an ale from the refrigerator. "I didn't mean to react the way I did tonight."

"Aye, I know."

"I guess this has me more on edge than I realized. I would like to find out more about who I am and where I came from, but quite frankly, for some reason, it has scared the hell out of me."

Pleased that he was confiding in her, Phoebe took some comfort. "When I first arrived in this century, I felt lost and alone. A six-year-old child can read and write better than I could. I was painfully aware of that fact, but you, Meg, and Shae ne'er gave up on me."

At the mention of his former wife, he frowned slightly. Although they had remained friends throughout the years, Shae had been the first to reopen his forgotten childhood memories of the seventeenth century through hypnosis. He took a swig of ale. "I'm not certain I understand the connection."

"I had a connection to this century through you afore we e'en knew about it. That connection can ne'er be severed. You must find what ails you from the past for you have lost your family and tribe. You have as much of a connection to the seventeenth century as I do this one."

"I never quite looked at it that way before." After taking another swig of ale, Lee set the can on the table. "Phoebe, I'd like to try the dreaming again."

Once again, she prepared. Soon, accompanied by the white hound, she walked through the mist to the dreaming realm. Bright lights filled the night sky. Cars rushed to and fro, and the walkways were crowded with people. She sucked in her breath. 'Twas the time when she had arrived in the twenty-first century and was struck by a car. "Lee, I don't wish to relive it."

His grip on her hand tightened. "Come with me."

Up ahead, the mist thinned, and she stepped forward. A two-year-old lad scribbled lines in the sand. His skin was brown and his hair, black. Lee, or Crow in the Woods, as he was known by at that time. As a lass of ten, she had often looked after him for his mother. She watched him play and smiled. But the peaceful scene shifted with the sudden advance of armored soldiers aiming their muskets. They fired. All round Phoebe, men, women, and children fell. Amongst cries and shrieks of pain, longhouses were set afire.

Nooo. She didn't wish to relive the memory, but she must be brave for Lee's sake. He was the reason she had been brought to this place in time.

Houses were ablaze, and swirling smoke filled her lungs. On her hands and knees, she scrambled for safety. As she crept along the ground, she nearly succumbed from the heat. She covered her ears to silence the dying wails. The wind fanned the flames. She coughed and sputtered. A wet tongue licked her face. Grateful to see her hound, she wrapped her arms round his neck, and he led her through the blinding smoke.

The smoke drifted and she spied a young lad. He crawled along the ground, crying for his momma. She bundled him against her 'til his cries quieted.

Far into the day, embers and smoke danced into the sky. The screams and shooting muskets came less often. Throaty sobs and moans surrounded her. The lad stirred. At the time, she hadn't known he was Crow in the Woods 'til she had wiped the grimy soot from his face. The lad *was* Lee. She had witnessed the English soldiers burn the Paspahegh town and annihilate its people.

Crow in the Woods babbled about his hunger. She rocked and comforted him. Barely more than a child herself at the time, she called for her momma. The duty to keep Crow in the Woods safe had fallen upon her shoulders. At nightfall she huddled with him in her arms, but sleep was too strong to maintain her grasp. She had failed to keep the lad safe. She heard his muffled cries in the darkness and stumbled after him. Brambles tore into her arms and legs. She ignored the pain. "Where are you, Crow in the Woods?"

Mist engulfed her, but the long-legged, white hound stood like a beacon on the path afore her. During the actual event, Phoebe had been too young to recognize the dog was a spirit. She followed him, but the mist grew thicker.

The lad's cries came from within.

"Crow in the Woods!"

His whimpers surrounded her, but she could not locate him. Then the mist vanished, and along with it, Crow in the Woods's cries. He was gone.

Phoebe blinked and found herself in her own living room with Lee seated across from her. Tears streaked her cheeks. " 'Twas as if the mist had swallowed you alive."

"In some way, I was." Lee moved closer and drew her into his arms. "I recall the screams, and there was fire all around me. I didn't remember the soldiers. They killed my mother, didn't they?"

"Aye."

There was a long silence afore he asked his next question. "What happened to my father?"

She withdrew from his embrace and dried her tears. "Most of the warriors were away on a hunting trip when the soldiers attacked. I ne'er saw him again."

"What was he like? I don't even know his name."

After all these years, he had finally asked about his father. "I didn't know him well. Men and women led different paths. He was tall, or at least, he seemed that way with me being a lass. His name was Black Owl."

His hand formed a fist. "And the goddamn English murdered innocent women and children." He unclenched his hand and lowered his head.

Phoebe let him grieve for the family he ne'er knew. She touched the arrowhead on the deerskin cord round his neck. "He made this for you."

Suddenly uncomfortable, Lee stood. "And this is what I'm supposed to make peace with? How?"

"Lee, e'erything in life is linked. You came to this time afore me, and when the time was right you called me here." She gripped his hand. "We are linked. The past will unveil the answers if we allow it to reveal the message."

He smiled slightly. "I've never known anyone with the knack for speaking in as cryptic a manner as you."

"Whilst I am a cunning woman, I cannot speak about what I don't know."

He kissed her on the mouth. "If we're truly linked, and I also believe we are, then I can face the journey, whatever it may be."

She hugged him even though her own worry hadn't faltered.

3

Lee

GUNSHOTS and screams surrounded me. Billowing smoke burned my eyes. A woman held me. She screamed and I was falling. I hit the ground, and she very nearly landed on top of me. I clung to her skirt. She lay still and unmoving.

Drenched in sweat, I woke from the nightmare that had plagued me for over two weeks. The dreaming had unlocked my memory of the annihilation of the Paspahegh. Even in waking moments, I would catch glimpses of the burning town or my dead mother. I buried myself in work, but Phoebe saw past my diversion. She suggested that we continue with the dreaming. I made excuses to avoid it. I didn't fool her, or myself either. I was afraid. Would I become like my parents—nothing more than a memory to Heather?

To be honest, my father wasn't even a memory. The only thing I had to remember him by was an arrowhead. I clenched it in my hand. No, that wasn't all. His name had been Black Owl. Why had I taken so long to ask Phoebe? And why hadn't I been totally honest with her about the skeleton's resemblance to myself? More than anything I wanted to believe that it had been nothing more than a sign to uncover more about my heritage.

The alarm went off, and I went through the mindless motion of showering and dressing. I kissed my family and waved goodbye, wondering if it would be the last time that I might see them. I barely made it to the station when I got a phone call from my ex-wife Shae.

"Lee, could you help me with a patient?"

As a psychologist, she had often helped me in cold cases through the use of hypnosis on the victims. "How?" I asked.

"She's witnessed a murder. It's taken months for her to work through the trauma enough to talk about it to anyone besides me. She wants to help the police, and I would like for her to speak with someone who won't make her feel like she's on a witness stand already."

A murder case—a great way to start the morning. Then again, what did I expect? I had been a Violent Crimes unit detective for several years. "You know I'll help, Shae. When and where?"

I wrote down the details and fortunately the rest of the morning was more routine, with me filling out a backlog of paperwork. Still, I kept thinking that I smelled smoke and imagining people fleeing through it. In the afternoon, I met with Shae at her office to speak with her patient.

The witness's testimony unlocked a case that had gone cold six months before. Although she was weepy and nervous, she held together to give me a statement. She departed with uniformed police, who would keep her under protection until we could safely lock the suspect away.

As I gave Shae a quick goodbye, she called me back. "Lee, how have you been? And Phoebe and the baby?"

Shae's blonde hair was shoulder length instead of down her back as I remembered from the days of our youth, and she had grown plump in the decade we had been separated. "Everyone is fine."

"You look like hell."

No matter the circumstances, I could count on her blatant honesty. "Thanks, I needed that. I haven't been sleeping well."

"Is Heather keeping you awake at night?"

Now I detected her psychologist's nose working overtime. "No, she sleeps through the night—and before you ask any further, everything is fine between Phoebe and me."

She waved at me to calm down. "I was asking as a friend."

Unlike most divorced couples, we could talk about our relationships, for which I was thankful. I let my guard down. "I remember what happened when I was two. I can't get the screams out of my head."

"That's common with such a trauma. Have you talked to anyone about it?"

"Who can I talk to besides you and Phoebe? No one else would believe me."

"Then talk. I'm finished with my patients for the day."

"Shae—"

"Lee, I'm serious. That kind of trauma can damage you permanently. You saw what my patient was like—and that was after months of therapy. I know you like to think of yourself as a tough guy, who can hold everything together, but everyone has a breaking point. You trusted me once before, and I'm partly responsible for the memory surfacing. Talk to me."

Three years ago she hypnotized me at my request. Brief glimpses of what had happened surfaced during the session. I sat in the chair across from her desk.

"Good," she said. "Now what triggered the memory?"

"The dreaming." She opened her mouth to say something, but I motioned for her to allow me to finish. "I know you've always maintained that it's hypnosis."

"I realize now that it's more than hypnosis. Please, go on."

I shrugged. "What's there to say? You know what happened. I saw my mother murdered."

"You're not all that different than my patient who just left. You're just better at hiding it. I bet you haven't fooled Phoebe."

"I haven't," I admitted.

"Then why haven't you told her?"

I debated whether to confide in her about the whole sorry mess going back to uncovering the skeleton. Besides Phoebe, she was the only person who knew that I originally came from the seventeenth century.

"Lee?"

"Shae, you know as well as I do that I shouldn't even be here. Both Phoebe and I should have died almost four hundred years ago."

"That's not true. You wouldn't be here if that were the case."

I met her gaze. "How can we know for sure that our presence in this time is permanent?"

"So that's it. Lee, you and Phoebe have been through some traumatic experiences, but time travel is a freak of nature."

"Is it?"

"Stop it. You're playing that game with me by responding to me with questions."

"That wasn't my intent. Hell, you might as well know . . ." Unlike with Phoebe, I went on to tell Shae the whole story about the skeleton, the recreation of his face that looked like mine, and my experience during the dreaming, which had led to the nightmares.

After I finished, she seemed to mull my story over and finally said, "I see."

"That's it? I spill my guts, and—"

"You didn't give me a chance to finish. I think Phoebe is right. Now that the memory has surfaced, you need to face your fear. I obviously can't tell you whether you're going to travel back in time, but the skeleton triggered something. It could be your mother's death and how you got here, or it could be something more. Only you can find out what it all means."

She often spoke as cryptically as Phoebe. I stood. "What do I owe you, doctor?"

"It's only friendly advice. Nothing more."

I uttered my thanks and headed for the door.

"Lee, if you need to talk, don't be stubborn. Contact me."

I assured her that I would, but she was right. I needed to listen to Phoebe.

For a change of pace, that night I arrived home before Heather had gone to bed. Phoebe relayed a bedtime story to our daughter about how she had saved a hound when she was a girl. Her Paspahegh father had wanted to relieve the dog of his misery after he had been mauled by a bear. But she had insisted on being given a chance to save him. With the help of her own mother, Phoebe had cleaned the blood away and sewn his gashes with deer sinew. She stayed by the dog's side until he was mended. For touching the dog's spirit, she had passed a test and was taught in the ways of *wisakon,* the art of healing.

Only when she finished did I realize she had spoken the entire story in Algonquian, and I hadn't stopped to think the translation through. My knowledge of my native tongue had grown. "Walks Through Mist," I said.

Hearing her Algonquian name, she smiled. "Bedtime, Heather."

We kissed our daughter goodnight and tucked her in. Once outside Heather's room, I grasped Phoebe's hand and took in her scent. I could no longer hold back. I tasted her mouth.

"Crow in the Woods," she murmured.

I let go of her hand. "Don't call me that."

" 'Tis the name you were given by your parents."

"It's a child's name." I silently cursed myself for spoiling the intimate moment, but she had easily spotted my anxiety over the past couple of weeks. I escorted her into the living room and began telling her about the nightmares and my visit with Shae, still leaving out the part where the skeleton had looked like me.

"I had hoped the job was what ails you. Lee, you know I will help in any way I can."

She didn't suggest the dreaming as I had hoped. Instead, she waited for me to say it. Why couldn't I? I checked my watch trying to think of some excuse to avoid it. Only a little past eight. I couldn't even use the reason that it was getting late. I thought about an assault case at work and almost said that I needed to call Ed. I couldn't lie to her. The case could wait until morning.

Then, I thought of Phoebe. It would be so easy to let go—the thought of touching her bare skin and making love with her in the bedroom. Or someplace more exotic?

"Lee?"

I let out a slow breath and turned toward the kitchen. "Would you care for a beer?"

She grasped my arm and drew me back. "Why do you tell me what's wrong, then run from it?"

"Actually, I was thinking of getting you naked. I figured a drink would help put you in the mood."

"You know I'm nursing Heather, and I don't need an ale to put me 'in the mood.' Your kisses and touches are pleasurable enough. You're avoiding your fear."

She saw right through me. She always had. Even Shae had acknowledged that, and she would have been all too familiar with my diversion as well. Of course, I couldn't admit that fact to Phoebe. "You're right, and I hope you'll hold that thought for later. Phoebe, I'd like to try the dreaming again."

"Aye, I expected as much." She failed to move from her spot on the sofa.

"Well?"

"I'll guide you, but 'tis time you learn your own path."

Only twice had I attempted the dreaming without Phoebe's guidance. Both times revealed little information, plus I had difficulty making sense of anything. "How will I interpret it?"

"I shall be along on your journey, but you will lead the way. Don't let it dissuade you. You're ready for the next level, and when it's time, you'll discover the answers you seek."

She made it sound so simple. With some reluctance, I went into the kitchen and nearly made a beeline for the beer—a pattern I had followed for my entire adult life. It would have been so much easier to silence my fears with a couple of drinks. After I married Phoebe, I drank less, but when stressed, I reverted and could easily drown my tension with a six-pack. I stepped toward the refrigerator.

"Lee, did you find the candle?"

Phoebe's voice had come from outside the kitchen. I quickly changed direction and opened a drawer, collecting the candle and matches. She entered the room, and I held up the candle to show her that I had found it.

She grasped the candle from me and returned to the living room. I resisted the urge for a beer and followed her. Phoebe lit the candle on the coffee table, and I sat across from her.

My hands shook when I reached out to grasp hers. For some reason, the thin webbing between the third and fourth finger on her left hand caught my notice. *A witch's mark?* It had never bothered me, but the seventeenth century was a superstitious time. "Phoebe, I love you."

"And I you. We shall make the journey together."

I took a deep breath. Even with her presence, I felt like a total novice.

"Absorb the flame."

Her words reminded me of the first time we had shared the dreaming. Initially, I had been unable to concentrate and could only think of her. While I didn't have that distraction now, I still couldn't concentrate. People weren't chattering in the hall and horns hadn't been honking like when we had lived in the apartment, but a car sped by with the bass vibrating. In the distance, a dog barked. I shook my head. "I don't think it's going to work tonight."

"It shall."

As usual, she wasn't about to let me give up. I stared into her blue-green eyes. They mesmerized me. It wasn't the first time they had given me a hypnotic sensation, but somehow I felt this time was different. I gazed at the lighted candle and reached for it, then passed my hand through the flame. The heat should have burned my hand, but I withdrew it unharmed. The sound of flapping wings came from nearby. "The crow," I said.

"Follow it."

The black bird settled on a nearby branch and cawed.

"It's not moving."

"What is it doing?" she asked.

"Preening."

The crow took flight, and I followed it and became engulfed in a thick fog. The bird cawed to let me know where it was. I moved toward the sound until the mist thinned. I stood in the middle of a clearing. Muzzle flashes and screams surrounded me. A woman held me to her body.

"Phoebe, I can't continue."

"You must."

Her face—I had finally caught a glimpse. Her black hair was pulled back in a single long braid, and she had bangs. "*Nek.*" Mother.

Her grip on me was so tight that I could barely breathe. All around me were licking flames. Longhouses were on fire, and smoke billowed. She screamed and I fell, striking the ground with a painful thump. My shoulder hurt, and she very nearly landed on top of me. I clung to her deerskin skirt, but she lay still and unmoving. She was dead.

At the time, I was only two and too young to understand. I touched her face. "*Nek.*"

More guns fired. The sound scared me. Alone, I crawled along the ground. Smoke nearly choked me, and I coughed. Still on my hands and knees, I crept blindly. Another woman—no, a girl—pulled me to her.

Phoebe.

I had seen her before, but my memory refused to recall the previous occasions. She spoke softly, and I huddled in her arms until I fell asleep. When I awoke, the guns sounded less often, and I was hungry. I tried to tell Phoebe, but the only thing that came out was childish gibberish. She rocked me. Gradually I calmed, taking comfort in her arms. The next thing I knew, her arms were no longer around me. I wandered aimlessly. Unsteady on my feet, I shuffled through the darkness.

"Crow in the Woods?"

Phoebe's voice had come from . . . where? I faced in every direction but was unable to locate her. I called out, but again, the only sounds I was capable of producing were baby talk.

"I'm coming, lad."

The crow cawed. Could it be? The bird might lead me to safety. I followed the sound.

"Where are you, Crow in the Woods?"

Confused, I halted. *Call out to her.* At the time, she hadn't gone by Phoebe and had yet to take the name Walks Through Mist. I struggled to recall her childhood name. Unable to communicate, I cried out in frustration.

The crow cawed from a nearby tree. Through the moonlight, I saw the bird resting on a branch. It cawed and took flight. I stumbled over a root when I tried to follow and became engulfed by mist. The mist got thicker. "Red Dog," I cried.

"Crow in the Woods!"

I whirled around, but I could not find her. The clammy dampness on my skin chilled me. I was lost.

In the distance, I heard the sound of flapping wings. The crow hadn't left me, but I couldn't see where I was going to follow. Then, it was above me, cawing to me. My arms and legs no longer felt small like that of a child. I stepped forward. On and on, I faltered, while the crow circled above me.

Up ahead stood a woman dressed in a long skirt and linen cap. Her back was to me, and her sides heaved as if she was crying. "Phoebe?"

The woman faced me with tears rolling down her cheeks. She had black hair and brown skin. "Help me."

Phoebe's daughter. I moved closer. "Elenor, what's wrong?"

"Momma said to contact her if I e'er needed her."

The mist swirled, and Elenor vanished.

Once again, the crow circled overhead. The mist grew thinner, and I emerged in a forest. A man with the top half of his face painted black stood before me. He wore a loincloth, deer-hide leggings, and a bear-claw necklace. The right side of his head was shaved, and on the left side his black hair was tied in a knot and held an osprey feather.

He looked familiar. I had that same sick feeling in my stomach as when the anthropologist had shown me the clay figure of the reconstructed skull. The warrior was me.

I blinked back the image. The nausea in my stomach remained. I waited for the discomfort to pass and glanced around the room.

Phoebe sat across from me. "You appear unwell."

The candle had burned to a nub. "What does it mean?"

"You saw the annihilation of your tribe. You have carried the memory with you, but you buried it because you were a young lad."

She almost sounded like Shae. The burning town, the firing of the muskets, and my mother's face were still fresh in my mind. Normally, I felt anger when I read the story of the Paspahegh, but with the memory's release I could finally grieve for all that I had lost. I lowered my head. If only I knew the death songs of my people, I would sing the words to Ahone, the Great Spirit. But that life had been ripped from me, and I had grown up never really knowing who I was.

"Lee . . ." Phoebe had moved next to me and placed a comforting hand on my arm.

I collected myself before glancing over at her. "I saw your daughter, Elenor."

Phoebe's brow furrowed. "Elenor?"

"You didn't see her?"

"Nay."

For a moment I debated whether I should tell her that Elenor had been asking for help. "I only saw her briefly." She looked at me as if she knew I was holding back. "After that I saw a warrior, and then, I was here."

"Did you recognize the warrior?"

"No," I lied. My response had come easy, and after all these years of interrogating chronic liars, I didn't like seeing that trait in myself, especially when it concerned Phoebe. I pretended my reason was to protect her. Throughout my career, I had experienced cold, raw fear, from viewing dismembered bodies to staring at a rifle barrel aimed directly at me. That paled in comparison to what I felt now.

4

Phoebe

"YOU HAVEN'T SAID BUT TWO WORDS all evening." Meg looked across at Phoebe.

As friends, they took turns caring for the children. Phoebe watched five-year-old Tiffany after school afore Meg got home from her nursing job. Her friend reciprocated, granting Lee and Phoebe the occasional "date." Recently, Meg usually stayed the night when Lee was late getting home. During this week, he was absent more times than not because he was consulting with another county's police department on a case.

She often felt isolated in the twenty-first century, so Phoebe enjoyed Meg's company. Because it was Friday eve, they had no worry about Meg needing to leave early for work the following morn. When living with the Paspahegh and Arrohateck, Phoebe had been surrounded by other women and their children. Even when she had lived amongst the English, her servant Bess had always been nearby. Meg's skin was a light nut brown compared to Bess's deep ebony, but she reminded Phoebe so much of her faithful servant.

Since her arrival, they had been friends. Both had lived at Colwell House, transitional housing for women, at the time. Whilst Meg had fought drug addiction and struggled to raise a child on her own, Phoebe had learned the nuances of a new century. The first lesson Meg had taught her was that Africans were commonly born on this side of the Atlantic.

"Shouldn't we put the lasses to bed?" Phoebe asked.

"Sure."

Tiffany slept on a cot in the same room as Heather. Afore tucking them in, Phoebe told her story of crossing the Atlantic in a wooden sailing ship. For Tiffany's benefit, she spoke in English. The lasses giggled when she made the rocking and rolling motion of the ship. They were too young to hear about the severity of the hardships she and her momma had faced upon landfall, the months of hunger after surviving the trip. "Next time, I shall tell you about our first meeting the Paspahegh."

Meg and Phoebe kissed the lasses goodnight.

Heather laid back and Phoebe resisted picking her up. On the nights when Lee was late, she was always tempted to take her daughter to bed with her as she had done when she had lived with the Arrohateck. Instead, she turned from the room and poured a glass of wine for Meg and water for herself.

Meg, who was nearly ten years younger than Phoebe, sat cross-legged on the sofa. "Now are you going to tell me what's bothering you?"

Phoebe sipped from her glass. "You haven't said how Tiffany is doing in kindergarten."

Distracted by the question, Meg beamed with pride. "She's learning to read and write. Drew a beautiful picture of a flower this week."

Even though she had learned the distinctions when she lived with the English, sometimes Phoebe still wondered why everything should be sorted into neat categories. To her a flower was a poppy or a daylily, and a bird was a thrush or a jay. Even Lee was referred to as an Indian, not by his tribe. Didn't such classifying individuals into such large groups make them seem less important?

"Phoebe, now that we're through chitchatting are you going to finally tell me what's wrong?"

" 'Tis Lee," she admitted. "I fear I will lose him."

Meg narrowed her brows. "You're crazy. He loves you and always has." She took a gulp of wine. "Phoebe, you're not trying to tell me there's another woman?"

To that question, Phoebe laughed. "Nay. E'en though warriors like him oft take other wives, he seems content with me."

"And you would put up with him if he decided to take another *wife*?"

"Would I have a choice?"

"Hell, yeah. In this day and age, women don't have to tolerate that kind of crap from philandering men." Meg eyed her suspiciously. "And you've conveniently changed the subject. Is it because of Lee's job that you think you'll lose him?"

"E'er since a skeleton was uncovered, he's been distracted. He thought it was a sign of his own death."

"I'm not sure I follow. Why would a skeleton signify his own death?"

" 'Twas a Native who had been buried for several hundred years. I told him it was more likely a sign that he needed to make peace with his own past."

"And he didn't believe you?"

"I think he fears the past."

"You're probably onto something. Tough guys like him don't want to admit such things."

Phoebe debated how much to share with her friend. 'Twas time to tell the truth. "Lee is also from my time."

Meg's mouth dropped open, then she closed it again. "Phoebe, ever since we've met, I've listened to your seventeenth-century stories. At Colwell House we were supposed to pretend we believed they were true, so that you could remember your past and get better."

Her heart sank. All this time Meg had only feigned belief. "Aye, and I did remember. I hail from the seventeenth century."

"I shared your tears," Meg continued, taking a deep breath, "when I discovered that you had lost a son and your first husband. I honestly thought that when you married Lee you would truly heal, but don't you think it's time to admit that the seventeenth-century world was only a way to help you through your grief? And now you want me to believe that Lee's from the seventeenth century too? He doesn't even have the same accent as you."

" 'Tis because he arrived when he was two. He nearly forgot his first language. He is Paspahegh. He came through the mist long afore I did, but because of his age, he didn't recall where he had hailed from."

Meg waved her hand. "Please stop. I can't deal with any more tonight."

"Meg, I can prove to you that I speak the truth."

Her friend shook her head. "Maybe later, but not now. I think it's time for bed."

As Meg headed toward the guest room, Phoebe thought of the time when she had recalled the loss of her son Dark Moon. For ten days, she had been unable to rise from her bed. Only Meg had taken the initiative to draw her from the dark depths of her mind—and now, she was walking away. Phoebe reached out to call her back, but no words came.

Instead she retired to her own room, tossing and turning for hours. She continued to ponder Meg's disbelief and anger. All this time her friend had only pretended to believe. Why had she not shown Meg the dreaming? Once again she thought about bringing Heather to bed with her. By the time she began to doze, Heather cried. Half asleep, she shuffled to her daughter's room when a man met her at the door with Heather in his arms.

She blinked. "Lee?" She hugged him and gave him a kiss on the lips. "I was worried when you didn't call."

"I meant to, but the situation prevented it. This case should be wrapped up in another week or two." He handed her Heather and rubbed his bloodshot eyes.

"It looks like you got e'en less sleep than I."

"Zero, and my last dose of caffeine is wearing off."

Glad that he was safely home, she hugged him once more. "I'll nurse Heather, then fix you breakfast."

A lass's shout came from Heather's room.

"I think I woke up the entire house," Lee said, pointing in that direction. "I'll get Tiffany."

Phoebe made herself comfortable on the sofa and began nursing Heather. When Lee carried Tiffany from Heather's room, Phoebe forced a smile. Tiffany was being raised without her father, and Phoebe viewed Lee as a good influence for the lass. She only hoped that after the previous eve, such times would continue.

When Meg plodded out from the guest room, Phoebe held her breath. Her friend came face-to-face with Lee and stared at him. "I need to speak with you."

"Okay." He put Tiffany down. "If it's about me being gone so much lately—"

"It's not." Meg glanced over her shoulder at Phoebe, then back again.

"She knows," Phoebe said.

Confusion spread across his countenance. "Knows what?"

"That you went through the mist afore me."

Lee looked in Meg's direction again. "I suppose it was only a matter of time."

"I don't believe any of this! First Phoebe, now you. How can you possibly stand there and tell me that you're Paspa . . . ?" She stumbled over the word.

"Pa-spa-*hay*," he finished for her. "My tribe was annihilated in the seventeenth century." He grasped Meg's arm and led her over to the sofa. Meg sank into the nearby chair and drew Tiffany into her arms. Rubbing his eyes, Lee sat aside Phoebe. "I didn't want to believe either, but I have the memories. I'll spare you the gory details for Tiffany's sake, but I never knew my biological parents because of the English. I recall the day my mother died."

"Meg," Phoebe interjected. "Allow me to show you the dreaming. I can prove to you that we speak the truth."

Meg's lower lip quivered. "The dreaming? I remember you mentioning it at Colwell House, but I thought that was only part of the fantasy."

"I didn't believe either," Lee said, "until Phoebe showed me the dreaming. And there's the fact that she speaks fluent Virginia Algonquian, a language that has been dead for nearly two hundred years."

"I've heard you speak it," Meg said with a quick glance at Phoebe, "but I didn't realize . . ."

"I have an old professor who can verify she speaks Virginia Algonquian."

"All right, I'll let you show me the dreaming—after breakfast." With a trembling hand, Meg grasped Tiffany's arm and guided her to the kitchen.

Lee gave Phoebe a kiss. "I don't know whether it was wise, but maybe it's for the best that she learns the truth," he said.

" 'Tis good to have another ally. You shall see."

He smiled, touching Heather's cheek while she nursed. "I missed the two of you."

"And I you."

He stood. "Heather was crying when I walked in the door. I need to lock my Glock away." After another kiss, he vanished into the bedroom.

When Phoebe finished nursing she went into the kitchen. Tiffany and Meg sat at the table, eating Raisin Bran. "Has Lee not returned?" she asked.

"Haven't seen hide nor hair of him," Meg answered, without looking at her.

Puzzled, Phoebe went into the bedroom where Lee sprawled on top of the bed—fast asleep. He had removed his suit jacket and shirt but left on his trousers. Deciding not to wake him for breakfast, she pulled a blanket over him.

Upon her return to the kitchen, Phoebe convinced Meg to stay 'til later in the day whilst the lasses napped. Throughout the morn they had some tense and awkward moments, and in the afternoon when the lasses were asleep and the house was finally quiet, Phoebe collected the candle to show Meg the dreaming.

"Listen, Phoebe, I'm sorry. I shouldn't have said what I said."

" 'Tis normal to be afraid."

"I'm not afraid. It's just . . . just—"

"If you would feel better, I can call Lee to join us."

Meg swallowed noticeably. "No, don't wake him. He's had a late night and needs his sleep."

"Good. Then let us proceed." As a cunning woman, Phoebe wondered if Heather would eventually play a similar role. For the present, she knew she must concentrate on Meg. There were no hidden secrets during the dreaming. If they continued, Meg would come to know the seventeenth century like she had lived during that time. Some people found the experience too intimate. She drew the drapes and darkened the room, afore setting the candle on the table and lighting the wick. She motioned for Meg to sit across from her.

Her friend sat. "Now what?"

Phoebe grasped Meg's hands and felt them tremble. "We seek my guardian spirit. He's a sleek white hound—a greyhound. He will guide us to the spirit world. Once there, you will find the proof you need to know that I speak the truth. Absorb the flame."

"How do I do that?"

"Look into it. Think of its heat. Let it become part of you." Phoebe had led others on similar journeys. 'Twas best to let them experience the first journey at their own pace.

Though her hands continued to tremble, Meg stared into the flame.

"Absorb the flame. Do you feel its heat?"

Meg gave a weak nod.

"Soon you will be engulfed by mist."

"I see it. Phoebe! I'm lost."

"Don't be frightened. I'm here." Phoebe tightened her grip on Meg's hand. "The hound will be nearby to guide the way." Walking through the mist with the hound leading the way, Phoebe kept a grip on Meg's hand. Her friend's shaking gradually subsided, and when they came out on the other side, Phoebe's mother stood afore her. "Momma?"

"Phoebe..." Momma opened her arms wide to embrace Phoebe.

"Momma..." Tears filled Phoebe's eyes. The last time she had seen her mother was afore the smallpox had taken her, along with many others. Her gray hair was blonde again and hung in a single braid down her back. She wore a deerskin skirt and shell-bead necklace. Dogwood-blossom tattoos encircled her upper arms. She looked like she had when they lived with the Paspahegh.

"How have you been, Phoebe? And your friend?"

"This is Meg, Momma. She was born in Virginia, not Africa. Like Lee, she hails from the twenty-first century."

Meg held out a hand. "I've heard a lot of good things about you, Mrs...."

Momma stared at Meg's hand with uncertainty. "I do not follow English customs. My husband is Silver Eagle."

Meg lowered her hand to her side. "Didn't mean to offend you."

"No offense taken. Any friend of my daughter's is a friend of mine. 'Tis a pleasure to meet you." Momma glanced in Phoebe's direction. "Tell me about yourself."

"Lee and I have married. We have a daughter. We call her Heather."

Momma smiled with pride. "I should like to meet my granddaughter. Did you honor her with an Algonquian name?"

"Snow Bird." Sadness crossed Momma's countenance, for Snow Bird had been her best friend. Together she and Momma had taught Phoebe the ways of *wisakon*. "Momma, Lee is Crow in the Woods."

Momma mouthed the name as if remembering that long-ago time, but she showed no surprise that Lee had gone through the mist afore her. "Does he recall what happened?"

"Aye. He saw his momma murdered."

"A child so young." Fog suddenly surrounded them. "We do not have much time. Lee must seek the past, and you must seek your kinsmen. Your friend here shall become a part of it."

Afore Phoebe could question further, the mist engulfed her mother. "Momma?" She blinked and Momma vanished. Once again, she was in the living room, and a wide-eyed Meg sat across from her, blinking, trying to make sense of what she had witnessed.

"Phoebe," came a man's voice from behind her.

She turned to Lee. His eyes were once again clear and he appeared refreshed. "I didn't mean to intrude," he said.

"You're not intruding. I saw Momma." As she told him what had happened, Meg joined them.

Meg shook her head. "I don't get it."

"It takes a while," Lee admitted. "Even now I sometimes question, but I think I'm beginning to understand."

"Understand what? It was like some weird trip."

Phoebe smiled and gripped Lee's hand. In time Meg would comprehend. Momma's words had assured her of it. To include her friend had been the right course. "We shall find the answers together—all of us."

5

Lee

EXHAUSTED AFTER A SIXTY-HOUR WEEK, I joined Phoebe outside Shae and Russ's split-level house. A decade before, it had been Shae's and my home. I was surprised that she hadn't moved when she had married Russ, but it had been her suburban dream house. I doubted she was plagued by memories that I had ever lived there. After all, my work schedule hadn't changed. I had seen as little of her then as I saw of Phoebe and Heather now.

So why had I allowed Phoebe to talk me into going out for a party when I would have preferred to spend the time with her and my daughter? Distraction was the only reason I could come up with. When I was home, I would hear the voices.

Phoebe rang the doorbell and Shae answered with a broad smile. "Phoebe, Lee. I'm so glad you could come." She waved the way inside.

As we stepped in, I handed Shae the bottle of wine I had brought. She thanked me but shot me a concerned look that I knew all too well. We couldn't kid ourselves. Even though we hadn't been to-gether as a couple in years, we shared a long history.

Shae looked at Phoebe and asked, "How's Heather?"

"She's fine. Meg is watching her this eve."

"Good. Let me get you some drinks."

Classical music played in the background. Shae had avoided the seventeenth-century music she usually played when Phoebe was a guest to make her feel more at home. Relieved, I glanced around the room and recognized a few of my former neighbors. One woman waved with a smile.

But there was something missing. Anytime I attended a party where I was the only cop present, someone always pulled another person aside and shouted, "They've come to get you!" Or raised their hands, screaming, "I didn't do it!"

"What's the matter, Lee?" Shae handed Phoebe a glass of water and me, a beer.

"Where are the cop jokes?"

"I warned everyone ahead of time. I don't think you'll hear any."

"Thanks, Shae. I owe you one."

"What's new? But who's counting?" She gave us a warm smile before running off to tend to other guests.

"Well, should we make our way over to the food table?" I asked. "I'm sure Russ has cooked up some delicacies."

Like Shae, Russ was a psychologist, but he was a gourmet cook too. Phoebe helped herself to a slice of strawberry cheesecake and began to mingle with the other guests. Even though she came from a different time period, she always found something in common to talk about. These days the conversations generally centered on kids.

I, on the other hand, found such gatherings uncomfortable. Not many sane individuals wanted to discuss dismembered bodies or what it was really like to face the wrong end of a gun barrel. Such topics made most people downright nervous. But if I decided to talk about *CSI* or *Law & Order* as if they were reality, everyone would be all ears. Instead, I kept close to Phoebe and quietly sipped my beer.

"You say you're from England?" a dark-haired woman with thick glasses asked Phoebe.

"Aye. I hail from Dorset."

The woman seemed intrigued. "I would have guessed Scotland from your accent. My ancestors were from the London area. They arrived here during the seventeenth century."

Phoebe exchanged an amused glance with me. I shook my head, letting her know that I didn't think discussing the seventeenth century from personal experience would be a wise move.

"And your husband?" the woman continued. "Where is he from?"

I pointed to myself. "What do you mean? I'm from Virginia, and my family was here long before yours."

A look of genuine disbelief spread across her face. "I'm quite certain Hispanics didn't arrive in Virginia until after the seventeenth century."

I opened my mouth to respond, but Phoebe poked me in the ribs with her elbow, reminding me that it was my turn to be polite. "I'm not Hispanic," I replied with as much grace as I could muster.

"You're not?"

Actually, it was a common mistake, but her haughty tone rubbed me the wrong way. "I'm Indian."

She raised an eyebrow. "A real one?"

"No, a fake one." Phoebe poked me once more, but I continued, "For the record, I don't live in a tepee, nor do I scalp people for a living. I do have a few feathers around the house and some buckskin moccasins. That last word is Algonquian. One of the native languages in this portion of Virginia, or Tsenacommacah as my family called it in the seventeenth century."

The woman's mouth formed an O. "It seems I was in error. I thought all of the Indians in Virginia were gone."

My mother's death scream echoed in my head. "Gone? They didn't simply vanish. They were forced from their homes or killed. Thankfully, a few survived to tell the story."

"You don't need to get huffy. I wasn't there." She did an about-face and moved to another group of people.

Even minus the cop jokes, I was an outcast. I glanced over at Phoebe. She understood my feeling all too well.

"Lee!" Russ strode over and shook my hand. He said hello to Phoebe, then continued, "I should have warned you that Margery's very proud of her family history, but I didn't think it would come up."

I shrugged. "I get that sort of thing frequently. At least you didn't have a costume party, or I might have been surrounded by fake Indians, who for some peculiar reason seem to think they're honoring my heritage."

"Shae's told me about some of the misconceptions. I have no doubt most of it is due to ignorance."

Russ had never been the sort to make small talk with me in the past, and I wondered what he was leading up to. "Agreed, which is why I'll continue to reeducate them when their stereotypical ideas are directed at me."

"As you should." Russ smiled slightly, then drew me aside. "Phoebe, do you mind if I borrow your husband for a few minutes?"

She arched a brow. "Borrow him?"

"Never mind," Russ said. "I'd like to speak with Lee in private, if you don't mind."

"Of course not."

Phoebe headed off to converse with some of the women while Russ led me to the den. He closed the door behind us.

"It's more serious than I thought," I said.

He ran his hand through his beard. "Lee, I'm fully aware that you can read people. I'm sure that's an excellent quality in your line of work, and I appreciate the fact that you're more patient with me than with my neighbor."

"I only tend to react when people piss me off. Besides, I'm sure the ability to 'read people' is useful to psychologists, too."

"Agreed," Russ replied. "I'll get right to the point. Shae's worried."

I was uncertain whether to feel betrayed, but I should have guessed that Shae would eventually confide in Russ. "How much do you know?"

"I believe—everything."

Preparing for the worst, I sipped my beer. "Everything?"

"She was having difficulty separating her personal and professional life. I've known about Phoebe for quite some time. When the two of you got married, I thought it was a little odd. You seemed so very different, but now it makes perfect sense."

"Not many couples can say they've known each other for four hundred years."

"Although some say it feels like it's been that long."

We shared a laugh. "You said you'd get right to the point," I reminded him.

"Shae thinks that between the stress of your job, a family, and the memories of your past, you'll do something foolish."

Either Russ didn't know quite as much about me as he thought or he was trying to psychoanalyze me. I gulped my beer. "Like what? It's a well-known fact that cops and Indians drink too much. I must be doubly damned."

"And I must have just pissed you off. I'm only trying to help."

I gave him credit. He could read me as much as I could him. I mumbled an apology and asked, "What does Shae think I'll do?"

"She's worried that you'll get distracted at the wrong moment and be injured—or worse."

"I appreciate her concern. Let her know that I'll do my utmost to be careful. And Russ—I'm glad she has someone like you that she can confide in."

He gave me a long look and finally said, "Thank you, Lee."

Before I could respond, the sound of glass shattering came from the other room. Russ and I exchanged glances before we followed the commotion. The woman with the thick glasses had dropped a plate. She sat in a chair insisting that she was all right, but her speech was slurred.

A twenty-something blonde giggled. "Someone must have spiked the punch."

My gut warned me that Margery's problem wasn't alcohol related. Something was very wrong. I moved closer.

Shae brought a glass of water. "Here, Margery. Drink this."

Margery reached for the glass, but her hand halted in midair. She seemed confused, and the pupils of her eyes were unequal in size.

"Call 9-1-1," I said. "She's having a stroke. Margery, you need to lie down."

All animosity from our earlier conversation had vanished. While Shae dialed 9-1-1, I made certain there was no broken glass nearby. Russ grasped Margery's left arm, and I got her right. We helped her to the floor. Russ placed a sofa cushion under her head and shoulders, while I removed her glasses. I checked her pulse and breathing rate. "Help is on the way. You're going to be all right."

She mumbled something that I couldn't quite make out. I glanced over at Russ. He shook his head that he didn't understand either. The left side of her mouth drooped. She uttered more slurred speech and grew frustrated.

"Just relax until help is here," I said.

"*Kenah.*"

Unlike the other words, that one had been distinct. She had thanked me in Algonquian.

Margery muttered a string of words, each coming faster and more frenzied. They were Algonquian. That much I knew.

"You understand her," Russ said.

"Some of it." Because of Margery's rapid pace and my infantile knowledge of the language, I couldn't quite grasp the meaning. I called for Phoebe. She bent down beside me. "What's she saying?" I asked.

Phoebe shook her head. "I don't know."

"It's Algonquian."

"Nay, 'tis gibberish."

"I'm certain . . ." I pressed two fingers to my temple.

Margery's words no longer made sense. Russ stared at me. Aware he was thinking that stress had caused a hallucination, I remained silent. He wouldn't believe me anyway, and Phoebe would only worry. I couldn't help but puzzle over what it all meant.

Two weeks later, I had received a thank you note from Margery in the mail. Her scrawl looked like that of a child learning how to write, but due to quick medical intervention, she would make a full recovery—in time. Between Margery's letter and the fact that I had finally wrapped up a serial rapist case that had kept me away from home consulting with detectives in a nearby county, I felt like celebrating.

Around two-thirty in the morning, I accelerated the Thunder-bird on the winding, twisting road toward Richmond. I was relieved to finally be heading home with the case closed. I should have given Phoebe a call before leaving, but with the baby teething and cranky, she needed her sleep.

Several miles later, a sleek animal darted across the road. I slowed. *A fox.* Safely past the animal, I increased speed again. Barely had I gone another mile when the headlights picked up another shape on the edge of the road. Before I could slow, the T-Bird slammed into a deer. The animal rolled off the fender, over the hood, and up the windshield.

Fearing the deer would come crashing through, I braked to a halt. The windshield held, and the deer slid off the hood. I was shaking. Thankful the air bag hadn't triggered, I checked for any injuries. I was numb from the accident but seemed to be in one piece. I grabbed my flashlight and hauled myself out of the car to check the damage.

Behind the car, the deer struggled to get up. Both of its back legs were shattered. Unable to let the animal suffer, I withdrew my Glock. As I aimed at the deer's head, I thought I overheard a woman's voice.

I fired.

The deer fell, then lay still.

"Momma . . ."

It *was* a woman's voice, and she sounded like she could have been injured. I holstered my gun. Shining the flashlight on what I thought was the source of the voice, I moved forward. "Are you hurt?" I shouted.

No response.

I made a sweep with the flashlight beam along the forest edge. No one. I had probably scared her half to death by taking out my piece and firing. "Ma'am, I'm a detective." I held out my badge. "The deer had two broken legs. I put it out of its misery."

My head hurt. Maybe I had hit it and imagined the voice. Following standard procedure, I took out my cell phone and called in the accident. Out here, between major cities, it would likely take a while for anyone to arrive. Before calling Phoebe, I returned to the T-Bird to assess the damage—a cracked windshield, a big dent in the fender, and a broken headlight. It certainly could have been much worse. Perhaps I should make the best of the situation and get a permit to keep the carcass. After all, Phoebe had been raised on venison.

"I need your help," came a female voice with a distinct British accent.

I made another wide sweep with the flashlight to no avail. "Ma'am, where are you? Keep calling to me so that I can locate you. Help is on the way."

The woman sobbed. "He's dead."

With a shudder, I moved toward the tree line, telling myself that I wouldn't get lost in the forest. "Who's dead? I'm here to help. Keep talking."

Another sob. "Help us."

"Keep talking," I repeated, heading in the direction of the voice. More crying.

Following the sound, I stepped among the trees. Instead of locating an injured woman, I became engulfed in a mist. *Follow the path.* Who guided me? I had only engaged in the dreaming without Phoebe on a couple of occasions.

Help us.

The voice was now in my head. I moved forward but stumbled in the thick fog. In the past, the greyhound had led the way. Could I summon it? I envisioned the dog in my mind, but it failed to appear. *What was happening?* Either I was having my own vision, or the deer had crashed through the windshield and killed both of us in reality. I laughed. And Shae had been convinced that I would die from a bullet.

Unable to see in any direction, I halted. *I am dead.* Then why was I still breathing? I touched my neck. My pulse was elevated but steady. Convinced that I was indeed alive, I took a deep breath and continued on.

From somewhere within the swirling mist, a crow cawed, reminding me of my true heritage. My Algonquian name translated to Crow in the Woods. I hadn't known the truth until after meeting Phoebe. Somehow I had reached through time and summoned her.

Hadn't Phoebe also traveled through the mist to reach me?

Help.

My duty was to protect and serve. Reminding myself that additional help was on the way, I fumbled farther through the fog. I couldn't ignore the plea. Then I heard a caw, and the mist cleared enough that I could see a crow on a nearby branch.

I *was* experiencing the dreaming without Phoebe's aide, for the crow was my spirit guide. The jet-black bird took flight, and I followed. Soon I was standing along the bank of the James River. Shae was hanging onto my right arm, and a gray-haired man in a police uniform stood before me. My father smiled and shook my hand. "Detective. Imagine that. My son, the detective."

"Dad?" Nearly nine years had passed since his death. I had almost forgotten the sound of his voice.

But the crow cawed, and I meandered along the river once more until I came to a pitched tent. I smelled fish roasting over a campfire. A grinning man sat in a camp chair. This time, my father only had a hint of gray. "Lee, I've got something for you." He handed me a deer-antler arrowhead.

The one I presently wore around my neck.

"You carried it when you were discovered lost in the woods as a toddler. It's part of your heritage."

Part of my heritage. My biological father had carved it.

"Only he can give you the answers you seek."

"Dad?" I reached out, but the mist engulfed him. And again, like the suddenness of death, my father had been taken from my grasp.

With more questions than answers, I wandered. The mist surrounded me, and I felt the dank air on my skin. The crow cawed. I followed the sound. The bird guided me through the camouflaged layers just as Phoebe's greyhound always showed her the way. Why had it taken me so long to realize the crow was my guardian spirit?

Another crow joined the single bird, then another and another, until a flock had gathered. They made a horrifying racket. I couldn't make up my mind which way they were guiding me. I stopped and listened. They cried a warning.

The mist cleared slightly, and I found myself standing beside a tree. The loud cawing halted as suddenly as it had begun. Numerous black birds watched me from the safety of the branches.

One crow moved closer to a nearby branch and made a series of clicks and rattles. *Crow in the Woods*.

The words weren't English or Algonquian, but I had heard my name in my head. "Did you speak to me?"

The bird clicked. *Danger*.

"What kind?"

Clicks and rattles were all around me. *You are seeking what once was.*

"How is that dangerous?"

Because you have answered the call.

"The call?"

The crows gave an alarming cry, and out of the mist, a man strode toward me. His skin was brown like mine and, although his shirt was wool, he wore deer-hide leggings and moccasins. A single eagle feather rested in his black hair, which fell down the length of his back. The prominent cheekbones and shape of his nose and mouth gave him an uncanny resemblance to me. He spoke in Algonquian.

Only grasping a few words here and there, I said, "*Nows.*" Father.

He waved for me to accompany him.

On and on I marched until the mist engulfed me in a fog. Black Owl continued speaking, and I followed the sound of his voice. "*Nows*, what happened?"

He halted and turned to me. "I will not abandon you a second time."

My mother's death scream echoed in my head. "Phoebe says you were away hunting at the time. You couldn't have known."

"Phoebe?"

What had Phoebe's Algonquian child name been? "Red Dog. She is my wife."

A hint of a smile crossed Black Owl's face. "Then you should be well prepared for the upcoming journey."

"Journey?"

But like my adopted father, Black Owl was swallowed by the mist. Once more, I was on my own.

A crow cawed.

No, I wasn't alone. The crow would guide me, if I let him.

The black bird flew overhead.

I traced my steps carefully and stretched my arms. The crow lifted me toward the sky. Exhilarated by the feeling, I rode the wind alongside the bird. The passage of time had little meaning here.

Voices whispered in the breeze. On the ground below me, Shae waved. Beside her stood my adopted mother and father. The wind currents changed, and I floated toward the light. Around and around in a giant arc.

"Lee..."

I floated to the ground, and Phoebe stood before me. She wore a long green skirt, a laced top with metal eyelets, and linen cap. She was dressed the way I had envisioned her during my first experience with the dreaming.

Glistening in the light, her fingers stretched toward me. "Come with me," she said.

I reached out to her. She whispered her love. Our fingertips nearly touched, but the shimmering light changed to a feathered wing. With a cry, the crow spread its wings and took to the sky.

My hand closed over emptiness. I let out an anguished cry. *Phoebe.*

6

Phoebe

WITH A SUDDEN START, PHOEBE SAT UP IN BED. Certain she had heard Lee summon her, she checked the other side. The sheets were cold neath her fingertips. "Lee?" The clock aside the bed read 4:55. She switched on a light. In her bare feet, she donned her robe and peered into the bathroom and called again. Turning on the lights as she passed, she searched the house. His car was absent from the garage.

Fearful of what might have happened, she placed a call to Lee's cell phone. Voicemail answered, and she left a message for him to call her. Then she dialed Ed. "Lee ne'er made it home, and he doesn't answer his cell."

A sleepy voice responded. *"That's odd. I talked to him this morning just before he left Williamsburg. It was around two. He should be home by now. Let me check further, and I'll get back to you."*

As she hung up the phone, she muttered her thanks. Unlike when she had lived with the Arrohateck, she felt so alone—always alone. There the women played separate roles from the men and consoled each other. In this time period she had no extended family. Neither did Lee.

Briefly she thought of calling Meg, but decided to wait. At any minute Lee might walk through the door, or Ed might call to say that he had been found. Heather would rouse shortly. She needed to remain brave for her daughter's sake.

When the clock struck seven, Phoebe fed and bathed eight-month-old Heather. She splashed and cooed, unaware that her poppa was late. Her eyes and skin tone were brown, her hair black like her poppa's. At eight, Phoebe heard a car on the road outside. Hoping that it was Lee, she ran to the window. As she parted the curtain, her hope sank. The car was red, not the dark blue of Lee's Thunderbird. At eight-thirty, the phone rang. She hurried to answer, only to be asked about a magazine subscription. At nine, she faced the four winds and said her prayers to Ahone. At nine-twenty, she heard another car. This time, it pulled into the drive. When Ed's bald head emerged from the car, her heart nearly stopped. 'Twas bad news. He wouldn't have visited in person if it wasn't. Fighting tears, she answered the door and invited him inside.

"Lee's car was found. He hit a deer and apparently called in the accident around 2:40 this morning. By the time the tow truck arrived, he was gone. The deer had been shot. Ballistics will verify if it was from his gun, but I suspect he put the animal out of its misery."

"Then where is he?"

"It's anyone's guess. There was a lot of blood at the scene, but we think it belonged to the deer. I'm making certain forensics goes over the area and car with a fine-toothed comb." She was puzzled why investigators would use such an instrument, but he continued, "There was no sign of a struggle. Although we can't rule out foul play at this point, he might have been injured and in a daze, then simply wandered off. In that case, rest assured, we'll find him soon and bring him home. The search dogs are trying to pick up his track as we speak."

Whilst Ed spoke in a comforting manner, she had already been a detective's wife long enough to comprehend what he left unsaid. His brow furrowed, making his bushy eyebrows appear more like a hairy caterpillar. His countenance alerted her that he was worried. "Ed—"

"Phoebe, is there anyone who can stay with you, or somewhere I can drive you? I don't want you to be alone until Lee's found."

He was more vexed than she had feared. "Aye," she responded.

"Then please make the call now. I won't leave until I know you're in safe hands."

She touched his hand. "I know you're worried, but he's not dead."

Not wishing to share his emotion with her, he pulled away. "Make your call, Phoebe."

His reaction warned her of his deepest fear. "Do you recall when Lee was shot and nearly died?" she asked.

His gaze came to rest upon hers. "How could I ever forget? He saved my life."

"I felt the shooting when it happened. This morning I heard him call out to me, but he hadn't died. I would feel it, if that were the case."

"I hope you're right. I'd still prefer you weren't alone until we find out what's happened. *I* would be able to do my job better knowing that someone was with you. If the situation were reversed, Lee would do the same for Marian. If you can't find someone to come here, then you and the baby can stay with us."

She thanked him and placed a call to Meg at the doctor's office where she worked. Ten minutes passed afore Meg returned the call.

"Phoebe, what's wrong?"

"Lee's missing." Phoebe went on to explain the situation as best as she could.

"I'll be there as soon as I can."

She hung up the phone. "Meg and her daughter will stay with me."

"Good. Everything's going to be all right."

He gave her a hug and kissed her upon the cheek afore parting. The action warned her how worried he was. But she had grown accustomed to waiting. Her first husband, Lightning Storm, had frequently gone on hunts and raiding parties. And Henry had sailed the Atlantic, often absent for months at a time. On his final voyage, he had contracted the smallpox and taken three years to return. For now, she must focus on her daily activities and pray that Lee would be found.

An hour passed afore Meg and Tiffany arrived. "Any news?" Meg asked, embracing Phoebe.

"Ed says he will call when he has more information."

Her friend squeezed Phoebe's shoulder. "He'll be all right, Phoebe."

Meg's presence gave her comfort, but throughout the day, Ed brought no word. After putting Heather to bed that eve, she went into the bedroom she shared with Lee. His jeans remained folded in the drawers, and his suits hung in the closet. 'Twas almost like he was on duty. A photograph rested on the dresser. It had been taken afore Heather's birth at a historical park in front of replica seventeenth-century sailing ships. "Lee, call to me again, and I shall find you."

The phone rang. She overheard Meg's voice in the other room. "I'll get her." A knock came to the bedroom door. "Phoebe, it's Ed."

She picked up the phone, praying that he had some news.

"I'm sorry I didn't call earlier, but there's nothing new to report. The dogs picked up a scent and lost it almost as quickly as they had found it. We can only surmise that he must have gotten a ride with someone, but what happened after that, we don't know."

Detecting something unspoken, she said, "Ed, be completely truthful with me."

"All right. Lee has vanished without a trace. So far, there are no leads— absolutely nothing. We'll need to wait for the lab results to see if anything turns up there, but my hunch is that someone followed him. They were likely armed, otherwise there would have been a struggle. We'll go through all of the cases he's worked on and see if we can find a likely suspect. I have a couple in mind that I want to question.

"Phoebe, there is one other thing I must ask, and please forgive me, but has everything been okay between you and Lee?"

"I don't under . . . aye, and e'en if he was angry at me for some reason, he would ne'er leave Heather. He adores her."

"Thanks. I'm certain I would have heard something from Lee if there had been difficulties, but I had to ask. I'll let you know when I have more information."

No closer to answers than she had been afore, Phoebe hung up the phone. How could she sleep? *Lee was gone.* For the first time since his disappearance, she truly realized that he might not return. Surrendering to her grief, she sank to the floor. She curled into a ball and sobbed.

"Phoebe?" Meg knocked on the door. Her friend sat aside her and drew her into her arms.

Phoebe cried on Meg's shoulder. "What if I'm wrong? He could be dead."

Meg hushed her. "I don't want to hear you talking like that. He's not dead."

"But Meg, Lightning Storm died in battle. Two days passed afore we discovered what had happened. A runner brought the news."

Her friend dried Phoebe's tears with a tissue. "Believe in yourself. You said you would know if he had died."

She squeezed Meg's arm. "Thank you, my friend."

"Will you be all right now?"

Phoebe nodded, and Meg stayed with her a few minutes longer, making certain that she was all right. Once more, Phoebe attempted to ready for bed. She changed into a thigh-length nightgown with thin shoulder straps and placed a hand to the bed where Lee normally slept. The spot was cold. She *must* do something—anything—to discover what had happened.

Instead of climbing into the empty bed, Phoebe returned to the parlor and placed a candle on the coffee table. After lighting it, she sat cross-legged on the floor and concentrated on the flame. Soon the mist engulfed her.

"Phoebe?"

At the sound of Meg's voice, she blinked.

"What are you doing?"

Phoebe focused on Meg's concerned face. "I'm participating in the dreaming to reach Lee's spirit."

"Then you think he's . . ."

Dead. Even though she hadn't said the word, Phoebe heard it all the same. "Nay, you were right. I would know, but if I reach him, he can tell me what has happened. Meg, afore all this, he called to me."

Meg's expression changed to puzzlement. "You know I want to believe you—"

"Then share with me."

Phoebe held out her hand, and Meg grasped it. "The dreaming again?"

"Aye."

Meg stared at the lizard tattoos upon Phoebe's upper arms. Her gaze dropped to the snake tattoos upon her thighs.

Though Phoebe wouldn't have been embarrassed, she was glad the serpent tattoos coiling about her breasts were hidden from Meg's view. "I got them when I became a woman," she said.

Meg sent her a nervous smile. "You'll have to give me the name of your tattoo artist."

The faith she had placed in her friend had been well founded. As she reseated herself, Meg sat aside her. There was no time to waste. Lee counted on her to locate him.

Phoebe stared into the flame, recalling the first time she had shared the dreaming with Lee. He had wanted proof that she hailed from the seventeenth century. She had memorized everything about his countenance, from his brown-skin tone to his prominent cheekbones. In the Algonquian tongue she was known as Walks Through Mist. Concentrating on the flame, she sought the other realm now. The white greyhound stood afore her, and she followed him through the mist. "Lee," she called as she traveled.

No response.

She continued walking. The mist failed to clear. She walked 'til her feet ached, but Lee ne'er answered her hails. She blinked, and the room came into view. Suddenly chilled, she put on her robe.

"What does it mean?" Meg asked.

Discomfited by not connecting with Lee, Phoebe attempted to hide her true fear. Mayhap she had erred. "He has not found a way to speak to me."

Meg placed an arm over her shoulder. "Then we'll try again later. He'll be fine. You'll see."

"Aye." But her response was half-hearted. *Lee, where are you?*

When the phone rang she rushed to answer, hoping Ed had something to report.

"Phoebe?" came Shae's voice. *"I saw on the news that Lee is missing. Is there anything I can do to help?"*

Shae had been instrumental in helping Phoebe cope when she had first arrived in the twenty-first century. "There's naught we can do but wait. Meg is staying with me." She went on to tell Shae as much as she knew. Afore she hung up, Shae reassured her to call if needed.

Meg stifled a yawn.

"Get some rest," Phoebe said. "One of us needs to be awake when the lasses arise."

"I'm going to tell my boss that I need a couple of days off."

"Don't be daft. I'll manage."

Covering her mouth, Meg barely hid her gape. "We'll talk about it in the morning. Just promise me that you'll wake me if you need or hear anything."

"I shall." After Meg shuffled to the spare bedroom, Phoebe hesitated, not wishing to return to the room she had shared with Lee. Due to the long hours he had kept, she often went to bed alone. Finally, she moved forward. Tonight was like any other. He was simply late. As she entered the room, she looked around to see if anything was out of the ordinary. *Had she missed any clues?* She had heard his call. Had it been a cry for help?

Exhausted, she went into the adjoining bathroom and readied herself for bed. As she did so, she envisioned Lee walking in circles. She returned to the bedroom and slipped betwixt the sheets. Other nights, Lee would have given her tender caresses, and they would have made love. *Lee, how could you leave Heather and me like this?*

Burying her face in the pillow, she cried, pounding her fists against the mattress. When her energy was spent, she dried her tears. She must place faith in herself. For she would know if Lee were dead. He *was* alive, and she would find him.

Hours stretched to days. Ed reported the blood on Lee's car had in fact belonged to the deer, and the animal had been mercifully dispatched by Lee's gun. Beyond that, there were no leads or clues as to what had happened to him. Phoebe requested Ed to take her to the scene of the accident. He showed her the skid marks and the dried blood on the road. Then he went to the other side of the pavement to point where the search dogs had picked up Lee's scent.

"We've scoured the area," he said. "There is no sign of him. The only thing I can guess is that he got into another vehicle. If it was voluntarily, we would have heard from him. Even if he had been injured and a good Samaritan had happened by, the hospitals would have reported his admission. No one fitting his description has turned up. I'm working on the angle that he had been forced into another car, but right now, I have no leads."

Aware that if a case wasn't solved within the first twenty-four hours it often remained that way, Phoebe appreciated that Ed no longer pretended Lee would be found safe and sound. She scanned the forest. She had heard him call. *But from where?* "Tell me about the normal routine aft such an accident."

"Okay, as you know, deer can shoot out of nowhere in a second. For the sake of argument, let's say Lee was uninjured. He still would have likely been shaken. When he recovered sufficiently, he would have gotten out and checked the damage, after which he would have seen the injured deer and put it out of its misery. Then he'd call in the accident. He did all of that, so we know he was coherent enough to follow procedure."

She listened to the rush of the James. Lee had been here. Why couldn't she sense him? She followed a path through the trees 'til reaching the banks of the river. "Lee?"

"Phoebe, the dogs scoured the area and never picked up his scent again."

"You're right." She retraced her steps along the path, and a crow settled in the tree and cawed. 'Twas the sign she had been looking for. The bird would lead her to Lee.

7

Lee

THE MIST CLEARED.

As I emerged from the fog, the crow vanished. The sunshine was warm, but the air was a bit chilly. To my surprise, I found no one. I must have traveled some distance. How long had I been walking in circles? Even the road wasn't in view. For some reason the cypress and poplar trees seemed taller and larger than usual.

Lost in a forest. I fought the growing panic of my childhood fear and took out my cell phone. No signal.

Keep calm. All I had to do was make my way back to the T-Bird and wait for help. But which way had I come? I was lost. I turned in every direction, wondering which way would lead me back to the car. Nothing looked familiar.

Relieved that I had changed out of my suit before leaving Williamsburg, I would be able to navigate the distance to safety in relative comfort. I heard the sound of rushing water and moved toward it. As I passed through the trees, I felt Phoebe's presence. "Phoebe?"

The feeling vanished almost as quickly as it had come over me. I made my way to the bank. The expansive James River loomed before me. If I followed the river downstream, I'd eventually come to a house or road. The gentle roll of the land appeared familiar. I had seen the lay of it when I had participated in the dreaming with Phoebe.

For some reason I shivered, but it wasn't from the cool air. I continued walking until I came to a pitched-roof house made of red brick. A black woman in a long dress was bent over in the garden, weeding. She looked vaguely familiar. "Bess?"

She straightened and turned toward me. Her skin was the color of ebony and her prominent cheekbones were decorated with tribal scars. "Mr. Lee?"

I had hoped that I was wrong. She wasn't just any black woman, but Phoebe's servant, who had come from Africa. Not wanting to think about what Bess's presence truly meant, I moved closer. "Bess, I don't know how I got here."

She showed me the way inside to a hall with wooden floors. A table was on one side, with candles on top and a mirror above it. On the other side was a staircase with a wooden handrail leading to the second story. "Miss Elenor, we have a guest."

A woman appeared at the end of the hall. She stepped out of the shadows. She was brown-skinned and had black hair like her Arrohateck father. Only her blue eyes revealed her mixed heritage. She clutched a handkerchief, and her eyes were puffy. I now knew who had called to me in the night. Like her mother, Elenor was a cunning woman. Her summons had been meant for Phoebe, not me.

"You called for help," I finally said, breaking the silence.

"I expected Momma."

Still not wanting to think about where I really was, I swallowed. "For some reason, I heard your call and was sent instead."

She placed the handkerchief to her face. Her sides heaved, but she uttered no sound.

When someone was in need, I could count on my police experience to hold my own emotions in check. "Elenor, tell me what has happened."

She looked up. "Master Crowley."

"Please, call me Lee. After all, your mother is my wife."

She showed me the way into the parlor and motioned for me to have a seat in a wood chair with tasseled cushions. She sat across from me near a spinning wheel. "My husband, Christopher, and Poppa's son, David, have not returned from England. I fear they have been lost at sea. Momma told me that if I e'er needed her, then I should contact her through the dreaming."

A simple cry in the night, and I had answered. But something else had happened. Normally the dreaming allowed those from different time periods to speak to each other in another realm. I didn't quite understand it myself, but something was very different this time. Once before, as a two-year old, I had done more than participate in the dreaming. "What year is it?" I asked, fearing the answer.

"1643."

1643? The date floated around in my head, and I clenched a fist. Hadn't I been born somewhere around 1608? I was only a couple of years older than what I would have been had I never traveled to the twentieth century in the first place. This time was alien to me. I wondered how I would survive. The skeleton that had been unearthed a few months before popped into my mind. I hadn't survived. I would die here.

"Mr. Lee . . ." Bess handed me a leather mug.

If I recalled correctly, Phoebe had called it a flagon. I took a sip. Spicy, yet sweet—an herbal tea mixture. The drink had a calming effect. "Thank you, Bess."

Bess sent me a comforting smile. "We'll find a way to let Phoebe know that you're here."

Phoebe. She had called me back, yet I had continued on. I blotted her image from my mind, or I would lose my semblance of composure. I turned my attention to Elenor. "I don't know how I can help. I don't know anything about sailing in the twenty-first century, let alone the seventeenth."

"You were sent here for a reason, Lee Crowley. Only time will reveal the answer to us."

She spoke as cryptically as her mother. Had I expected anything different? These people would help me. That much I knew. I took a deep breath. "For whatever reason, I'm here. I'll do whatever I can to help you, but I do look a little out of place for 1643."

Both women eyed my short hair, T-shirt, and jeans. "Aye," Elenor finally said. "And there will be no hiding the fact that you are Indian."

I had entered the dreaming often enough with Phoebe and studied sufficient history to realize that I had entered a more prejudiced time than the one I had left. Though Elenor was racially mixed, she lived a colonial life and had married an Englishman. While I suspected her life had been no more free from racism than mine, she seemed to blend in. Even with coaching, I doubted that I could ever pass as a convincing colonist. "What do I need to know?"

For the first time since my arrival Elenor smiled. "I shall send a messenger for Charging Bear."

Phoebe's brother. "Then what?"

"Trust us. We shall show you how to fit into our time."

As a matter of fact, I did trust them—and I wasn't the sort who trusted others easily. For better or worse, I was home.

Over the next few days, I stayed at the plantation and became acquainted with the rest of the family. Elenor had three children, two boys and a girl. They ranged in age from two to seven. Only the eldest, Christopher, showed any hint of his Native heritage. Nicolas was the youngest, and the girl, Elsa, reminded me of Phoebe with her blue-green eyes, reddish hair, and freckles. Seeing the kids, only made me think of Heather and how I was missing every precious moment in her life.

Bess also had a teenage son, named James after her late husband. Although the women were unafraid of heavy, hard work, James performed the lion's share. Then there was Henry, Phoebe's second husband. He must have been in his early fifties, but with gray cast throughout his hair and wrinkles near his eyes and mouth, he looked closer to sixty.

During the dreaming, I had witnessed sailing to Virginia through his eyes. In that long-ago lifetime, he had loved Phoebe and was instrumental in her escape after she had been tried as a witch. Without his aid, she would have never joined me in the twenty-first century. For his selfless act, I was forever indebted and doubted that I could ever repay him.

In the evenings after the chores for the day had been completed, the family gathered in the parlor. Bess told tales from Africa, and Henry shared stories from his sailing days. Elenor refrained from saying anything about her husband and Henry's son in a brave attempt to hide her fear from the children. When my turn came to speak, the kids were fascinated about my life in the twenty-first century.

After the kids went to bed, Elenor guided me through the dreaming. Night after night I was unable to reach Phoebe. In silence, I cried my sorrow. To the others, I maintained an image of self-control—an appearance I had perfected over the years working as a cop. After all, was my predicament really any worse than Elenor's?

For some reason, I recalled my first dreaming experience when Phoebe sat across from me. While there were no noises to distract me, I couldn't concentrate any more than I had then.

Absorb the flame.

Unable to focus, I looked over at Elenor and shook my head.

"Do not give up," she said.

"I won't, but I'm not going to reach her tonight."

She smiled in a way that reminded me of Phoebe. Everything made me think of Phoebe. I longed to see her, touch her silky skin, and breathe in her sweet herbal scent.

As if reading my mind, Elenor squeezed my hand. She reflected a similar anguish in her eyes.

"How long has Christopher been gone?" I asked.

"Nearly a year," she replied. "Poppa tells me that I must be patient. He says on his last voyage, three years passed afore he returned."

My eyes widened. On that particular voyage Henry had contracted smallpox.

"You know of the time I speak?"

"I do," I admitted. "I've seen much of your lives here through the dreaming. So why can't I contact Phoebe now?"

" 'Tis oft easier to channel what was in a person's life. Momma is a powerful cunning woman. She will find you."

"Just as you will find your husband."

I had taken an instant liking to Elenor and finally realized my mistake. Except for the couple of times that I had been successful entering the dreaming on my own, Phoebe had accompanied me. Some of those journeys were sexual in nature. My feelings for Elenor were like those for a daughter, and not being able to lower my inhibitions meant I could not experience the dreaming.

I got to my feet. "Thank you, Elenor, but from now on, I must try to reach Phoebe on my own."

A knowing smile crossed her face. "I was wondering when you would seek the truth."

"The truth? You mean you knew all along?"

"Aye. You are connected to my mother, not me."

"But I care . . ."

"Aye." She stood across from me and pressed her hand to my chest. "You are connected to her in here and in spirit. 'Tis not a chain that can easily be broken."

Her words brought comfort. "I wish I could do more to help you."

"You shall, aft you have learnt why you are here. 'Til then, you must leave us."

The thought of leaving my haven suddenly struck sheer terror in my heart. "Leave?"

"You are not safe here, Lee. Momma would ne'er forgive me if anything should happen to you in my care. Charging Bear should be here afore long. He will show you how to adapt as an Indian in our time."

Amazed by her wisdom, I nodded. "Your mother would be proud, and I strongly suspect that she's not the only powerful cunning woman in the family."

" 'Tis wise to remember that it runs in the blood. You have a daughter of your own."

Heather, a cunning woman? Only time would tell, and for the first time since my arrival, I had the feeling that I would see her and Phoebe again. And true to Elenor's word, Charging Bear arrived three days later by foot.

Phoebe's brother was nearly as tall as me. Attired in a loincloth and deer-hide leggings, he wore his hair in the traditional warrior style with the right side of his head shaved. On the left, his black hair stretched the length of his back and was tied with a leather cord.

Two eagle feathers were braided along the side, and the hair on top of his head stood upright.

The kids rushed out to greet him and squealed with delight when he gave them hand-carved toys in the shape of a bear, owl, and a deer. He intertwined his index finger with mine in an Indian handshake and said in fluent English. "My brother, at long last, you have returned home."

Although I had only met him during brief encounters of the dreaming, I felt like I had known him all of my life. "Phoebe's told me much about you."

"Walks Through Mist," he said in Algonquian.

"Walks Through Mist," I agreed.

"You are Paspahegh?"

"I am."

"Few Paspahegh and Arrohateck survive. The Appamattuck have taken me in. They will accept you as my brother."

Like me, Charging Bear had lost his tribe in the English wars. Only with that thought did I realize I stood on what used to be Paspahegh land. Was I near where my mother had drawn her final breath? Thankfully, her death scream did not haunt me. Instead, I was drawn to these people, who had given me shelter when I needed it, and Charging Bear was like finding a long-lost brother.

Before we set off on our journey, Charging Bear visited and had a meal with the family. A few hours later, we waved goodbye, and he led me away from the mist-covered river to a forest trail. A flock of green birds with yellow heads chattered. In awe, I watched the Carolina parakeets.

Charging Bear smiled. "Life must be very different where you come from."

He accepted my story completely. How much time had passed before I had truly believed that Phoebe had traveled across the centuries? "It is. Why do you believe me?"

"Because Walks Through Mist would only marry an honest man. What is your Paspahegh name?"

I fidgeted on my feet before responding, "I only have a child's name."

"For now, does it matter? Does your English name have meaning? Your parents honored you aft you were born."

I had never quite thought of it in that way before. Hell if I knew what Lee or Crowley meant. They were just names like any other. "Crow in the Woods," I said.

Charging Bear nodded his approval, and we continued our journey. Although I was physically fit, I had difficulty keeping his brisk pace. I became drenched, and he barely broke a sweat. After several miles, the trail led to the riverbank. He tossed ferns aside to reveal a dugout underneath. Together, we shoved the canoe from the bank and got in. Charging Bear showed me how to paddle. Going upriver, I felt the ache in my muscles soon after leaving shore. Twice, we came ashore after spotting colonial boats, and at sunset, we landed for the night.

We built a fire, and Charging Bear shared some freshly caught fish and parched cornmeal with me. After eating, I fell asleep in an exhausted heap. The next morning, we set out at dawn. Even after pulling numerous double shifts, I had never worked as hard as paddling a dugout against the current. A few times when we encountered swifter current, we tied lines to the dugout and walked alongside on the banks. In shallow areas, we had no choice but to enter the bone-chilling water and lead the boat as if it were a dog on a leash.

Two days passed before we reached a town of arched houses covered by woven mats. Upon our entrance to the town, the Appamattuck sent up a shrill cry. Men in this society proved their warrior status. Would I be capable of passing their tests? I envisioned myself running a gauntlet, but the chief introduced himself and gave a speech. He welcomed me as Charging Bear's long-lost brother. When Phoebe spoke Algonquian, she usually enunciated words slowly and carefully to help me understand. In my present environment I was at a loss, except for a few words here and there.

The chief finished speaking and motioned for me to accompany a couple of women.

I looked to Charging Bear for guidance.

" 'Tis all right, Crow in the Woods," he said. "You must be cleansed to reclaim your birthright."

For safe keeping, I unstrapped my holster, where I kept my Glock hidden beneath my shirt, and handed it to Charging Bear. "It's a gun from the twenty-first century. Please keep it holstered. I don't want anyone accidentally hurt or killed."

He assured me the weapon wouldn't leave his hands, and I followed the women to the river. For some reason, I thought of Phoebe. She and her mother had gone through a similar purification ritual. Only ten at the time, she had believed the stories from the colony that Indians cooked children and ate them.

We reached the river bank, and the nearest woman told me to undress.

A group of people gathered along the bank, waiting for me to do as I was instructed. After all of the years of being given dreamcatchers, arrowheads, and medicine pouches from tribes that weren't mine, I was suddenly embarrassed to claim my heritage. Was I white or Paspahegh? With renewed determination, I removed my shirt, shoes, and socks.

I hesitated once more, and the men laughed.

Aware they were goading me, I stripped my jeans and briefs and entered the chilly water. Without a stitch of clothing to protect me, the ball-numbing water nearly sent me into shock, and I overheard a round of laughter when I gasped. The women had accompanied me, and one began to wash me.

Laughter surrounded me.

"I can do it myself," I insisted and dunked myself underwater.

Coughing and sputtering, I resurfaced. Although my fingers were nearly frozen, I scrubbed myself. Neither of the women moved any closer. *So cold.* But I continued washing. My mind wandered, and the crow lifted me toward the sky. The wind carried me higher and higher. Phoebe called me back to her.

"Crow in the Woods."

I blinked. It had been a man's voice, not Phoebe's.

Charging Bear stood on the bank, and the women waved for me to follow them. As soon as I was out of the water, I was handed a fringed loincloth and moccasins. Thankfully because of the dreaming, I spared myself further embarrassment and pulled the soft hide between my legs, letting the fringed material flap over a strip of leather that I tied around my waist. I slipped on the moccasins, and a mantle covered with duck feathers and shell beads was draped across my shoulders.

The chief offered me a leather necklace decorated with feathers.

"I'm honored, sir," I said in my best Algonquian.

He placed it around my neck. "Your people welcome your return. Join us on this joyous occasion."

The townspeople had formed two lines, and I traveled the path away from the river. Some bowed their heads and others shouted a salute. I was escorted to the largest longhouse, where another group of people had gathered. Inside the longhouse, about twenty people lined the walls, and I was introduced to each individual.

The chief took his place at the end wall of the house and sat on a wood frame. His two wives sat beside him. I was shown to a mat near the frame on his right. The others were seated on mats in rows in front of the chief. In turn, each person stood and welcomed me. Many gave lengthy speeches that I barely understood.

Following the lectures, we had a feast of venison, fish, corn, and beans. I had never seen so much food in one gathering. After dinner, a pipe was passed around. Barring a few joints in college, I had never been a smoker of any kind, much less a pipe smoker. When my turn came, I puffed quickly and felt a stinging sensation on my tongue. A warrior near me showed me how to take slow breaths.

Not wishing to offend my hosts, I tried again. While the experience wasn't exactly pleasant, I managed to keep from burning my tongue.

"Did the English try to scalp you?" one man asked.

My short hairstyle seemed to be a great source of amusement when I replied in the negative.

Others were curious about my life with the English. Even if I fully understood the concept of time travel myself, I didn't know the correct words to explain it. Instead, as best as I could, I relayed a couple of adventurous police tales to a captive audience.

After the pipe made several rounds, drums beat outside the longhouse. I was escorted to another house where Charging Bear joined me and handed me my Glock. He motioned for me to sit near the fire. "I will show you how to paint your body and face." He brushed and sponged on black and red paints. When he was finished, he handed me an English mirror.

I barely recognized myself.

Charging Bear smiled. "Now we shall dance." He showed me to the door where the people had gathered. The drums beat in rhythm. Men, women, and children danced in a circle around a fire to the tempo of the drum.

Charging Bear showed me the steps. At first, I was awkward, but I copied his movements. Round and round I went. No one made fun of my clumsy gait, and suddenly the steps seemed familiar. My mother had shown me. The beat of the drum lived inside me. My heart pounded, and when the people sent up a shrill cry, I joined them.

At long last, I was home.

When the dancing ended, I was shown to a guest house with turtle shells, gourds, clay pots, and woven baskets. Unlike the Native houses I had seen at historical museums, I spotted a few metal pots that had been obtained from trading with colonists. Wooden frames with mats covered with animal skins and the occasional wool blanket served as beds. An open fire crackled in the middle with a smoke hole cut away in the mat above it.

Thankfully, I was too exhausted to think of all that had happened or my present situation. I would try to contact Phoebe after I had a few hours' sleep. I barely got settled on the sleeping platform when the door rustled.

A woman stood at the entrance, and I sat up. She wasn't just any woman, but a beautiful one with long black hair, black eyes, and full lips. She wore a necklace of glass and shell beads. One breast remained exposed from her deer-hide covering. She moved closer, and my body reacted. "I'm Falling Rain," she said. "I was given the honor to welcome you."

"That won't . . ." My voice cracked, and I stood, clearing my throat. "That won't be necessary," I said with as much conviction as I could muster.

She frowned. "Do I displease you?"

I thought of Phoebe, and how much I wanted to hold her. An awkward moment passed in silence. I reached out and nearly took

Falling Rain into my arms but dropped them back to my sides. "No, it's nothing like that."

She lowered her gaze, and I wondered if she could make sense of my Algonquian. Finally, she turned and left the house. Relieved that I had fought off temptation, I breathed deeply and stepped outside. Except for night sounds, the town was now quiet.

When I reached the river, I sat along the bank. The moon cast a gentle glow, reflecting off the water. Could I enter the dreaming here?

A soft tread of footsteps came from behind, and Charging Bear stood beside me. "Have we offended you, Crow in the Woods?"

"On the contrary, you have honored me in every way possible. I miss my family. I've tried contacting Walks Through Mist but have been unsuccessful."

He gripped my shoulder in understanding. "When you are ready, return to us."

"I will."

Charging Bear left my side. In the distance, an owl hooted and a fish splashed. In my mind's eye, I spotted the flame. *Concentrate.* No familiar mist appeared before me. Why couldn't I break through the barrier?

A gentle breeze blew in my ear. With it, I thought I heard voices. The wind picked up, and the voices faded. *Phoebe.*

8

Phoebe

LIKE ON THE NIGHT LEE HAD VANISHED, Phoebe heard him call her name. The sound carried like a whisper on the breeze. "Lee?" But his voice had already faded. Even she had begun to doubt herself. How many weeks had passed since his disappearance? Three? Or had it been four? Ed no longer called with updates, for there were none. The trail had gone completely cold.

During the day, Phoebe went through the motions of caring for Heather. Each night, she entered the dreaming searching for answers—to no avail. Throughout her life, she had suffered many losses—a son, a husband, even her world—but she had ne'er truly been alone afore. Meg stayed with her when she wasn't at her nursing job. If it had not been for her friend, Phoebe would have forgotten the simplest of tasks—such as sleeping and eating. But many empty hours passed that she was alone.

When Dark Moon and Lightning Storm had died, other women were always nearby to help her through her grief. Her mind was sinking, and she surrendered to her worst thoughts. What if Lee *was* dead? Mayhap his call had been from the afterlife.

She tried not to believe. If he was dead, Ed would have found some clues. So why could she no longer believe that he was still alive?

A tapping sound brought Phoebe out of her melancholy thoughts. The sound came again. *The door.* Only a few days earlier, she would have raced to it, hoping to find Lee on the other side, ne'er giving a thought as to why he simply would not have used his key. Another rap, and Phoebe reached the door, opening it to Shae.

"Phoebe, I'm sorry for not coming sooner. I..."

Shae's eyes were puffy and swollen, reminding Phoebe that she too had loved Lee. She motioned for Shae to step inside. "There was naught you could have done."

Shae dabbed a tissue to her eyes. "I'm not so certain."

"What do you mean?"

"Before his disappearance, Lee came to my office to help me with a patient who had witnessed a murder. Afterward, I asked how everyone was. He looked like he hadn't slept in a week and admitted that he was having nightmares of his mother's death. I tried to tell him that such problems were normal after reliving a childhood trauma. I also urged him to seek professional help, but he said that he couldn't because only the two of us knew the truth about him. I honestly thought he'd tell you..."

Phoebe recalled Lee saying that he had visited Shae. "Tell me what?"

"A couple months ago, a Native American skeleton was uncovered."

"Aye, Lee told me about the skeleton."

"He thought the skeleton was himself."

"Himself?" Phoebe tried to make sense of Shae's words. The skeleton couldn't have been Lee, unless... why hadn't she paid more attention to the signs? The skeleton hadn't been a warning of Lee's death, but that he would return to *their* time. With a sick feeling in her stomach, she placed a hand over her abdomen. Lee would be as lost in the seventeenth century as she had been in the twenty-first. "Tell me all that you know."

"They called in a forensic anthropologist to determine the age of the skeleton. She claimed it was historic..."

Shae's story matched exactly to what Lee had told her, except for the part that he had visited the anthropologist and saw a mirror image of himself in the recreation of the skeleton's countenance. He had confided in Shae, not her. None of that mattered now—only finding Lee. "Shae, will you accompany me to see Dr. Kelsey?"

"You know I will."

The following day, Phoebe carried Heather in a backpack, much like she had carried Dark Moon and Elenor on a cradleboard. Shae met them on campus, and they proceeded to Jan Kelsey's office. After a round of introductions, Jan asked, "I wish we could have met under better circumstances, but what can I do for you, Mrs. Crowley?"

"Please, call me Phoebe."

"If you'll call me Jan."

"Aye. A couple of months ago, my husband worked on a case where a skeleton had been uncovered. You were called in for an evaluation."

"I was, and it's a case that I won't forget. Here, let me show you." Jan led the way from her office to a lab. "Even though the find fell under the jurisdiction of Historic Resources and not the police, I called Lee about it. I thought he'd be interested in seeing our reconstruction of the skull because it's a Native American male who had been buried for over two hundred years. Well, that's only a partial truth. Here, let me show you."

At the back of the lab sat a clay facial reconstruction. Though the black wig had been fashioned in a traditional warrior style, the eyes staring back at her were none other than Lee's. "Lee?"

"The resemblance is uncanny, isn't it?" Jan said. "I thought he might be an ancestor to Lee."

Phoebe stared at Lee's countenance. At least now she had some idea as to where to search for him.

"Phoebe, I've put the girls to bed," Meg said, joining her in the parlor. "Now, are you going to tell me what you've found out?"

"Lee has returned to the seventeenth century."

"How is that possible? I'm having a hard enough time trying to figure out how you got here in the first place."

"As am I, but I must find him and return."

"How?"

"I don't know how, for I don't fully understand how I got here. 'Twas like entering the dreaming, but that time, I traveled physically. If I can discover what was different, I can travel to him."

"Or he can return to you."

Phoebe hadn't thought about that possibility afore.

"What about Heather?" Meg asked.

"If I return to the seventeenth century, she shall accompany me. I will not leave another daughter behind. Will you join me in the dreaming?"

Over the weeks, Meg's fear had faded. She freely joined Phoebe in the dreaming.

The mist became an impenetrable fog, engulfing them. With the spirit dog guiding the way, Phoebe latched onto his collar. Meg walked aside her.

Phoebe found herself in bed, unable to rise. An iridescent dragonfly hovered round her.

Meg tugged on her arm, pulling her to a sitting position. "Get up."

"Nay." She fell back to the bed.

"I've already told Lee not to call here anymore."

Phoebe sat up under her own power. 'Twas the time when she had recalled Dark Moon's death, and she had nearly forsaken Lee. Meg hadn't truly said those words to him. She had said them to get Phoebe's attention. "We must travel much farther, Meg. This is a recent happening."

Meg swallowed. "They kept my people as slaves during the seventeenth century."

"I vow that no harm shall come to you. And many were indentured servants, who were later freed, like my beloved Bess." Phoebe held out her hand, and Meg grasped it.

Together, they continued forward. As they walked, Phoebe felt a long skirt against her legs. Up ahead, the mist thinned. When they emerged, she found herself standing on the bank of a river. 'Twas the James.

Dressed similar to Phoebe, Meg spread her skirt in disbelief. "Where are we?" she asked.

"Near Henry's house." Phoebe followed the river downstream.

Meg's eyes widened with fear. "Are you certain we're still in the living room and haven't traveled through time?"

"Aye. The lasses are asleep in their beds."

"But it seems so real."

" 'Tis the way of the dreaming. Come with me."

Alongside the river, they walked until arriving at a brick house. When Phoebe had lived there, the house had been wood, surrounded by a palisade to keep the Indians out, the very people she most identified with.

Upon seeing them approach, Bess squealed and rushed toward Phoebe with open arms. "Phoebe . . ."

They hugged and cried in each others' arms. Finally, Phoebe stepped back and made introductions.

"Did Mr. Lee bring you here?" Bess asked.

Her heart pounded. "Then you've seen him?"

"Aye. He came here 'bout a month ago, not knowin' how he got here."

"Momma?" Elenor stood inside the door frame of the house. She ran toward Phoebe.

After more hugs and cries, and another round of introductions, they went inside. Phoebe greeted the children. Henry and Bess's son James were on a hunting trip. The group sat in chairs round the parlor.

"I tried to contact you, Momma," Elenor said, "but Lee came instead. Both of us tried to reach you through the dreaming, but he said he wouldn't be successful 'til he was strong enough on his own. Charging Bear took him upriver to the Appamattuck."

Her daughter went on to tell the story of how Lee had arrived and spent several days with them. The times that Phoebe had heard his voice, he had called to her, and where she had felt his presence, he had traveled through time. Now, she knew where to find him. More determined than afore, Phoebe went outside, accompanied by Elenor and Meg. But the hound stood near the bank of the river, where a fog spread. She gripped Elenor's hand. "I'll see you again."

"I know, Momma."

Phoebe embraced her daughter once more. "I love you, Elenor." But the fog engulfed her and Meg. Phoebe blinked. She was back in her own parlor.

Wide-eyed, Meg sat across from Phoebe. "It continues to amaze me."

"I must contact Lee."

"Tonight?"

"Aye."

Meg gave her a warm smile. "I think I'll say goodnight. Say hi to Lee for me."

"I shall."

Again Phoebe entered the dreaming, and this time, she found herself in a moonlit forest. She came to a stream and cast off her shoes, dipping her toes into the cool water. Even the white hound had not accompanied her—and the crow was a day spirit.

Phoebe.

She gazed in the direction of the sound but only spied shadows cast by the moon. Deeper and deeper into the forest she traveled until blackness surrounded her. A breeze kissed her face.

Phoebe.

The gentle wind grew stronger, and she fought against the air-flow. Up ahead, she spotted a light and moved toward it.

A man stood at the center of the light. His hair was slightly longer than the last time she had seen him, and he wore a wool shirt and breechclout. Round his neck was his father's arrowhead and a feathered necklace. Black feathers hung from his ears, and he carried a bow.

"Lee?"

He smiled. "Phoebe, I've been trying to reach you."

For some reason, the wind wouldn't let her reach his side. "And I you. I knew not where to find you."

He reached for her, but the wind buffeted her from side to side. She was like a bird caught in a wind tunnel. He caught her hand and pulled her toward him. The wind was stronger and pulled them apart.

"Lee!"

But she was back in the parlor, and Meg was soon aside her.

"I saw him, Meg."

"Was he all right?"

"Aye, he was fine. He has reclaimed his birthright."

9

Lee

PHOEBE HAD REACHED ME through the dreaming. Although I took comfort in seeing her again, I yearned to hold her. The following morning, I told Charging Bear of my experience and how the wind had kept us apart.

"Have you talked to the wind and asked why it keeps you separate?" he asked.

Talk to the wind? Why did my own culture seem alien to me? Recently, my days were filled with learning how to be Appamattuck. I no longer roomed in the guest house, but had moved in with Charging Bear and his seven-year-old son Strong Bow. Charging Bear had lost two other children during a smallpox outbreak, and his wife had died giving birth to Strong Bow.

Normally, the women taught young sons how to use a bow until they were big and strong enough to accompany the men on a hunt, but Charging Bear had decided not to marry again, and with the help of a few adopted aunts, to instead raise the child himself. He was much too proud a warrior to admit that he still grieved for his wife. In this way we could commiserate together, without acknowledging the true source of our sorrows. As it turned out, his arrangement worked ideally for me because I could learn my lessons alongside Strong Bow.

My awkwardness gave me an inkling of what Phoebe had endured when she first traveled to the twenty-first century. She had lamented over the fact that a six-year-old could read and write better than she could, and I felt inept when a seven-year-old could out-shoot me with a bow and arrow. How much easier it would have been if I could draw my Glock, but I kept the gun safely tucked away on my waist. My woolen shirt nicely covered my gun belt.

In the beginning, I kept slapping my bow arm with the string, creating nasty bruises, but I persevered and got the hang of it. Nearly a month had passed before I successfully hunted my first turkey. Now the time had come to prove my worth. Charging Bear insisted that I attempt to bag a deer.

In order to hunt deer, I wore a stuffed deer head with a skin draped over me. In this way, I approached a grazing doe. My prey immediately looked up, flicking her white tail. I attempted to move my fake deer in a natural manner, but the skin billowed with my movements.

The doe bolted, and Charging Bear doubled over laughing.

More determined than before, I tracked down another doe. I sweltered from wearing the fake deer garb. In my hurry to be rid of it, I shot off an arrow, cleanly missing my target.

As the deer bounded off, Charging Bear snorted another belly laugh at my expense. "You are in too much of a hurry, Crow in the Woods. On the morrow, we shall bring Strong Bow. He will assist you."

Once again, I had been upstaged by a kid.

"Do not be discouraged," Charging Bear said.

"It's difficult relearning everything."

"Aye, but Ahone has given you the task for a reason."

A reason—I only wished Ahone or whoever would reveal what that reason was to me. We started the long walk back to town. I had no real grasp of the distances involved, but we must have traveled several miles. Charging Bear had me lead in order for me to learn the routes. Sometimes, I wondered why. I had traveled through time twice. Who was to say that I was in this time period permanently? Then, I remembered the skeleton, reminding me that I would die in this time period. The thought of not seeing Phoebe or Heather again depressed me further. If I could have blended in with the local colonists, I would have sought out the closest tavern for an ale or two.

After about a mile, Charging Bear tapped my arm in warning. He pointed.

Up ahead, three colonists, carrying flintlock rifles, wandered in our direction. We sought cover in the tall brush and waited until they were well past our hiding spot before returning to the path.

"What would they have done if they had seen us?" I asked.

"Unknown. Some are friendly. Others are not. 'Tis best to be wary."

No doubt Charging Bear expressed wisdom, and the chance sighting made me truly aware of the world I had traveled to. While I had encountered overt racism in the twenty-first century, few wanted me dead simply because I was Indian.

Once back at town, Charging Bear greeted his son, and we had a potpourri meal of corn, beans, and some sort of chewy meat that I was afraid to ask what it might be. Young boys hunted small game, and just about anything that crawled, flew, or slunk ended up in the cook pot. Fortunately, a couple women, including Falling Rain, were tolerant of my lack of hunting and fishing skills and shared their food with me. At the same time, I suspected I was the butt of numerous jokes and expected to be dubbed Rabbit Chaser or Trips Over Own Feet any day now.

At dusk, drums beat rhythmically, and the evening dancing began. Only since my arrival had I learned that each dance told a story. For a short while, I participated, but on this night, my heart wasn't in socializing. Although I wasn't a total outcast here like I had been everywhere except among cops, I longed to see my family. One woman nursed a baby, reminding me of Heather, and even though there were no red-headed women, I kept seeing Phoebe.

I returned to the mat house I shared with Charging Bear and stoked the hearth fire. Since I was alone, I decided to try and reach Phoebe through the dreaming. I stared into the flame and concentrated. I managed to enter the mist easily for a change.

A crow flew overhead. The bird settled on a branch and communicated in clicks and rattles. *You have traveled and now you are seeking where you came from. Why?*

"I wish to speak to Walks Through Mist."

What prevents you?

"I'm not certain, but the last time the wind interfered. Charging Bear says I should speak to it, but how does one talk to the wind?"

Like me. Crow in the Woods, you are capable. The wind can carry you anywhere, like it does me.

"Anywhere?"

I thought I heard the bird laugh. *In time you will understand. Follow me.*

The crow took flight, and I attempted to follow as best as I could. I walked along a path through the forest, when the wind started blowing. The bird buffeted in the turbulence. *Talk to the wind.*

"I must speak with Phoebe—Walks Through Mist."

The wind roared like a raging voice, and the black bird nearly slammed to the ground.

"Why are you angry with me?" I asked the wind.

Another gust nearly swept me off my feet, then the wind died down. The crow settled on a branch and preened his disheveled feathers.

"Crow, I don't understand. What did the wind say?"

You may now see Walks Through Mist.

"Lee?"

Unable to locate Phoebe, I hurried toward where I thought I had heard her voice. Brambles cut my arms, but I ignored the pain.

"Lee." Up ahead stood a white greyhound. Beside the dog was Phoebe dressed in her familiar long green skirt, laced top with metal eyelets, and linen cap. She ran toward me, throwing her arms around my neck. "I missed you."

My mouth pressed against hers. Tears formed in her eyes, and I gently brushed them away. "Phoebe, I have never loved anyone as I do you."

More tears. "I thought you had died."

No longer able to resist her lips, I kissed her in a burning hunger. The separation had been almost more than I could bear. Quickly undressing, we touched and explored each other's bodies before sinking to the ground. Mad with blind lust, I nearly rushed ahead but caught myself. I wanted to savor her. Breathing in her herbal scent, I stroked the length of her body.

Her panting breaths and soft moans were more than I could stand. I clutched her hips and plunged inside her. She opened herself wider. She was all around me, driving me further. With each of my thrusts she arched up to meet me. Our rhythm grew faster and more intense until our energies were spent. Still inside her, I gazed upon her contented face. We kissed and hugged. She possessed me—body and soul. After one more kiss, I rolled to her side.

"Come see Heather. She misses her poppa."

I nodded and reached for my clothes. Instead of a loincloth and woolen shirt, my jeans and T-shirt were piled by my side. Could it be? I had come home. Hurriedly, I dressed and watched Phoebe as she did the same. Hand in hand, we walked along the path until we reached the house.

In the living room, Meg waited with Heather in her arms. "Lee!" She placed my daughter in my arms.

Heather squealed with delight, and I hugged her to my chest.

"Are you home for good?" Meg asked.

Outside, a crow cawed, and the wind picked up, sending a shiver down my spine. Not wanting the moment to end, I glanced around the room at the familiar chairs, coffee table, and sofa. Everything was part of the dreaming. Reluctantly, I handed Heather to Phoebe.

A tear formed in Phoebe's eye. "Lee, please stay."

A gust howled through an open window, and I fought to maintain my own composure. "I wish I knew how. Apparently my work isn't complete, but we'll see each other again. I know that now."

Phoebe held out her hand.

Before I could grasp her slender fingers, I blinked and stared into the flame. I wore a loincloth and woolen shirt, but I believed my words to Phoebe. I had to, or I would not be able to face what was being asked of me.

The following morning, with the help of Charging Bear and Strong Bow, I was once again on the trail of a deer. I was a little more adept at fishing and almost wished we could have worked on that food-gathering technique instead. But Charging Bear insisted that I learn to hunt big game. Unlike most of the men, I felt no need to impress the women with my hunting prowess, but I did understand the need for everyone to contribute their share, if physically capable.

Draped in my fake deer costume, I watched Strong Bow, similarly attired. Already the boy could mimic the movements of a deer, and I tried to copy him when he approached a stag. Even though I had never hunted in my previous life, I wondered if trying to take on a nine-point buck was a sensible idea for two inexperienced hunters.

Charging Bear said nothing, and I hoped that was a good sign.

Before I could think of my next move, the buck charged Strong Bow. The deer trampled the boy and stabbed him with his antlers.

Instead of shooting an arrow, I reached for my Glock and fired. The buck toppled. I replaced my gun in its holster, and we checked Strong Bow. The boy's feet were bruised. He moved them freely, and at a quick glance, I didn't think anything was broken. His left arm had taken the brunt of the buck's antlers. A neat hole pierced cleanly through his arm.

Charging Bear pressed some moss to Strong Bow's arm to control the bleeding, while I wrapped vegetation around the wound. Even though the wound must have hurt like hell, Strong Bow didn't dissolve into tears. No doubt existed in my mind. He was one strong kid.

After the wound was packed, and the bleeding halted, Charging Bear said, "You did well, Crow in the Woods."

"I cheated, but it's the weapon I know. Hopefully I'll learn how to use a bow before I'm out of ammunition." And twice in as many months, I had unintentionally killed a deer. At least this one would feed and clothe people instead of being dumped in some landfill.

Several women greeted us when we returned to town with the injured Strong Bow and deer carcass. One older woman saw to Strong Bow's injury. Pleased with my hunting progress, the other women immediately started processing the deer. The fact that I had shot the deer with my Glock didn't seem to alter their perceptions of my contribution. Several warriors had flintlocks, and they viewed my gun as a variation on the colonial weapon.

That evening, I sought Phoebe through the dreaming. As before, Crow interpreted what the wind said, but I found the entire process a little easier. As I traveled, I felt a tightness around my neck. I wore a suit and tie, like I had so many times working as a detective. The suit felt heavy and uncomfortable, and I loosened the tie. Already I had become accustomed to wearing deer hide and moccasins.

But Crow led me to an office. Ed sat behind a desk. When he looked up, shock spread across his face. "Lee?" He stood and thumped me on the back. "Lee, where have you been? We've been looking all over for you."

"I'm sorry, Ed."

"Sorry, what do you mean you're sorry? You go missing for six weeks, suddenly reappear, and that's all you have to say."

"I don't think I'm coming back."

"Not... I don't understand." His eyes flared in anger. "What about Phoebe and Heather? You stupid fool, you can't just give up on everything that you've worked so hard for. Who's paying you? You're the last one I would have expected to sell out."

"I haven't sold out to anyone, but my life is more complicated than any of us could have guessed."

"For Christ's sake, Lee. Tell me what's happened. We're more than partners. I thought we were friends."

"We are. I think that's why I'm here now."

His anger faded with the realization of what I was trying to tell him. Over the years, we had been witness to some horrific scenes from mangled bodies to charred corpses. In all that time, I had never seen him lose control, but tears entered his eyes.

He gave me a bear hug, like a father to his son. "You stupid bastard. I never thought it would end like this."

I stepped back and shook his hand. "Bye, Ed."

"Will I ever see you again?"

"I don't know, but I must see Phoebe before I leave." I turned, and the office faded. Crow guided me to what had once been my home.

Unlocking the door with my key, I entered the darkened house in which only a small lamp was lit. Almost as if I had been working late, I crept toward the bedroom. Through the partly open door, I saw Phoebe sound asleep in our bed. I closed the door behind me, stripped down to my underwear, and joined her. Our relationship had certainly matured over the years. Though I still desired her like crazy, my first thought was to let her rest. Content just to breathe in her scent, I snuggled next to her, but my movement woke her.

"Lee?" She touched my face to see if I was truly beside her.

"I'm here for now. I just want to enjoy being next to you."

She switched on a light and sat up. Her long red hair was in disarray, but for some reason, the modern nightgown seemed out of place. I grasped her hand and kissed her fingers. "Walks Through Mist," I said in Algonquian.

Though she tried to be brave, tears formed in her eyes. She brushed them away, hoping that I hadn't seen them. "Which time is ours?" she asked.

The skeleton had warned me. "I'm sorry, I didn't tell you everything. The skeleton we found some time ago—it was me."

"Shae told me," she whispered.

I should have known that I could count on Shae. Someday I would need to thank her for telling Phoebe when I hadn't been strong enough to do so myself. For now, though, I told Phoebe about my encounter with Ed, Charging Bear, and how his son had been injured by the buck.

"Many warriors were hurt by the hunted."

So many times, she had told me stories about the seventeenth century, but that's what they had been—mere stories. Now, I lived it, and they had become reality. In the twenty-first century, I hadn't known my heritage until Phoebe entered my life, but in the seventeenth century, I felt out of place. Charging Bear encouraged me, but I couldn't live without my family. "I want you and Heather to join me."

"I don't know how."

I had traveled through time twice and Phoebe once. What made those occasions different from the dreaming? "We'll find a way."

She wrapped her arms around my neck. " 'Til then, we will share moments like this."

Only with our pact did I truly realize, the seventeenth century was now my home.

10

Phoebe

"PHOEBE, MAY I COME IN?"

In the past, a personal visit from Ed would have ripped at her heart. With Heather on her hip she opened the door, allowing him to enter. "You have news of Lee."

Without so much as looking at Heather, he gazed at Phoebe gravely. "Not solid evidence. In fact, I don't quite know how to explain it."

"You saw him last night."

His brow furrowed. "How . . . ? How did you know?"

"He told me."

"He said he was going to see you, but none of it seemed quite real. I thought I had dreamed it."

"You did. He hailed you in the only way he could."

Ed's mouth dropped open. "Phoebe! First Lee, now you. I can't figure out what in hell is going on. He said that in all probability I wouldn't see him again. Is he dead?"

"To this world, he may be."

"You're not making much sense. Either he is or he isn't. In either case, I need proof. And how can you stand there smiling at me if he's dead?"

"I'm smiling to hide my tears."

Ed hugged her and Heather. "I'm sorry, Phoebe. I didn't mean to make you more upset than you already are. I'm just trying to make sense of what's happened."

When she had arrived in the twenty-first century, Lee had been skeptical too. "I want to believe your story, but there is no evidence," he had said. For a moment, Phoebe entertained the idea of explaining the dreaming to Ed. Shae knew about it, and even Meg, but they were intertwined in the circle. Lee had said goodbye to Ed for a reason. That way of life was no longer part of Lee. In the coming days, she would be tested. She must stay strong and believe that she and Heather would join him in the seventeenth century.

"Ed, he came to you as a friend. Accept his visit for what it was."

"If I do that, then I must accept the fact that he's dead." He shook his head. "I don't believe it—not without a body."

A shudder coursed through her, and she debated how much to tell him. "Some months ago, a skeleton was uncovered."

"I don't see what that has to do with any . . . the skeleton was a Native American man."

"Aye. Talk to the anthropologist about what she discovered. If you still have questions afterwards, then contact me again."

Like a protective father, he placed his hand on her shoulder. "Phoebe, if you need anything, please, don't hesitate to call me."

"I shall, but I have Meg and Heather with me."

He turned and went down the walkway to his car.

If Ed had come any earlier, she would have been devastated, but she had also seen Lee the night afore, and she would continue to seek him through the dreaming 'til they could be together again.

The following afternoon, Phoebe traveled to Shae's office. How many times had she gone there for therapy sessions? Through hypnosis, Shae had helped her recall her memories from the seventeenth century. She owed Shae to inform her of the latest event.

When she arrived, Shae hadn't finished with her last patient of the day. Phoebe waited in the outer office, flipping through out-of-date magazines. Her mind wasn't on the pretty pictures but Lee's words. On the occasions they had traveled physically through time, what was the difference?

"Phoebe?" Shae quickly said goodbye to her patient, then ran for a tissue. "Oh God, you found him. Don't say it. He's dead. You wouldn't have made a personal visit otherwise."

"Shae . . ." Phoebe stood. "Pray let us talk."

Shae escorted Phoebe into her office and closed the door behind her. She dabbed her eyes with the tissue. "I'm sorry. That wasn't fair of me. It's just . . . just . . ."

Phoebe squeezed Shae's hand. "You can say it. You still love him. That's why I came to tell you what I know in person."

"Not many women would be as kind as you to an ex."

"I know the love betwixt the two of you has changed."

Shae dabbed her eyes once more and collected herself. "I should be comforting you—not the other way around. Please—tell me what's happened."

"Last night, Lee came to Ed and me through the dreaming. He has said goodbye to Ed."

Shae bit her lip afore speaking. "I don't get it."

"It means he's not returning to this way of life."

"Then, he has returned to the seventeenth century?"

"Aye, and when we discover how we have traveled, Heather and I will join him."

Shae's brow furrowed as if attempting to take in what she had been told. "Do you think he'll say goodbye to me too?"

"When the time is right."

"I don't know whether to be relieved or cry." Shae hugged her. "Coming here couldn't have been easy for you. Thank you for doing so. I hope you'll keep me informed."

"I shall."

Parting ways, they said goodbye.

Over the next several days, Phoebe contacted Lee through the dreaming. Or he sought her first. But they talked, shared meals, went for walks, and made love—much as they had afore Lee had returned to the seventeenth century. Strong Bow had recovered from his injuries, and Lee had hunted his first deer using a bow and arrows. When he told her the news, his proud smile reflected that he had accepted how things had come to pass.

"What if I'm unsuccessful in returning to you?" she asked.

"We'll find the answer," he assured her.

She wished she could be as certain. "When I traveled to this century, you called to me."

A thoughtful expression crossed his countenance. "There could be a connection. Your daughter called to me, except...who would have called to me when I first traveled to the twentieth century?"

No one. Another path that led nowhere. They must be overlooking something significant.

Lee grasped her hand. "We *will* figure it out and be together again. Remember, I used to be a detective. It's a matter of fitting the clues together and discovering the answers."

Afore she could respond, she heard the crow caw and the wind rustled the drapes. Anytime Lee appeared to her through the dreaming, those two elements accompanied him. Like her hound, the crow was his guardian spirit. Of that, she was certain, but the meaning of the wind eluded her. Sometimes, it was peaceful. Other times, it blew like a gale. Their time grew short. She kissed him on the lips, and he vanished.

On the following eve, Meg joined Phoebe in the dreaming. As they entered the Appamattuck town, the drums beat. Phoebe's heart quickened. Beside Lee stood Charging Bear. Though years had passed since she had last seen her brother, she recognized his broad shoulders. "*Mat*," she said. Brother. She hugged him and stepped back. "Please meet my friend, Meg. Meg, Charging Bear."

"A charming African," he said with a smile.

"Born in Virginia," Meg replied, "and you speak English."

"Aye. My mother and sister taught me. 'Tis been handy to know o'er the years."

The other Appamattuck greeted them. After a round of introductions, they feasted. During the dancing, Phoebe could no longer hold back. So many years had gone by since she had last taken part. She moved to the drum's tempo, showing Meg the steps in a circle round the fire.

From the sidelines, Lee watched her. No longer cropped short, his hair covered the back of his neck. He wore a woolen shirt, a breechclout, and moccasins. How different he looked from the man who had worn a suit and tie nearly every day—but during the dreaming, she had often envisioned him as a warrior. Only now, the Appamattuck *were* his world.

Phoebe left the sacred circle and joined Lee. "I have gone o'er in my head about what differed the first time you traveled. Mayhap your mother sent you from harm. She knew the ways of *wisakon*. Like a cunning woman, she might have known magic as well."

He reached a tender finger to her cheek and traced the length of her face. "If you had suggested such a thing a couple of years ago, I would have thought you were mentally ill."

"And now?"

"You and the others here have shown me that I knew very little about the world. I'll see if I can contact my mother through the dreaming."

"E'en if she can offer no aid, 'twould be good for you to know her." His brow furrowed, and she gripped his hand. "If you come to know her, mayhap you will recall more than her death."

"That would be nice," he agreed.

He glanced beyond her, and Phoebe turned to see what he was watching. Charging Bear had introduced Meg to Strong Bow. Behind them, she saw the hound, and she turned to kiss Lee goodbye. The dreaming ne'er gave them enough time together.

Phoebe blinked. Meg sat across from her in the living room.

Her friend smiled. "You never told me that your brother is handsome."

"I ne'er thought of him in such a light."

Meg broke into a wide grin. "And he's not married."

"He lives in the seventeenth century," she reminded her friend.

"Details. You contact Lee through the dreaming. I don't see why I can't do the same."

"Meg, the dreaming is not a game. I contact Lee that way because I have no other choice."

Meg slid into the seat aside her. "Phoebe, I know it's not a game. I only want to see Charging Bear again. It's been a long time since I thought any man could be special."

Worried that her friend might get hurt, Phoebe said, "If you continue to accompany me in the dreaming, there is a danger. You are of this time."

"And you may be too. I also want to be there for my friend, in case she needs me."

Phoebe smiled. "I was so very lucky that our paths crossed when I came to this time."

Accompanied with Meg and the lasses, Phoebe traveled south of Richmond to locate the home of the Appamattuck. Anytime a bridge spanned the James, she thought how easy the river was to cross compared to navigating it by dugout. In some areas, little had changed. Trees hugged the banks, but the marinas quickly reminded her what century she was in. Near the town of Hopewell, they located a historical marker for Opposunoquonuske alongside a major road. "She was the *weroansqua*," Phoebe said.

"A weroan-what?" Meg asked.

"*Weroansqua*—female chief. She retaliated after Lord de la Warr destroyed the Paspahegh town. The English sought revenge and burned her town."

Even though the day was hot, Meg rubbed her arms and shivered. "I don't know how you lived through such a time."

"I had no choice, and many died."

"Shall we continue? If she was run out, we won't find the Appamattuck here."

"Aye."

They drove on to Petersburg. Some of the town had run-down brick buildings, but Old Towne had a quaint charm of antique stores and gift shops, celebrating the history of the area. Even then, many of the shops remained empty. What had she been thinking? Like the Arrohateck and Paspahegh, the Appamattuck had been annihilated. They had survived a century beyond the other tribes, but there would be no locating them in the modern world.

"I was a fool to bring you and the lasses here," Phoebe said.

Meg squeezed her arm. "Don't give up. You'll find him."

After lunch at a delicatessen, Phoebe carried Heather on her back, and they walked along a trail near the Appomattox River. The waterline was low and rocks projected above the surface. Sycamore trees surrounded them, and they strolled along the path through the shrubby vegetation of tall grasses. Warblers flitted through the branches, and hummingbirds sipped nectar from orange trumpet-shaped flowers. On the trail's border, large white flowers bloomed with a bright red center.

"What a beautiful flower," Meg said.

" 'Tis swamp rose mallow. The leaves and roots are used for soothing dysentery."

Meg cracked a grin. "You know all of them, don't you?"

"Aye. 'Twas my duty as a cunning woman."

"I thought I had learned a lot about health care when I became a nurse, but your knowledge puts mine to shame."

"Why shame?"

"They don't teach anything about herbs or plants in nursing school."

Tiffany ran on the trail ahead and pointed at a heron fishing along the river edge. A dragonfly landed on Meg's arm. Her friend giggled, and the insect flew away. 'Twas beautiful scenery, but that hadn't been the reason why they had come to this place. *Lee.* Phoebe's heart ached. Except for the dreaming, the distance in time was too great. If only she could find some evidence that he had been here.

Ready to turn back, Phoebe felt a breeze brush her cheek, almost as if she were being lightly caressed. In the gentle wind, she could almost imagine him calling her name. "Lee?"

"Do you sense something?" Meg asked.

The feeling that had seized her vanished as quickly as it had come. " 'Tis gone now. There's naught here." Disappointed, Phoebe headed back in the direction of the car.

"Phoebe . . ." Meg caught up with her and called for Tiffany to join them. "You will be together again. I *know* that."

Aware that her friend's words had been meant to cheer her, Phoebe wished she could manage a smile. Instead, an inner voice warned her that all of her strength would be called upon in the coming days. In a sense of defeat, she returned to the car in silence.

After driving home, Phoebe went through the normal motions for the remainder of the day. She nursed and fed Heather, changed her diapers, and told her a bedtime story. When the lasses were both safely in bed, she and Meg entered the dreaming. They traced their steps along the same path they had earlier in the day. Now mat-covered houses stood in the distance.

They continued toward the town. By the time they reached it, Meg was immediately drawn to Charging Bear, but Phoebe couldn't locate Lee. She followed the hound. He led her on an erratic path through the town. A couple of women stirred a cook pot and chatted, while other women weeded. Men made arrowheads and nets.

At the edge of town, she spotted the crow in the tree. "Lee?"

"Phoebe . . ."

"Lee, where are you?" She whirled around, and he stood afore her. Her arms went round his waist, and they kissed.

"I thought I reached you earlier."

She *had* heard him call her name. "I wasn't certain I had found the town."

"You did."

For some reason, she felt awkward and had no clue as to why. "Lee—"

"Phoebe, it'll be a while before I'll be able to talk to you again."

Her fear had come to pass. "Why?"

"I must become a part of my people."

"Has the tribe not already accepted you?"

"They have, but I need to know who *I* am."

For the past three months, Phoebe had attempted to remain strong, but her world crumbled. *He really wasn't coming back.* She failed to notice Lee's arms going round her. Like a frightened child, she clung to him. For ages, she stood there, hanging on tight.

Lee kissed her. "I promise—"

She pressed her fingers to his lips. "Don't make vows that you cannot keep."

"But I do promise that I'll return for you and Heather."

The words had been uttered, and she feared they would only bring bad luck. So lost and alone, she clasped him tighter and listened to the steady rhythm of his heart, but the wind picked up, and they were thrown apart.

"Lee!" Phoebe struggled to reach his hand. She blinked and stared into the candle flame.

Meg sat across from her. "What happened?"

"He's gone."

11

Lee

I HAD GIVEN PHOEBE MY MESSAGE with a heavy heart. Over the past six months, I had been instructed in the ways of the Appamattuck. Though I had a long way to go, I had learned much. I wasn't proficient in any of my tasks. Far from it, but I was confident that in time I would learn the necessary skills, for I could approximate the time of day by the sun, follow tracks, estimate distances, fish and hunt, and I was beginning to make tools by hand.

The one thing I had bypassed was to go through the *huskanaw* as adolescent boys did to become men. Because I had returned to my roots as an adult, no one expected me to partake in the grueling ordeal that covered many months in the wilderness. Hell, just a few years shy of forty, I was nearly regarded as an elder in this society. Even though I had remained fit, the rigors of the *huskanaw* were not something I would choose to endure. But I wanted to participate in some sort of initiation and discover my adult name.

My wishes were well known among the people and met with their approval. Even though I would not undergo the *huskanaw*, my chosen path would not be an easy one. In preparation, Charging Bear told me to fast and pray. I had never been much of a praying man and wondered to whom I should pray. Ahone the Great Spirit? Or the Christian God as my adoptive parents had taught me? Caught between cultures my entire life, I found it easier in day-to-day life to ignore all religious teachings. But the Appamattuck had taught me that spirituality was an individual matter. Because of what

I had witnessed since meeting Phoebe, I approached the ceremony with an open mind. Ultimately I sought the four winds as I had often seen Phoebe do.

I started by facing the east and held out my hands with my palms facing up. My people had often given thanks for the new day in such a way. I faced the south and promised myself that I would devote myself to the good of the tribe. I turned west. In the shadow of the setting sun, not only would I commit myself to the tribe but also give back in whatever way I could. Finally, I faced north. I would accept what had gone before and reconcile with the past, which would give me harmony and return me to the east.

For some reason I stood motionless, contemplating what I had just done. By facing the four winds, I had made a circle. Everything was a circle—the days, the seasons, life. *Time?* Unsure what had hit me, I comprehended the sacred circle. My chosen path was the correct one, and I would learn much in the coming days. Ready to meet what lay ahead, I stepped out of the circle.

Resembling a ghostly apparition, a *kwiocos* met me. The *kwiocosuk* were regarded by the English as priests. They were much, much more. Not only were they spiritual leaders, but they were medicine men and tribal councilors too. Charging Bear had informed me they were spirits in the form of a man. This man was painted black and stood a couple of inches shorter than me. His head was shaved on the sides. In the center his black hair stood upright. Instead of a simple loincloth, he wore a cloak that resembled a baggy shirt made from deer hide. Around his waist hung a leather bag, which no doubt held his herbs and tobacco.

"Are you ready?" he asked.

"I am."

"Then follow me." He led me from town to the forest.

The *kwiocosuk* lived on the perimeters of town in the forest, but he wasn't leading me to the *quiocosin*, or the temple. Instead, we traveled farther into the forest until arriving at a cleared section where we joined another *kwiocos*. A fire burned in the center.

"Your name?" the first *kwiocos* asked.

"Crow in the Woods," I replied, even though he was fully aware of my name.

His dark eyes met mine, almost as if he could see through me and into my soul. "Your mother grieves; for Crow in the Woods is dead." He turned to the fire, and the *kwiocosuk* sang.

While my knowledge of Algonquian had expanded exponentially since my arrival, I couldn't make out their words. During the *huskanaw* boys died symbolically and returned to the town as men. I presumed the death of Crow in the Woods was something similar.

The song ended, and the second *kwiocos* stepped over to my side. He held a wooden bowl in his hands. "Are you prepared to cast out the past and relearn your life anew?"

Uncertainty crossed my mind.

Picking up on my change of heart, the *kwiocos* asked, "Do you doubt what is being asked of you?"

"I do," I admitted.

"Because you were raised by the *tassantassas*, I will grant you leeway. Why do you question yourself?"

"I cannot imagine casting out my wife and daughter."

"If they are meant to be in your new life, they shall be."

Simple as that, and I no longer questioned. The circle *would be* complete.

The *kwiocos* handed me the wooden bowl. "Drink."

The other *kwiocos* sang and gave an offering of tobacco to the fire. I raised the bowl to my lips and took a few sips. The tea tasted bitter. I lowered the bowl.

"All of it," he said.

Was the potion really any worse than a person's first beer? Pretending the drink was beer, I finished the rest but had difficulty to keep from gagging. Overhead, clouds billowed, and I heard the cry of the hawk.

Before long, the last rays of the sun descended in the sky, and I felt a little dizzy. Music, a recorder playing, sounded in the distance. I had heard the notes before but couldn't recall where. The instrument changed to a piano. I thought it was Beethoven but couldn't be certain.

Suddenly, a stream of people poured in. Everyone I had ever known seemed to be present—my mother and father, my adoptive parents, my cousins, Shae, Phoebe and Heather, Meg, Ed, even kids and teachers I had known in school and had not seen since. All talked at the same time, and I couldn't make out what any of them were saying.

My mother, Snow Bird, stepped forward and wailed. "My son is dead."

What I was seeing couldn't be real. Hadn't she been the one who died? I had promised Phoebe to try and reach my mother through the dreaming, but this experience was nothing like that. Could I reach her now? I extended my arm. "Mother."

Blinking back her tears, she gazed in my direction but didn't appear to see me. "The vengeful spirit Oke tricks me. I hear my son's voice on the wind, but it's not possible, for he is dead."

My adoptive mother, Natalie Crowley, joined Snow Bird. She was no longer the frail, bone-thin form that I had buried, but a vibrant woman in her forties with dark brown hair. "He's not dead. He was found wandering in the woods. I thought you had abandoned him, and I raised him as if he were my own flesh and blood."

Snow Bird hugged her. "I would never have abandoned him."

They stood before me chatting. How could this be? Neither knew the other's language.

"Mom."

Both women looked in my direction, but Phoebe stepped between them, wearing a cloak about her shoulders. Instead of her youthful appearance, she had deep wrinkles in her face, and her red hair had gone white.

"Phoebe?"

" 'Tis the wind."

"The wind?" Through the crow I had spoken with the wind during the dreaming. Is that what she meant?

The group of people embraced each other and sobbed in unison. "He's dead."

The *kwiocos* had said Crow in the Woods was dead. Was Lee dead as well? The voices vanished, and I felt myself falling. I struggled to remain upright, only to be pulled in another direction. I shifted and again I was thrust another way. Finally I gave up. Instead of falling, I floated. Moonlight showered me in a cool warmth.

By morning, clouds gathered and pelted me with rain. Wet and shivering, I waited until the day nearly ended when a *kwiocos* gave me another tea. Once again, I drank the concoction. After downing the bitter drink, I set out and roamed the forest. My moccasins suddenly felt heavy, and I kicked them off.

The voices returned. Only this time, they belonged to the trees and animals. A large branch had broken away from a sycamore tree, and I heard it crying. "What happened?" I asked.

"A gust swooped through and snapped my branch away."

I inspected the damage. A bird's nest had fallen with the downed branch. Inside the nest were four down-covered, lifeless nestlings. A mother robin cried for her babies over my shoulder.

"Why do I keep seeing death?"

"Death is part of you," said the tree, "and it is necessary for re-birth."

As a detective, how many deaths had I investigated? Over the years, I had lost count of the bodies. I had viewed them in every state of decomposition and delivered the news to their grieving families. On one occasion I had killed a man myself. That time I recalled the deaths of my people, only to blink back the vision to see the suspect in front of me holding a gun. Both Ed and I had fired. Ballistics verified that my bullet had been the fatal one.

From a distance, a mountain lion approached me. Nimble-footed, she moved with a flowing grace. Her eyes and ears remained alert, yet she stalked as if performing a ballet. Spellbound, I watched her until I realized that she was merely a shadow. Dancing shadows surrounded me, and I joined them. First, we danced to recorder music, then the piano. Finally, came the rhythmic drums. The cycle continued. I was part of all of them, yet none of them.

On the third day, the *kwiocos* asked, "Do you now understand?"

Uncertain that I believed the significance of what I had been seeing, I contemplated his question. Like the shadows, one or both of the *kwiocosuk* were always with me. "Crow in the Woods died with the Paspahegh."

For the first time, he smiled.

"Lee Crowley was born," I said.

He handed me the wooden bowl. "Your wife grieves. Lee Crowley is dead."

And for the third time, I drank the bitter potion. The skeleton unearthed might have been mine, but he had no longer been Lee, for I was dead. I returned to the forest and wandered along. Shortly, I came across a white greyhound. The dog's long legs and sleek frame were made for coursing. Having seen him often during the dreaming with Phoebe, I followed. Perhaps he would take me to her. As I neared his side, he raced off.

Huffing and puffing, I chased after him but couldn't keep up. I lost the greyhound and bent down to see if I could locate any tracks. Nothing. Disappointed, I stood.

Once more, I wandered through the forest. Branches scraped my arms. Because I had kicked off my moccasins the day before, brambles cut into my legs. Up ahead, I heard whining. I followed the sound and located the greyhound.

The dog gazed at a dead crow on the ground.

Death, again. I picked up the lifeless body and held it in my hands. Was the crow meant to be me? I *was* dead. I carefully placed the dead crow on the ground and covered the body with leaves.

The greyhound took off again with his feet barely touching the ground.

I followed, and he led me to a tunnel in the midst of the forest covered in a rainbow of light. The shadows performed their dance inside. I moved toward them, when one of the shadows waved for me to follow.

I stepped inside only to be met with a blast of wind. At first gales howled around me, then they were at my back, blowing me farther and farther inside. After several feet, the wind grew more intense. I reached a branch in the passageway. To my right, I spotted my birth parents.

My mother reached out. "Crow in the Woods."

Before I could respond, she screamed and sank to the ground. My father bent down and stared at my mother's body. "I couldn't save her." He raised his eyes and handed me an arrowhead. "Nor could I save you."

The wind pushed at my back, and I clenched the arrowhead in my hand. On and on I went until I came to another passageway. My adoptive parents stood before me. I showed them the arrowhead.

"You carried it with you when you were found," my mother said.

"I hadn't realized how much a part of me it is. It's who I am."

My dad smiled. "Nonsense, Lee. You're a detective."

"A detective? Why would a detective need an arrowhead?"

"A detective doesn't. I'm so proud of you."

Another gust hit me, and my parents were gone. I struggled to keep from floating away. At another branch, I briefly saw Shae, but my momentum didn't stop until after I blew past her. I groped around in the dark. Certainly, I would see Phoebe next.

The tunnel was more like a maze, and that feeling of being lost and abandoned crept through me. Passageway after passageway—I had no idea which way I was going. Nothing gave me a clue as to the way out. I fought to remain calm and kept moving forward. What seemed like hours passed, and I still had no clue how to find the way out.

"Lee."

"Phoebe?" I called.

Finally, I spotted a light and knew what I must do. Once I reached the light, I would find her, so I raced toward it. I kept running and running, but the light stayed the same distance. Out of breath, I halted. The light taunted me. Why couldn't I reach it?

In my hand, I still clenched the arrowhead. I traced a finger over it, feeling tiny ridges where pieces of antler had been chipped away to form it.

"Lee."

"Phoebe, tell me how I can get out of here."

No answer came. Had I really heard her voice or had I become delirious?

Again, I had that overwhelming sensation of being lost. *Fight it.* The feeling was nothing more than a childish fear. Then, it dawned on me. How was the endless tunnel that much different than the mist during the dreaming? When I was a two-year-old and captured in the mist, I had been alone and afraid. I moved forward.

Phoebe had been known as Red Dog, and I had left her side and wandered away. Had the crow guided me? A gentle breeze rippled through the tunnel. Could the wind help me? I summoned it to guide me.

A tailwind gusted, carrying me toward the light. *Phoebe, we'll be together again soon.*

Closer and closer, the light brightened, nearly blinding me. I pressed my hands to my eyes. No use, the light failed to dim. I passed from the tunnel over a precipice into the glaring light. Downward, I sailed. I called for the wind, but my body was no longer my own.

The light faded, and the sensation of moving ended. Beneath a night sky, I counted the stars, realizing all had a name and purpose. The moss was cool under my feet. From a nearby tree, an owl hooted, and near a stream, frogs croaked. Everything around me was alive. In awe of my discovery, I stood still, watching the stars and moon until they faded to a rosy morning light. The day creatures awakened. A cardinal trilled, and a crow cawed.

A man, his body painted black and with a partially shaved head, approached me. "What is your name?"

"My name?" I asked. He repeated the question, and I searched my memory. I could recall nothing but standing under the starlit sky and waiting for dawn. "I don't know my name."

The man smiled. "Come. You will relearn that which you have lost."

12

Phoebe

THE WATER GLASS SLIPPED FROM PHOEBE'S hand and crashed to the floor.

"Phoebe?"

"He's dead," Phoebe cried.

Meg rushed over and held her. She shoved the stray hair from Phoebe's eyes. "What was it you felt?"

Tears streaked her cheeks. "Lee's gone. He's dead."

"How can you know?"

"I felt him die." She barely noticed Meg taking her arm and guiding her to the living room and over to the sofa.

Meg sat aside her. "I'm not certain I understand. What happened?"

"I don't know—only that he's gone." Phoebe reached for the phone. "I need to tell Shae."

Meg grasped the phone from her hand and replaced it in its cradle. "Shae can wait. You need to take care of yourself and Heather first."

When would she wake up from the nightmare? After her loss of Lightning Storm, Lee had been the one to help her feel again. She choked back a sob. What would she do now?

Day and night blended. Phoebe had difficulty keeping track of which was which. Meg stayed with her when she wasn't at her job. But her friend had already taken too much time from work that her boss was no longer sympathetic. Phoebe went through the motions of caring for Heather, but even her daughter, young as she was, could tell something was amiss.

She struggled through the hours. At Meg's request, she continued to participate in the dreaming, but each time, the answer remained the same. Lee's voice had vanished.

"Don't give up hope," Meg repeated after each session.

"I won't," Phoebe vowed, but she failed to believe. She would have known *somehow* if he were still alive. Then one eve, she entered in the dreaming on her own. The mist engulfed her, and she accompanied her spirit dog. As she walked, a long skirt brushed her legs. Up ahead, the mist thinned, and when she emerged she found herself standing on the bank of the James River.

She recognized the gentle roll of the land and headed downstream 'til coming to a familiar brick house. "Elenor?" she shouted.

Bess spotted her and shrieked with joy. With open arms, her friend ran toward her, and they hugged when they met.

"Bess, 'tis good to see you," Phoebe said.

"What's wrong?" Bess asked, stepping back.

She should have known better than to think pretending enthusiasm could hide anything from Bess. "I have been unable to contact Lee. I believe he's dead."

Bess escorted her inside. "We haven't seen him in months, not since he went with your brother to the Appamattuck town."

"Aye. I've spoken with him through the dreaming, but his voice has gone silent."

Once inside, Elenor squealed, but she quickly picked up on Phoebe's sadness. "Momma?"

Bess explained what had happened.

"I can try and contact Charging Bear," Elenor suggested.

"Pray do. Thank you, Elenor." Phoebe grasped her daughter's hands. "Not a day goes by that I don't think of you."

"I know, Momma, and I'm happy to help in any way I can."

"And your husband?"

Elenor shook her head. "No word."

She had hoped her daughter would be spared the anguish of losing a husband. Before she could hug Elenor, she found herself in her own home facing a candle. 'Twas the way of the dreaming sometimes. Over the next few days, she attempted to contact Elenor and Lee with no luck. As Ed had said, there was no body, therefore no proof. From the beginning, the skeleton had been a warning. It haunted her. *What if it was Lee?* At least someone had cared enough to give him a proper Paspahegh burial.

For the first time, she truly thought of Lee as being dead. Why couldn't she cry? His suits hung in the closet. But he hadn't reported for police duty in several months now. Should she give the suits away?

Afore now, the dreaming had kept her hopes alive and the ability for her to face each day. Now what? She had cried her tears when Lee had gone missing, and like when she had lost Lightning Storm, she had to remain brave for her daughter's sake. But when Lightning Storm was killed, she had been surrounded by others to help her in her grief. Now, with the exception of Meg, she was alone.

13

No Name

WITH THE HELP OF THE *kwiocosuk*, I recalled my experience with the jimsonweed tea, which was spiritually enlightening. My memory slowly returned. I contemplated Lee Crowley's life as if viewing it from the outside, rather than from within. My symbolic death had been necessary in order for me to move forward and understand what it meant to be Paspahegh. Although the Appamattuck had graciously taken me in and accepted me as one of their own, in this century, I was not the only member of my tribe. The few remaining alive had been forced from their land, and my ultimate mission would be to seek them out.

Before I embarked on such a mission, I pondered Lee's life in greater detail. Caught between worlds, he had never quite fit in either. His adoptive parents had tried to show him his culture with gifts of Indian trinkets and artifacts, but they could never have guessed the tribe he originated from. As a result, they had groped blindly in their teachings.

In college, he had married his high school sweetheart. *Shae...*

I caught myself. My reflection was meant to be *his* life. He had been heartbroken when she had divorced him. Neither would understand the real reason for their separation until many years later. After I had completed the next step in my life, we would be friends again.

With fondness, I remembered Phoebe. No matter how hard I attempted to think of her as part of Lee's past, I couldn't imagine a future without her. She had been my light and love, and we had a daughter. In time, I hoped the passion we shared would be ours yet again. "I have failed," I admitted to the *kwiocos*.

"In what way?" he asked.

"I can view all of Lee's life as being separate from me, except for my wife and daughter."

He gave me a thoughtful look without staring. "Have you not considered the possibility that you are bringing them into this life as well?"

For a moment I had feared he would say that I needed to repeat my jimsonweed experience, as boys who remembered their past life too soon had to repeat the *huskanaw* experience. Instead, I simply needed to complete my transition before contacting her. "I hoped that might be the case," I said.

"You have been given a special gift."

"I've known from the beginning that I have traveled through time for a reason. But it can also be a curse."

"Why do you say that?"

How could I tell him that the way of life for the Appamattuck that I had freely joined would be gone in less than a century? "Because I know of tragedies that will come to pass."

"Perhaps that knowledge will be useful in a way to help your people."

"How?"

"Like your brother Charging Bear, you speak both languages. Unlike Charging Bear, you have lived their way of life. You might be able to bridge the gap to help avoid misunderstandings."

"That way of life was very different from the colonials."

"Did you not say that your wife had traveled through time too?"

"She did." But I already knew better than to point out that the two of us were separated by four hundred years. I had the means to contact her and would avail of it when the time was right.

Meanwhile, the *kwiocosuk* continued to guide and instruct me in the ways of my people. As the days passed, I recalled Crow in the Woods's life in the same fashion as Lee's. He had been a toddler when his mother and most of his people had been murdered. Anger boiled within me. No matter how I viewed the slaughter, I could not pretend I held no rage.

Once again, I felt I had failed.

"You will eventually close the circle on your previous lives," the *kwiocos* said. "When that time comes, you will know it."

If I found Phoebe's cryptic manner baffling, the *kwiocosuk* totally bewildered me. While I remained a novice Algonquian speaker, I doubted my confusion stemmed from that fact alone. But for now and for the first time in my life, I truly felt as if I belonged somewhere. My former lives would remain a part of me, but they would no longer hinder me.

"Come, my friend," he said. "It is time to prepare for the naming."

Three days later, I stood in the forest where I had drunk the *kwiocosuk's* potions. Four warriors were positioned in the cardinal directions. These men would guide me in the days—and most likely, years—to come. Charging Bear had taken his place in the south and wore red feathers. A *kwiocos* spread herbs and tobacco in a circle around us, and the chief smudged us with tobacco and blessed us with an eagle feather. Overhead, a hawk flew, making the moment seem all the more special.

The chief faced me and gave a speech. Occasionally, I had difficulty understanding every word, but I grasped enough for the meaning. He talked about my experiences with the *kwiocosuk*, and how I had arrived to this world on the wind. The wind was often the carrying force of life. Birds, insects, bats, and seeds traveled upon it, like I had. He went on to tell a story about how great winds could do much damage without someone to talk to them.

Finally, he announced, "*Kesutanowas Wesin.*" Wind Talker.

I bowed in appreciation. "I am honored."

From a nearby branch, a crow cawed as if cheering in celebration. I was pleased to see the crow would continue to guide me in my life ahead.

After receiving a summons from Elenor, Charging Bear and I traveled down the James River. Paddling downstream took less than half the time than our trip to the Appamattuck town. A couple of times we brought the dugout ashore to dodge colonial ships. I had so little contact with the colonists that they almost seemed mysterious to me, yet I never doubted the seriousness of an encounter if our paths crossed. In addition to my Glock that I kept tucked in its holster, I carried the weapons of the Appamattuck. Although awkward with them, I knew should the occasion arise I was capable of using deadly force, if necessary.

We passed a forest. In my former life, I had never learned the different types of trees beyond the more common types. Now, I knew them all in Algonquian. As we approached a tobacco field, I shivered. Without having been told, we had passed onto Paspahegh land. Here, was where my mother had died, but I was able to avoid the negative thoughts. After all, it was also where I had met Walks Through Mist. Soon, I would contact her.

Near sunset, the dugout rounded a bend. Enough daylight penetrated the sky for us to see the familiar pitched-roof house. Charging Bear and I brought the dugout ashore and carefully covered it with branches and leaves. We carried furs toward the house to trade for English goods.

A musket raised in our direction but was quickly lowered. "Charging Bear and . . ." Henry smiled. "Lee? I almost didn't recognize you. You look like an—"

"Indian," I finished for him. "Or were you thinking in coarser language?"

He thumped me on the back in friendship. "You should know me better than that. After all, you saw the world through my eyes."

"I did," I agreed. "I go by *Kesutanowas Wesin* or Wind Talker, now."

"Wind Talker it is."

I finally smiled and shook his hand. "Good to see you, Henry. Is Elenor here?"

"She is." He greeted Charging Bear, and we went up to the house.

Before we reached the door, Elenor stood in the frame. She squinted her eyes as if not recognizing me. "Lee?"

"He goes by Wind Talker now," Henry said.

She smiled in understanding and welcomed Charging Bear and me. We set the furs down, and Henry began to inspect them. "We shall talk business later, Poppa," Elenor said, then waved at us. "Come inside and have a meal. Tell me about your time away."

"Elenor, has your husband returned?" I asked.

Sadness spread across her face. "Nay."

"I'm confident you will hear from him again."

My words were meant to inspire hope, but Elenor's expression revealed her uncertainty. I had my own, but I seriously doubted I had traveled to the seventeenth century to find out what had happened to the two missing men. How could I when there was an ocean between us and no plane travel? And if locating them was merely a matter of contacting them through the dreaming, Elenor would have been successful without my help.

Elenor showed us to the table and dished out pottage stew into metal bowls with bread. The meal was a welcome relief from our journey. The family gathered around, including Bess and her son, and we brought each other up to date since my leaving. Henry worried about his son who had yet to return from England with Elenor's husband. The kids roared with laughter at Charging Bear's stories about teaching me to hunt.

"What can I say?" I said with a shrug. "In the twenty-first century I had no need to hunt. I went to the local grocery store for food."

"What's a grocery store?" Elsa asked.

When I tried to explain the rows and rows of food to the five-year-old girl, her blue-green eyes widened.

After the meal, Charging Bear went outside to barter the furs for goods with Henry, and the children followed them. I started in the same direction when Elenor said, "I didn't want to say anything in front of the others, but Momma fears you have died."

Phoebe. What needless worry had I put her through? "I couldn't contact her before now, but I'll do so soon."

"Good. I hope that you and Charging Bear will stay the night."

"I can't speak for Charging Bear, but I'd like that."

In the company of what seemed like family, I realized the time had arrived to contact Phoebe. While Charging Bear traded, I wandered the land to locate the right place to enter the dreaming. Instead of the solitude I sought, seven-year-old Christopher ran after me and joined me. I accepted the interruption as a sign that the dreaming should wait, and he told me how he often roamed the woods on his own when he wasn't tending to chores. Amazed at the liberties youths of this time were allowed, I let him show me the area.

In spite of Christopher's young age, he knew every trail like the back of his hand. He warned me of the dangers like bears and copperheads. On a more peaceful note, he showed me where a pair of pileated woodpeckers had carved a nest hole in a tree during the spring. A screech owl had taken up refuge after the original inhabitants had moved out.

"Do you ever find evidence that the Indians lived here?" I asked.

From his pocket, he produced an arrowhead. "I've found pots too, but I like the arrowheads best."

"Not surprising."

"And bones."

"Bones?"

He shuffled his foot in the sandy soil as if he was embarrassed by the admission. "Grandpa says we should let them rest in peace, otherwise their ghosts might haunt us."

"Why would they haunt you? You're not responsible for what happened here."

"Grandpa says their spirits are unsettled."

"They most likely are, but I can't imagine why they would scare innocent boys. Can you take me to them?"

Christopher hesitated, but he led me on a trail through the forest. We traveled a couple of miles, and he showed me to a section that had smaller growth than the surrounding trees. As we neared it, I had the same chills running up and down my spine as to when I had viewed the skeleton. I didn't need to be told. I stood in the spot where a massacre had taken place.

Guns fired and smoke billowed. The death screams came from every direction. Forcing away the cries, I thanked Christopher for bringing me there. "If you don't mind, I'd like to be alone for a little while."

"Did I do something wrong?"

Always the innocent, but I had been that innocent boy once too. "No . . ." My voice cracked, and I tousled his hair. "You did nothing wrong. This place is something I need to face on my own."

"The bones are over yonder." He pointed in the direction of a fallen cypress tree and ran in the direction of the house.

Ignoring the cuts from the brambles on my arms, I made my way through the overgrowth to where Christopher had indicated. More panic-stricken screams and shouts pierced my mind. I spotted part of a femur and a bony hand. Ribs, jaw bones, arms—most were partially buried in the loose soil. Whether the bodies had been hastily buried by the surviving Paspahegh in their flight or interred in a mass grave by the English, I didn't know.

The bones were what was left of my people, and I wondered if my mother was among them. More than thirty years had passed since they had been mass murdered. More gunshots echoed in my head, and soldiers had set houses on fire. Most of the warriors had been away, and the town had been left all but defenseless. Elderly men, women, and children had died and been buried in one stinking mass grave.

I sank to my knees. Only because of a freak accident had I not been buried with them. No wonder the tortured screams haunted my sleep as well as my waking moments. Why had all of these lives ended senselessly and I lived?

Phoebe. She had saved me, and then the mist had captured me.

But my mother *had* died. I called for her.

No response.

Had I really been expecting one? My gaze came to rest on a skull. The dome had a bullet hole. I didn't need a forensic anthropologist to tell me the cause of death. Unable to withhold my grief any longer, I lowered my head and wept.

By the time I returned to the house, nighttime had arrived. Under the moonlight, Charging Bear and Henry sat outside on a couple of logs smoking a pipe. "We were growing worried," Henry said. "Christopher said he had taken you to the graveyard."

"He did."

Henry stood. "I told him to stay away from there."

"I asked him to take me. If you're angry with anyone, blame me."

Both men moved closer. "There's no reason to be angry at anyone," Henry said. "I suspect you had your reasons for going there."

Suddenly pissed, I clenched my hands. "You live on Paspahegh land, or have you forgotten?"

Charging Bear tensed his muscles, ready to restrain me in case I made any foolish moves. "Nay, lad," Henry said. "I've not forgotten. Whilst I was ne'er a soldier, I brought some of those responsible to this land. For my services I was deeded a piece of it. I can't change the past, but I thought 'twas appropriate that Elenor and her babes are a part of the land."

I unclenched my hands and headed in the direction of the river. "You're right."

"Wind Talker." Charging Bear came with me. "Except for Strong Bow and you, I too have lost my family and tribe."

I faced him. "Me?"

"You are my brother, and one day, I hope, my sister will rejoin us."

He truly *was* my brother. "Thanks, Charging Bear."

We walked out to the river and sat along the bank. The moon reflected a glow off the water. Charging Bear told me about the English goods he had received from Henry—cast iron pots, English cloth, metal tools, and some copper. Protocol would prevent him from asking me about my experience, unless I brought up the topic myself. Still numb, I was uncertain what to say and was actually comforted by the custom of not forcing small talk just for the sake of something to say.

Finally he bid me goodnight, and I was alone. For a while I listened to the night sounds, then pictured the candle in my mind. I focused on it. Flapping wings approached me in the gentle breeze. Both the wind and crow were present. Good.

14

Phoebe

"Lee?" a man's figure formed near the mist. For nearly a month Phoebe had tried to reach him through the dreaming, and she blinked in disbelief. Was his appearance wishful thinking? He moved toward her. His hair was longer than she remembered, but it was definitely him. "Lee!" She ran to greet him.

Their mouths met in an intimate kiss. He brushed her hair away from her face and smiled. "I missed you."

She hugged him again, making certain he was real. "I feared you were dead. Lee—"

"I'm Wind Talker now."

"Wind Talker," she repeated, taking a step back. At long last she comprehended why he had been absent. Men rarely shared such transitions with women, and she grew vexed by the meaning. "Are we still married? Or have you taken another?"

He drew her to him and kissed her again. "There is no other in my mind or heart."

Relieved, she cried on his shoulder. "I thought you had died when your voice vanished."

"I needed to complete my journey before contacting you again. Come, I have something to show you. I suspect you'll find it as disturbing as I did." He grasped her hand and led the way.

Afore long, the forest surrounded them. As they walked, she spotted human bones—legs, arms, feet, even skulls. The grief that crossed his countenance warned her what she had already guessed. "Snow Bird?" she asked.

"I don't know if she's here."

Phoebe bent down and touched the sandy soil. Throughout the day, she had heard the screams and firing muskets. Tears streaked her cheeks. Most of the townspeople had died. But the two of them had survived. Wind Talker's mother, Snow Bird, had been among the fallen.

Smoke nearly engulfed her. She choked back a cough. The smoke drifted slightly enough for her to see behind her. Wind Talker had vanished from her view. Skulls grinned and bones rattled. Beyond them, the smoke remained thick. In the swirling cloud stood a woman, but Phoebe could not make out her features. "Snow Bird?"

"Red Dog, why have you summoned me?"

Hearing her childhood name, Phoebe felt as if she were ten again. "Your son wishes to speak to you."

"He lives?"

"He does. I have married him, and we have a daughter. She was honored with your name."

Snow Bird stepped out of the smoke. The skin on the left side of her face was stretched and bubbled in bright red burns. Her ear was gone and a hole remained where it should have been. "Tell me what has happened."

Sadness crossed Snow Bird's countenance when Phoebe relayed the death of the Paspahegh, but the features on the right side of her face brightened when she told her about traveling through time and meeting Lee. As the story progressed, Snow Bird's face transformed to the kindness Phoebe remembered. The burns vanished and her ear was whole again by the time Phoebe had finished.

Snow Bird craned her neck, looking from side to side. "Where is he?"

"He was aside me when we started. Mayhap the time is not right."

"I'm here," he said.

Wind Talker stepped aside Phoebe. She clasped his hand and felt it tremble neath her grip.

He moved closer to Snow Bird. "I have longed to meet you."

Snow Bird smiled. "You were but two winters old when I last saw you. You have grown into a fine man, Crow in the Woods." He didn't correct the name. "I'm pleased," she continued, "that you and Red Dog have married, and I have a granddaughter. Has life been difficult for you?"

"Sometimes," he admitted. "Until recently, I knew very little of my people."

A tear streaked Snow Bird's cheek. "Red Dog has told me that you were raised by *tassantassas*. I'm sorry—"

"You have nothing to apologize for. It wasn't your fault."

"Was your adopted family good to you?"

"They were. Although we had some awkward moments, they never treated me as someone inferior."

"That's good." Snow Bird reached out, and Wind Talker grasped her hand. "I'm proud of you, my son."

With those words, Snow Bird vanished. Wind Talker lowered his head, and Phoebe placed a hand on his arm. "You have finally met the brave woman who birthed you. She taught me much."

He glanced over at her. "I wanted to see you before now, but I had to wait until the time was right."

"I know that now." She waited to see if he would elaborate.

Finally, he said, "When Lee died, I feared I would lose you, but you were a constant in my visions."

She placed a hand over his heart. "I too went through the transition. Red Dog became Walks Through Mist. E'en so, Phoebe remained with me."

"I should have known that you would understand. What do you suggest?"

"Keep both names. 'Twill allow you to walk in both worlds."

His countenance grew pensive as if contemplating her words. "Are you saying you're not part of my world?"

Phoebe gripped his hand. "If it weren't for the dreaming, I wouldn't be able to hold your hand or kiss you. 'Til I find my way back, dreams are all that we share."

With some reluctance, he nodded in agreement. "And usually our time together is very limited. I've tried to work out what was different when I traveled the first time, but because of my age, I don't recall the details."

"Mayhap Shae can help."

Afore Lee could respond, the crow cawed and the mist spread.

Phoebe threw her arms round his neck. "I love you." But she found herself in her own living room. At least, Lee was alive.

15

Wind Talker

BEFORE DAWN ARRIVED, I TRAVELED alone to the mass grave. As the sun rose, I sang a welcome to the new day. With the added light, I could clearly see the outline of bones. They surrounded me, and I sung louder. My mother, the giver of my life, was buried among them. Of that I was now certain. When I was Lee, I often wondered if I would know her if she passed me on the street. At the time I thought she had abandoned me; I couldn't have imagined the sacrifice she had made in order that I might live. After I met Phoebe, I had learned the truth and cleansed myself of the anger I had bottled inside.

"Mother, you asked for my forgiveness, but can you ever forgive me? I blamed you when you weren't at fault."

Only a chorus of crickets responded to my question. I stayed there awhile longer before turning toward the settlement only to be met by three warriors. I stood ready in case they were from an enemy tribe. Then again, how would I know if they were enemies without Charging Bear's guidance?

None of us uttered a sound. Like mine, the warriors' shirts were wool. They wore loincloths and deer-hide leggings. The one on the left had his skin painted with ornate feather designs. His hair was in the traditional upright style with it braided down the back, while the man on the opposite side had his face painted black and had his hair tied in a knot.

Finally, the man in the center stepped closer.

Relaxing slightly, I blinked. His hair was still quite black, but there were streaks of gray running throughout. He was almost as tall as me, and his prominent cheekbones and the shape of his nose and mouth had an odd familiarity. If I had been closer to sixty, I could have sworn I was looking in a mirror at myself. He wore a bear-claw necklace and his hair held an osprey feather.

"Forgive me for intruding," he said in Algonquian, "but I heard your song."

"My mother was among the fallen here," I replied.

"As were my first wife and son."

Doubt lingered in his eyes, but neither of us voiced our thoughts aloud. I reached for the leather cord around my neck, and the two younger men went for their clubs. I held up a hand to show them I meant no harm. Slowly, I removed the arrowhead from around my neck and gave it to the older man. "I believe you made this."

He fingered the arrowhead and closed his eyes. "I am Black Owl."

My father. My mother had led me here so that I might meet him. "I was Crow in the Woods."

The two men stared at me, but their gazes had changed from distrust to curiosity. Black Owl raised his eyes, and I spotted a hint of a tear. "I thought you were dead, my son."

"I know and understand. I'm Wind Talker now."

"This is your brother, Wildcat, and your sister's husband, Swift Deer." He reached out and intertwined his index finger with mine, then he pulled me close and embraced me. The other men joined him in welcoming me to the family.

"How did you survive the attack, Wind Talker?" Black Owl asked, taking a step back.

"It's a rather long and complicated story. Come, we'll talk more at the house."

"The house? Are we welcome?"

"I married Red Dog. They are my family too."

A smile crossed Black Owl's face.

Like most Indian groups, we traveled in near silence so as not to alert anyone who might be passing by. When we reached the house, Bess's son raised a musket but lowered it again when he recognized me. The others soon joined us, and we made a round of introductions. Charging Bear and I translated between the groups for everyone to understand our conversations. I told Black Owl and my brothers how I had survived the colonial attack. Like others when they first heard my story, they were in awe that I had traveled through time, but accepted it.

After the death of my mother, Black Owl had sought vengeance against the colonials, but more colonists kept arriving from England, swelling the numbers beyond his comprehension. Only a handful of Paspahegh had survived.

Anguish crossed Henry's face.

"You weren't to blame," I reassured him.

"You know that's not true," he replied.

Black Owl exchanged a questioning glance with the others. "Henry brought soldiers and guns to Virginia," I explained.

"Did you fire the guns at my people?" Black Owl asked. Charging Bear quickly translated.

"*Matah*," Henry replied. No.

"Then how are you responsible?"

Not caring for the idea of a potential war erupting in Elenor's living room, I finally exhaled the breath I was holding. "Henry, you saved Phoebe's life. Without your aid, I would have never met up with her again."

"*Kenah*," he said. I thank you. "All of you, for not bearing a grudge."

Heads nodded and smiles were exchanged. Soon, we resumed our conversation. Black Owl told me how he had eventually sought refuge with the Sekakawon tribe where he had met his second wife. While I had studied much about my past, I had not heard of the Sekakawon before. That alone warned me the tribe hadn't survived into the twenty-first century.

At that point, my brothers joined in. Both had families of their own. Wildcat had a son and daughter, and Swift Deer had twin sons. My sister's name was New Moon.

By the time all of the talking halted, night had settled. Elenor and Bess prepared a dinner of roast venison, corn pone, and apple pie. After the meal, the men retreated outdoors and passed a pipe. Although I remained no expert at pipe smoking, I could now do so without burning my tongue.

Finally, I asked Black Owl, "What became of the remaining Paspahegh?"

He shook his head. "Besides Red Dog's mother, who sought refuge among the Arrohateck, three women went to live with the Chickahominy. All have gone to the afterlife. I'm unaware that any had daughters."

Unlike the English, all of the Algonquian-speaking people traced their lineage through the women. My dream of seeking the remnants of my people vanished. "And the men?" I asked.

"Most of us died fighting the colonists. I believe you and I may be the only warriors left."

In the twenty-first century, I was the only Paspahegh. Although I was disappointed that more of my people hadn't survived, I took comfort that my father was among the living in the seventeenth century. We spoke long into the night, even after my brothers had bedded down.

Soon after Black Owl retired for the night, I sought Phoebe through the dreaming. Each time, the presence of Crow and the wind accompanied me. If only I could understand what the wind said without the bird's interpretation, I would likely be closer to the true meaning of my name. Instead of my familiar home, Crow led me to an office, reminding me of the time I had spoken with Ed. This time was different though. A blonde-haired woman sat behind the desk.

Sensing my presence, Shae looked up in wide-eyed fright and pressed a hand to her chest. "My God, Lee, you nearly scared the crap out of me. You've come here to say goodbye, haven't you?" A soft choking sound came from the back of her throat as if she struggled to keep from crying.

"No, I haven't come to say goodbye."

"Then what?" She kept staring at me as if I were some sort of space alien.

"You can relax, Shae. I haven't taken up scalping, and even if I had, it's considered bad manners to scalp an ex."

"You bastard . . ." A hint of smile crossed her face. "What can I do for you, Lee? Or have you taken some Indian name?"

With her question, I understood what Phoebe had meant about keeping both names. In Shae's world, I was Lee and always would be. "I have taken another name, but you can call me Lee."

"Nice of you to be considerate. I probably couldn't have pronounced it anyway."

"Probably not," I agreed.

"A trip back in time certainly hasn't improved your annoying disposition."

"What can I say? You bring out the best in me."

She laughed. "Thank you for distracting me, but I've recovered from my initial shock. Why have you come to see me?"

I resisted the temptation to continue sparring and became serious. "You helped me unlock my memory of my two-year-old self. Over time, I've recalled more, and since then, I've met my mother in the same way that I'm standing before you now." At one time, even mentioning the dreaming would have set Shae off that it was nothing more than hypnosis. She finally seemed to have accepted the dreaming for what it was. "Is there a way that I can remember my actual journey to the twenty-first century?"

"I could try hypnosis, but you were a difficult enough subject when you were physically present. I don't know if it would work at all during the dreaming."

An interesting thought: hypnosis within the dreaming. "I'm willing to try."

"You can't be serious. What's so important about that particular memory?"

"I need to know the details of how I traveled through time so Phoebe and Heather can join me."

"I see," she said, letting out a weary breath. "Why would you want to remain in the seventeenth century?"

"It's who I am."

"And you want to subject your family to it too? Need I remind you, the Indians lost."

As if I needed a reminder. To my dying day, I would carry the memory of my mother's death scream. "Shae, I don't expect you to understand, but I am Paspahegh. Phoebe was aware of that fact when she married me. She identifies with the seventeenth century, not the twenty-first. As for Heather, I won't leave my daughter behind."

"You saw the skeleton. You will die there—all of you."

"Everyone dies. Does it really make any difference as to which century?"

"It does to me."

How foolish I had been to think that we could truly ever set the past aside. "I'll come to visit you on occasion. I'll even bring the family. If you like you can bring Russ, and we can have a big picnic at the beach."

"You're doing it again." But a smile crept to her face. "Okay, sit down and make yourself comfortable. We'll give it a try."

As she had instructed, I sat in the chair across from her and settled back.

"Close your eyes."

Again, I obeyed.

"Good. Now relax. Breathe in. Now out."

Together, she guided me through several breathing and relaxation exercises. Like the time she had tried to induce hypnosis before, nothing happened. "It's not working."

"I didn't really expect it to. Lee, I can't really offer anything that you can't do by yourself through the dreaming."

"Try again," I insisted, then lowered my voice, "please, Shae."

"Your stubbornness is the same in both centuries." Deep in thought, she tapped a pen on her desk. "When we were successful the time before you saw a crow."

"The crow is my guardian spirit."

"I don't pretend to understand anything about guardian spirits, but that's what guides you during the dreaming, I presume?"

I didn't like where her question was leading. "It is," I admitted.

"You see. I've never hypnotized you. You merely relaxed enough to enter the dreaming."

"You helped me focus."

She tapped her pen once more, and a few minutes passed before she spoke again. "Okay, let's try the relaxation exercises again.

You're already in the dreaming, so if I can somehow channel your concentration to the time you traveled to the twentieth century, you should have your answer."

"Thanks, Shae."

One more time, she led me through a series of exercises. When I called for Crow, the sound of flapping wings came toward me. I held up my arm, and a glossy black bird landed on it. "Lead the way," I said.

As the bird took flight, I glanced at Shae.

"Go, do what you must," she said. "Isn't that why you're here?"

Leaving Shae behind, I followed Crow along a street. This wasn't the seventeenth century, and I arrived outside a restaurant, where Shae and I had frequented when we were married. I hadn't been back since . . . *go with it*. There must be a reason why I was here.

I stepped inside and spotted Shae at the table in the corner that we had claimed as ours. Her hair was longer and she was thinner. Her head was bent studying the menu. I slid into the chair across from her. "Sorry, I'm late."

She looked up. Her eyes were red and puffy, as if she had been crying. She lowered the menu to the table. "There is no easy way of saying this, so I'll say it straight out. I want a divorce."

Dumbfounded, I stared at her, feeling like she had kicked me in the gut. As a detective, I prided myself on seeing clues that most people missed, but I had missed all of the signs leading up to this moment.

A tear trickled down her cheek. "Say something. Anything."

Too numb to speak, I clenched my shaking hand.

She grasped my hand. "I didn't arrive at this decision lightly."

I withdrew my hand from her grip and snapped, "Then why? I don't understand. Surely, we can talk this through, but not here—"

"I'm keeping the house. I'll reimburse you for your share, and–"

"For Christ's sakes, Shae. Tell me what happened."

"Nothing happened. We're mismatched."

"Mismatched?" I bit my tongue on an angry retort.

A waitress delivered water glasses to our table. Instead of taking our orders, she obviously sensed something amiss between us and scurried to the next table.

Resorting to my stoic detective stance, I calmed myself enough to speak evenly. "After more than ten years together, how can we suddenly be mismatched?"

"It's not sudden." Her words jumbled as she cried into a tissue with her reasons.

With the long hours and me almost never home, my job was mostly to blame. I managed to keep my impassive appearance, but inside I was being ripped apart. "Dammit, Shae. I love you. I always have."

She broke down sobbing. "And what do I do when I receive the call that you've been killed in the line of duty?"

There *had* been signs that I had missed. In the past, she had voiced her fears of me being shot, and I had dismissed them with a joke that I was more likely to be killed while crossing a street. But I couldn't believe our marriage would end like this. "And just like that," I finally said, "we throw away our lives together."

"Lee, reliving this point in our lives won't give you the answer you're seeking."

At the sound of Shae's voice, I blinked and saw her as her usual plump self, not the woman I remembered on that traumatic night. I was experienced enough with the dreaming to realize there had to be a reason why I had revisited this moment in my life. After that night, I had spent nearly two years in a daze, drunk more often than sober. "You broke my heart," I said.

"I broke my own too, but you know it was meant to be this way. I never saw inside your soul and realized how much you hurt from being denied your heritage. And let's face it, I wouldn't follow you to the seventeenth century."

She was right, and in so many ways, we were better friends than when we had been married. But I was already aware of that point and wondered why I had focused on the event. I sucked in my breath. "I *am* here to say goodbye."

"I was afraid of that."

"Shae, you don't understand. Goodbye doesn't necessarily mean that we can never speak, but that I have truly left my life in the twenty-first century behind. You are my only remaining connection to it because Phoebe isn't of your time."

"I'm not certain I understand."

"Like on the night you said you wanted a divorce, I'm severing my ties to your century. It will always be a part of me, like our marriage will always be a part of the both of us. But after that night, we led separate lives as a couple."

"Then, I will see you again?"

"I'm not sure. If you're afraid that I won't be able to pop in again and see you, there is another alternative."

"And that is?"

"You and Russ can join us, and we can all be part of the seventeenth century."

To that suggestion, she gave me a dismissive wave. "Not a chance. I happen to like central heating and air conditioning."

In the distance, I heard Crow caw. The time had come. "Bye, Shae. You were my first love, and nothing can ever change that fact."

"Bye, Lee."

Her voice carried on the wind, and I found myself overlooking the James River, where I had entered the dreaming. Like when Shae had asked for the divorce, I was numb, but I was a much stronger person now. I refused to drown myself in alcohol.

Phoebe had been right. Shae had helped, but not in the way either of us suspected she would. I had severed my last tie to the world I had grown up in.

16

Phoebe

LIKE THE TIME ED HAD COME TO TELL Phoebe that he had spoken with Lee in a dream, Shae's visit came as no surprise. She recounted her dream from the night afore. Lee had given his final farewell to the twenty-first century. For the first time Phoebe truly believed that her stay in this century might only be temporary.

"It seemed so real," Shae said.

Many who had never experienced the dreaming afore, made the same claim. " 'Twas a dream," Phoebe replied, "for he no longer hails from this century."

"Before I met you, I would have never believed time travel even possible, but now—"

"Now you know that it is, and I'm no wiser on how it happened. I can't return 'til I do."

"As I asked Lee, why would you want to? If time travel works both ways, can't he return here? Phoebe, you've studied enough history. To say that it doesn't go well for the Indians would be stating it mildly. Not only would you jeopardize your life, but your daughter's too."

"What about the skeleton?"

Shae's brow furrowed. "I hadn't forgotten about it, but does it necessarily become fact if he returns here?"

With so many unknowns, Phoebe only grew more confused. "We need to discover the secret of what caused us to travel through time afore making any decisions, but Shae, e'en aft three years, I feel like a stranger in this century. I can read and write, use all of the fancy machines to cook and clean. I had also planned on finishing my nursing degree when Heather got a little older, but to what end?"

"I'm not certain I understand."

"I'm more isolated and alone here than I have e'er been."

"With Lee's hours, I had wondered when you moved to the country if it was a good idea," Shae admitted.

" 'Twasn't because of Lee's hours. I'm used to the men being away. E'en in the city, I can be surrounded by people and still feel alone."

"What about your friend Meg?"

"I'd be lost without her companionship, but in the seventeenth century, I was rarely alone. Women worked together throughout the day, and we took turns looking aft the children. Someone was always nearby, no matter the circumstances."

"That's why we have cars and phones. We can always drive over and see our friends, or talk to them on the phone."

Shae truly didn't comprehend. "Not while they're working, 'less you have the same job."

"I think I see what you mean, but life could be very short there—for all of you."

Over the years, Phoebe had come to think of Shae as a good friend. Without her help, she would have been totally lost in this century. "In spite of your technological advancements, there is no guarantee for a long life in this century either."

"You're so right," Shae finally agreed, "but you still haven't said anything about Heather. Here she can be a doctor, lawyer, or just about anything she chooses."

"Aye, and in my time, she can grow to be a cunning woman as I did, and my mother afore me, and her mother afore her. Is that lesser than any of those occupations?"

"I didn't mean to imply . . . it's a proud tradition, and I shouldn't have tried to interfere."

Phoebe placed her hand on Shae's. "Thank you for being such a good friend. You will let me know if Lee comes to see you again, won't you?"

With a weak nod of her head, Shae said, "I will, but I don't think he'll visit again. He wouldn't have said goodbye otherwise. And you must promise me that when you do get back, you'll find a way to let me know that you made it safely."

"I vow that I shall. Shae, I have another request."

"Anything."

"Will you hypnotize me so that I may learn how I got here?"

"As I asked Lee, what can you learn from hypnosis that the dreaming won't tell you?"

"The dreaming doesn't always focus on what we are seeking at any given moment. Because I was hit by a car soon aft my arrival, I have avoided that moment in my life as much as possible whilst I'm in the dreaming. My guardian spirit knows my fear and may believe that I'm not ready to face it yet."

"Are you?"

"Aye," Phoebe said, hoping her hesitation wasn't visible. At first, Shae failed to respond. "Shae, one of the first things you told me about hypnosis was that it would help me focus on what happened—in a relaxed state."

"I did," Shae agreed, "and I suppose it's appropriate. The last time I hypnotized you was the same memory, when you recalled that Lee was from the seventeenth century as well. Of course, I'll do it."

"Thank you." Phoebe settled back on the divan and closed her eyes.

"Relax. Breathe in. Now out."

Shae went through several breathing exercises, and Phoebe felt the tension in her body begin to fade.

Shae's voice continued, "Now I want you to imagine your right big toe."

The script proceeded through Phoebe's foot and leg. Her lower body relaxed.

"You're in a boat, riding on a gentle wave. The waves reach your feet and legs."

Waves and waves—the boat gently rolled upon the water. A pleasurable tingling sensation entered Phoebe's fingertips. Her body was bathed in a glow, and she drifted and floated in peace.

"Phoebe, focus on when you came to the twenty-first century. Do you see it?"

"Aye."

In the woods, Henry called after her. For a moment, she contemplated whether she should continue forward or turn back. Her back stung from the whip's lashes. He called once more. She quivered with indecision, but a voice inside her urged her on. She feared what lay ahead.

"Do not fear it. You will be reunited with what once was."

At the time, she had thought it was Lightning Storm's voice, but she could clearly hear him now. It had always been Lee. She called to him in Algonquian.

"Forward," he urged.

Phoebe forded the stream. The water churned, and near the middle, the swift current swirled about her waist. She slogged through it and reached the other side, when suddenly she was lost. She stumbled through the gigantic roots of the forest. "Where my love? Where am I to go?"

A mob was upon her, and raging shouts came from the opposite bank. She could see their torches, and her breaths quickened.

"Walks Through Mist, follow my voice."

His words continued upon the breeze. She followed them until the white hound stood afore her. He would show her the way. Deeper and deeper, they traveled into the forest. She sought shelter in the opening within the roots of an immense oak. Like so many times during the dreaming, a thick mist engulfed her. A clammy dampness upon her skin raised the hairs on her arms. She latched onto the dog's leather collar. A ship rocked and swayed neath her feet. A wave of nausea overcame her, and she clutched her stomach with her free hand. The hound failed to break stride.

From a nearby branch, a crow cawed. 'Twas a sign that Lee was nearby. She continued walking along the arc.

"Walks Through Mist . . ."

Phoebe signaled the hound to halt, but he kept going. Lee's voice faded.

On and on she faltered through the fog with the dog tracing a huge circle. Their love was a circle in time—first, in innocence as children, then as adults, husband and wife. Naught could change the past or what was meant to be. The mist grew thinner.

"Follow the light," he whispered in her ear.

Up ahead, she spied her first glimpse of the city—what looked like thousands and thousands of torches. She emerged from the fog, and the dog vanished. Lights upon lights, swarming with people. And clattering noise. She covered her ears to block out the racket.

She stepped into the road to escape. More lights chased after her, blinding her in her tracks. *The car!* A sudden screeching of brakes, and the earth trembled. She struck the pavement and closed her eyes to the pain.

Phoebe blinked. "*Kesutanowas Wesin.*"

"Phoebe?"

Shae's perplexed countenance appeared afore her.

"Did you see something this time that you haven't before? I didn't understand what you just said."

"Wind Talker," Phoebe translated. " 'Tis Lee's Algonquian name."

"That's something new, isn't it? The time before you learned that it was Lee calling to you. Maybe it's something as simple that he needed to complete the transition. He did that by cutting his ties with me. If you'd like to try again sometime, we can see if we can focus on the exact memory when you traveled."

"Aye, I'd like that."

"Let me know when you're ready. I know you were hoping for more clarity this time, but I think if we keep trying, you'll find the answer you seek." Shae squeezed Phoebe's hand. "You will rejoin him."

Phoebe hugged Shae. "Thanks, Shae, for e'erything." They hugged once more and said their goodbyes. With new hope that she would travel to the seventeenth century, she waited 'til the eve to share the experience with Meg. After the lasses were tucked in bed, they entered the dreaming. They followed the river downstream 'til arriving at Elenor's house.

A group of Indians stood out front. "Wind Talker?" Phoebe called.

One of the warriors turned toward her.

Unable to contain her joy, Phoebe ran into his arms. They hugged and kissed. Finally, Lee stepped back. "I'd like to introduce my wife Walks Through Mist, and her friend Meg."

After Lee completed the introductions, Black Owl said, "You were but a girl when I last saw you, Walks Through Mist. I am pleased to welcome you to the family."

Out of respect for an elder, Phoebe kept her eyes lowered. "I'm honored."

"You do me the honor. I'm told you have birthed a granddaughter."

"Aye. We call her Snow Bird."

His dark eyes squinted as if he were suddenly in pain.

"Forgive me. I have reminded you of that long ago time. I only meant to honor your wife's spirit. Not only was she Wind Talker's mother, she taught me in the ways of *wisakon*."

"You *have* honored her. She was a gifted healer."

The group gathered round, and they talked late into the night. Phoebe learned about her new family amongst the old. As members gradually dispersed, Meg wandered off with Charging Bear. Phoebe grew uneasy for her friend. Even through the dreaming, love could seem very real.

As if reading her thoughts, Lee grasped her hand. "She'll be fine." He went on to tell her about his visit with Shae.

"Aye, she told me, and I must do the same."

"The same?"

Phoebe glanced in the direction where Henry smoked a pipe with Wildcat and Swift Deer. Lee nodded that he understood, and she moved in their direction. "Henry, may I speak with you?"

He stood and bid the warriors goodnight. He showed her round to the side of the house, where a candle from inside cast enough light to see each other. Unlike her, he had some gray in his hair, and wrinkles had formed near his eyes. If she had stayed continuously in this time period, she reminded herself that she would look much the same.

"By the laws of the colony, would we still be regarded as married?" she asked.

"E'eryone thought you were dead. I remarried too and have a son. Phoebe, I would ne'er attempt to come betwixt you and Wind Talker. I did not comprehend the ways of the Indians when I came to this land, nor how much you were a part of them. Your father vowed your hand to me. At the time, I thought I was doing my duty, but time has a way of showing us our errors. Your father's bones are turning to dust, and I knew when I helped you escape from gaol that you would seek your life with another."

Henry had always been kind. He *had* loved her, and she had given so little in return. "Were you happy?"

"Aye. Mary was taken from me way too soon. 'Tis going on nearly three years now since her passing, but we were happy."

For that much, she was thankful. "Then you are at peace with our lives having gone separate ways?"

"I was at peace with that decision when I helped you escape."

After she had been tried for being a witch. "Thank you, Henry. I doubt that I can e'er repay you."

"You already have. Elenor is the daughter that Mary and I were ne'er blessed with. I couldn't love her more if she had been my own flesh and blood."

"You know I wouldn't have left her if I had been given a choice."

"Aye, but she always knew you would return."

The feelings she had for Henry must have been similar to those Lee had for Shae. She kissed Henry on the cheek. "Thank you for helping Lee when he first arrived in this time."

He shrugged. " 'Twas naught."

"But it was, Henry. If there's anything I can do for you . . ."

"Only if you can find out what has happened to David."

His son. "I shall try," she vowed. As Phoebe turned, the mist formed afore her. She blinked her eyes. Instead of standing beside Henry's cottage, she found herself surrounded by the familiar living room of the twenty-first century. Across from her was Meg.

A radiant smile formed on her friend's lips. It was the smile of a woman in love.

17

Wind Talker

WIND KICKED UP, TOTALLY SURROUNDING ME. By now I recognized its meaning. I reached out my hand, but the mist captured Phoebe, once again separating us by time. Lowering my arm, I clenched my hand and worried that I'd be unable to unlock the secret of how we had traveled through time.

Charging Bear thumped me on the shoulder, and I turned. Sympathy registered in his eyes. Had Phoebe's concern about Meg falling for her brother been a valid one? Before either of us could speak, Henry approached me. "She has bid me goodbye."

Like I had Shae. "Thank you, Henry—for everything."

He shook his head. "As I told Phoebe, 'tis naught."

His modesty amazed me. If only I could be as humble. If nothing else, I was learning patience among Phoebe's family and my own, a trait that had frequently escaped me during my time in law enforcement. After bidding each other goodnight, we retired for the evening.

In the morning, after saying goodbye to Elenor, Henry, and the rest of the family, I set out with Black Owl and my brothers. We stopped near my mother's grave to pay our final respects. Afterward, Charging Bear separated from us to return to the Appamattuck and Strong Bow. I promised him that I would return in a few weeks, but I wanted to meet the rest of my family. Swift Deer and I were loaded with packs of supplies on our backs that Elenor had provided for us, and we began the journey to where the Sekakawon called home. In my head, I had difficulty picturing where the tribe lived, but from Black Owl's description, I thought it must be somewhere in the Northern Neck region, making the trip over sixty miles on foot.

Although Charging Bear had always maintained a brisk pace when traveling in the woods, I had only accompanied him for short distances in comparison. These warriors kept a similarly steady rate, and I struggled to meet their strides. In an effort to keep up, I shifted my pack to Wildcat's back. The switch only slowed him slightly, and my lungs burned in agony.

The first time we met another traveler, I didn't realize that the proper etiquette was to stop and chat. Thankful for the rest break, I relished a few minutes to catch my breath. I quickly learned that a chat meant smoking a pipe, learning the latest news, and sharing any available foodstuff. Several hours passed before we resumed our journey. After two days and making our third encounter, I envisioned several weeks passing before we arrived at our destination.

By nightfall, when we rested for the evening, I fell into an exhausted sleep and had no energy to contact Phoebe through the dreaming. I worried she would think I had abandoned her yet again. On the third night, I struggled to stay awake to make contact but drifted off before I could enter the misty realm, only to wake in the early dawn to Wildcat standing over me with an ear-to-ear grin.

"My brother has the vigor of an Englishman," he said.

What I wouldn't give for a hefty dose of caffeine. "Surprise," I replied and struggled to my feet. "Since I was raised by them."

"Sad—they don't improve their stamina over the next four hundred winters."

With a stretch, I groaned. "If anything, it gets worse. I'm fitter than most."

Shaking his head, Wildcat laughed in amusement. "Then we have little to worry about. A true enemy is a physical match."

If only that were true. My knowledge of history was better left unsaid. I sought an inconspicuous spot and relieved myself. By the time I finished, the others were already giving thanks and saying prayers, welcoming the new day. Over the months, I had grown closer to my heritage, but for some reason I held back in joining them. What was worse, I couldn't even think of a reason as to why.

Then I spotted a crow in a nearby branch, and I felt comforted.

Black Owl's gaze met mine. So many questions. In time, I knew they would be answered, but one topic gnawed at my gut. "I don't even know when I was born."

"You were born during the first moon of *cohonks*."

The Algonquian word for winter sounded like a Canada goose honk. The woodland tribes marked the season with the return of the migrating geese. My adoptive family had celebrated my birthday in August because that was when I had been found wandering alone in the forest. They had been off by a few months, and I had never observed the date they had chosen for me. Even though my family had tried, I had been the only kid in school who never had a real birthday. Now that I knew the approximate date, I didn't know what to think. "Thank you," I finally said.

Black Owl nodded, and as we started off on our journey, he told me about my mother. "Snow Bird was a gifted woman in the ways of *wisakon*. After she met Walks Through Mist's mother, they traded each other's knowledge. Together, they became more learned than the *kwiocosuk*. Only the two women knew how to heal gunshot wounds."

He went on to tell me about when I was born and how blessed my mother had felt upon my arrival. The snow had been deep that winter, but she always kept a warm hearth. As we walked along, he continued. There was no doubt in my mind, he had loved Snow Bird very much. When he reached the fateful day that the warriors had set off on a hunting trip before the massacre, he fell silent.

Too easily, I recalled the death and destruction. "She saved my life."

Black Owl halted and closed his eyes. When he reopened them, tears had entered them. "As I would have expected. She was a brave woman and a good mother."

The rest of the morning, we traveled in silence. About midday, another traveler appeared on the trail ahead. Everyone reached for their weapons.

"Pray don't shoot," the colonist shouted, raising his hands.

I translated what he had said, and they lowered their weapons gradually.

"You speak English?" he asked, directing his question to me.

"I do. I'm Wind Talker."

He held out a hand. "William Carter."

I shook it, while my brothers watched him closely. His brown hair was shoulder length and wildly astray. He wore a tattered linen shirt with an equally torn wool overcoat and breeches. His face was smudged with dirt, and he smelled like he hadn't bathed in weeks. I guessed him to be in his late teens to early twenties, and his hand trembled beneath my grip. Returning my hand to my side, I made a round of introductions.

"I'm lost," William admitted. "I'm thankful to happen across friendly Indians."

At least, he hadn't resorted to the use of the word "savages," but I detected something he had left unsaid. In any case, Wildcat brought out the pipe and welcomed William like any traveler. The encounter was my first time serving as a translator without the help of Charging Bear. I was fairly comfortable with Algonquian, but even after having been around Phoebe for nearly four years, colonial English could sometimes be difficult to comprehend, especially since William's accent was slightly different from hers and her family's.

Black Owl shared the last of Elenor's rations with William, and he gulped down the dried beef like he hadn't eaten in days, all the while muttering his thanks. Afterward, the pipe was passed around with Wildcat and Swift Deer doing most of the talking. Totally distracted from the conversation, William kept peering around as if he was expecting someone.

I exchanged a glance with Black Owl, and it was almost as if I was working with my partner Ed again. Both of us had spotted William's distraction. "Why are you really here?" I finally asked.

William swallowed and looked me straight in the eye. "I've run off."

"From where?"

"From York County. I'm indentured to Joseph Pierce. He paid my way to Virginia."

Slavery by any other name. Although I had witnessed people being held against their will, I had never experienced legal slavery, even if only for a specified length of time. I translated what William had said to my father and brothers. Finally, Black Owl said, "You're welcome to join us."

Again, I translated.

"I'm indebted to you, but . . ."

His eyes were wide with horror, and I recalled a tale that Phoebe had told me when she and her mother had first encountered the Paspahegh. "We don't cook and eat Englishmen."

"But I've seen the atrocities."

"Brought on by your own people. My father—" I motioned to Black Owl. "—and I are the last of the Paspahegh. I was only two years old at the time, and the men were away hunting, leaving elderly men and the women to defend the town. I only recently discovered that my father is still alive."

William closed his eyes. "Forgive me."

Without waiting for a translation, Black Owl placed his hand on William's shoulder. "You weren't there on that day."

Their gestures and sympathetic smiles were enough for each to comprehend the other. William got to his feet. "I'd be honored to join you."

As we returned to our journey, I learned that my initial hunch was correct. William was eighteen. He had sailed the Atlantic at sixteen and had been living as an indentured servant to an abusive master since then. Without any idea where he was heading, he had run off after he had been whipped for a minor infraction.

"My wife was whipped," I said.

"Is she—"

"She's English." I relayed the story of how Phoebe had come to Virginia.

Over the next three days, we learned more about our young companion, and he came to relax in our company. At first he was a little dubious about bathing daily like the rest of us, but our assaulted noses were relieved to be rid of his stench. Whether due to modesty or some other reason, he refused to strip his linen shirt or the lining to his breeches while bathing. For the time being, we accepted his behavior as a quirk.

As we got closer to the Sekakawon, crows greeted me along the way, and another day passed before we finally reached their town. Like the Appamattuck, arched houses were covered by woven mats. Lines of people greeted us. This time when we entered, I understood most of the chief's speech. He welcomed me as Black Owl's long-lost son, along with our guest William. Because William was a visitor and not joining the tribe, he didn't endure the dunking I had faced in the river.

We were escorted to a longhouse, where another group of people lined the walls. Wide-eyed with fear, William kept glancing over his shoulder as if he expected the worst.

"Relax," I said. "As long as you treat everyone fairly, they won't hurt you."

The chief introduced us to each person. New Moon was among them, and I was thrilled to finally meet my sister. When we reached the end wall, the chief sat on a wood frame. His wife sat beside him. William and I were shown to a mat on his right, and the rest were seated on mats in rows in front of the chief. Each person stood to welcome us, and I translated for William as best as I could, given the circumstances.

After everyone had taken their turn, some with lengthy speeches, we feasted on oysters, fish, and corn. Only when I had been greeted by the Appamattuck had I ever seen such a lavish spread of food, but over the months I had learned all guests were treated in such a manner, even if the townspeople had little else. Following dinner, a pipe was passed around, and stories were told.

When my turn came, I told how I had come to live with the Appamattuck and meeting Black Owl. Then, all eyes turned to William, and he suddenly went pale.

"Just tell them a story," I said, attempting to reassure him. "Any story will do—how you met us, or crossing the Atlantic."

"Thank you," he whispered. He went on to tell us about his voyage to Virginia.

His tale sounded so much like Phoebe's when she had crossed the ocean. Even with my fairly cast-iron stomach, I got a bit queasy thinking of crossing on rough seas. He had landed in Jamestown and met a number of the colonists. I detected one must have been a girl on whom he had developed a crush before being sent to the Pierce plantation as a servant. After another round of stories, drums beat outside the longhouse. William had a familiar worried look.

"There will be an evening of dancing," I explained. "Afterward, you'll be escorted to a guest house for the night and will be given female companionship should you desire it."

His expression went from anxious to completely panic-stricken. "But I have ne'er lain with a woman."

Recalling my own first time with Shae, I couldn't help but laugh at his youthful innocence. "Then you have a momentous occasion to look forward to. Shall we join the others?"

We went outside, where many of the townspeople had already gathered and danced to the rhythmic drums. Swift Deer showed William the steps. The young man easily caught on. For some reason, I sensed he wouldn't easily leave the town. Like Phoebe and her mother, he was already being accepted as part of the community. I wondered curiously whether, if I hadn't traveled through time, I would have been taken to the Arrohateck tribe with Phoebe or somehow ended up here with Black Owl. Contemplating the possibilities, I decided I didn't like either scenario. In that realm Phoebe was eight years older than me, and we would have most likely followed separate paths forever. By traveling through time we were closer in age and, almost from the beginning, I could not help but love her.

Throughout the rest of the evening, I could think of nothing else but to contact Phoebe. After a couple of hours, most of the dancers finally dispersed. Some lingered. A couple of men escorted William to the guest house, and Black Owl approached me. "You are welcome in the guest house."

His underlying meaning was understood. Unlike at the Appamattuck town, this time I was aware that sexual partners were presented to all guests. "You may not understand my reasons, but I have no need for anyone but Walks Through Mist."

He placed his hand on my arm. "Many years passed before I could care for anyone the way I did your mother." He lowered his arm. "You are welcome at my hearth."

"You honor me. I will join you later."

He gave me a nod, and as I had when I had first arrived in the Appamattuck town, I wandered toward the river and sat along the bank. I had no idea what the river was called in the twenty-first century, but I knew that it emptied a short distance away into a larger river, which I guessed was the Potomac. Seasons had changed and a cold wind blew. For a moment I longed for central heating. Still sensitive to the nippy air, I rubbed my hands together. Although I craved a hot pot of coffee, I had come a long way. I no longer desired beer. In my mind's eye, I concentrated on a flame from a campfire, and its heat began to fill me. No longer numb, I stretched my fingers closer to the fire.

Darkness faded, and Crow landed on a nearby branch.

"Except through you," I said, "I have yet to learn how to talk to the wind."

In time you will. Were you not honored with the name Wind Talker? Patience is the key.

Patience eluded me. I thought back to a previous conversation with Crow. "You said the wind can carry me anywhere."

I did.

I had been approaching the puzzle all wrong, and a new thought came to me. "Through time?"

The bird cackled. *One step at a time. First, you must learn to talk to the wind.*

Crow's response suggested that time travel might be possible again, and my heart pounded. "Where do I begin?"

At the beginning.

I should have known better. There would be no jumping ahead, and for now, the crow would continue to guide me. "I wish to speak to Walks Through Mist."

The bird gave a series of clicks and rattles, then took flight. I attempted to follow and stretched my arms. I felt like I was a bird. Together, we rode the swift air currents, flying high into the sky. The warmth of the sun permeated me and warmed my body as the cool air lifted me toward the clouds. Higher and higher I flew. A light mist enveloped my being, and I soared higher. The past was gone, and the future struck me with clarity, piercing straight through my soul.

I envisioned Phoebe in my mind and called her name.

18

Phoebe

"Lee?" TWO WEEKS HAD PASSED since saying goodbye to Henry and parting with Lee. During that time, Phoebe and Meg had tried unsuccessfully to contact him through the dreaming. Phoebe sat up in bed, rubbing the sleep from her eyes. He stood aside the bed. His black hair was now long enough for him to tie back. He wore a woolen shirt and a buckskin breechclout. She corrected herself. "Wind Talker."

He sat on the bed and kissed her full on the mouth. "It doesn't matter which name you use. You were right. Both are part of me." He kissed her again while tracing a hand down her side. "I missed you."

Returning his caresses, she touched and fondled him. Afore long her nightdress and his clothes were on the floor, and they lay on the bed together—naked. She spread her legs. His breath was hot on her neck, and his heart beat rapidly against her breast. The warmth of his *pocohaac* pressed against her skin, and he plunged inside her. In a steady rhythm, her body joined with his in perfect unison.

Phoebe floated amongst the layers of sensations until they fell to the bed, exhausted. He rested aside her, and she nestled in his arm. He told her about traveling to the Sekakawon and that his true birthday was during the first moon of *cohonks*.

"I should have recalled the time of year that you were born," she said.

"Nonsense. You were only ten winters yourself."

Each time she saw him, more and more of the detective faded. Although their separation was painful, she was elated that he had learned about his true heritage—*their* heritage.

"I'd like to see Heather," he finally said.

Phoebe got up and dressed. "She'll be walking soon."

A pained expression crossed his countenance as he adjusted his breechclout. "I'm already missing her milestones. How much longer? I'm not any closer to discovering how we have traveled through time than I was six months ago."

Six months? Only three-fourths of that time had passed for her. Even so, sometimes it seemed like an eternity. She moved closer and kissed him on the lips. "We must believe." She grasped his hand. "Let's go see Heather."

They went into their daughter's room. Lee halted aside the crib and stared at Heather. Careful not to wake her, he picked her up. "Snow Bird," he whispered in Algonquian.

Heather gave a soft cry. He rocked her in his arms, and she quieted. He glanced round the room. "Where's Tiffany?"

"She and Meg did not stay last eve."

"It's probably a good thing. I might have terrified her."

Phoebe smiled, taking in the sight of him snuggling Heather in his arms. "You might have surprised her, but I doubt she would have been terrified."

"I have changed my looks," he reminded her.

"Aye, and each time I see you I think you're more handsome than afore."

"And you, my love..." He kissed her on the mouth, and Heather stretched with a shrieking cry.

Both laughed at the interruption. The scene could have almost been a normal day after he had been working late, and she had arisen early to care for Heather. Almost normal—if they weren't separated by nearly four hundred years. Phoebe took their daughter into her arms. "She's hungry." She moved into the living room and got comfortable on the divan.

Lee watched her whilst she nursed. He stroked Heather's chubby cheek.

"I shall go to the home of the Sekakawon," she said.

"There won't be any trace in this time. I had never heard of them until I met my father."

She had that sick feeling in the pit of her stomach. "Another tribe that has been massacred?"

He gripped her hand. "You're aware that only a few tribes have survived into the twenty-first century. I survived because of an anomaly, and now that I've left, there are no Paspahegh in your time."

A slight breeze came betwixt them, signaling that their time together grew short. "Lee, I think the wind may be the key. E'ery time we speak, it interrupts us."

"I know, but . . ."

And he was gone. Her breath caught in her throat, but she had no tears left to cry.

Phoebe had not visited the place where she had been struck by the car since the event itself. She recalled little, except for the blinding lights in the night sky, and the sidewalks swarming with people. Now in daylight, she could easily see a flower shop, a restaurant, a bank, and a jewelry store amongst others.

"Does anything look familiar?" Shae asked.

"Nay. E'en if I had arrived in the light of day, I wouldn't have known what any of the shops were at the time."

"It's what I suspected, but I thought if you saw the place, it might trigger something the next time we use hypnosis. Why don't we go over to the restaurant and have a bite to eat? I bet they have cheesecake."

Phoebe couldn't help but laugh. Her discovery of cheesecake had unlocked a dietary weakness, but as they stepped into the street to cross it, she halted, half expecting a car to strike her. She trembled. "Shae . . ."

"Are you remembering something?"

Follow the light.

Lights had been everywhere, and she had wondered which one she should follow.

Shae grasped Phoebe's hand and led her across the street.

No car sped toward her, but she heard the piercing sound of a horn and the screeching of brakes. Recalling the pain, she closed her eyes. *Soon my beloved, I will join you.*

"Phoebe?"

She opened her eyes and discovered she was safely on the other side of the street.

"What just happened?" Shae asked.

" 'Twas here that Lee called to me. I told him I would join him."

"Let's go inside and talk more." After making themselves comfortable in a booth and ordering lunch, Shae continued, "Your memory of the event is strong. There's no doubt in that respect. If you'd like, we can go to my office after lunch and see if hypnosis works this time to focus on what you're seeking."

"Aye, I'd like that."

Shae sipped from her water glass. "What do you mean that you told him you would join him? You haven't said anything about that before."

"When I came to this century, Lee said that I should follow the light. There were so many I didn't know which one. I stepped into the street. The car struck me. I thought I was dying and would join him in the afterlife. I'm uncertain whether I spoke the words aloud or merely thought them, but I said, 'Soon, my beloved, I shall join you.' "

"I see."

The waitress brought their sandwiches. "Is there anything else I can get you?"

"A slice of cheesecake," Shae said, pointing to Phoebe, "for my friend."

"One cheesecake, coming up."

Phoebe stared at Shae and giggled, then she became serious again. "I saw him this morning."

"Lee?" Shae asked.

"Aye."

Shae took a bite of her burger and swallowed. "I thought you said you haven't been able to contact him."

"I haven't. He reached me."

"I see. Did he say anything that may help?"

"He has traveled to the Sekakawon with his father and brothers." Except for the intimate details, Phoebe relayed what had transpired during Lee's visit.

"Can't say that I've heard of the Sekakawon. Are you certain he can't return to this time?"

"Nay, I'm not certain of anything. I only want my family to be together again."

Shae reached across the table and patted Phoebe's hand. "That's understandable, and I'll see what I can do to help."

"Thank you, Shae. You're a true friend."

"We've been through a lot together, haven't we?"

"Aye." Lee had introduced her to Shae. In turn, Shae had found her the transitional housing where she had met Meg. All had been instrumental in her adjustment to the twenty-first century.

After lunch, Phoebe settled in a chair in Shae's office and closed her eyes. Shae coached her through the familiar breathing exercises, and her body relaxed. Again she was in the forest, running from the mob. Henry called after her. Her back stung from the whip's lashes, and she feared what lay ahead, 'til hearing *his* voice.

"Wind Talker," she said.

"Forward."

Obeying his directive, she crossed the swift running stream but was lost. "Where, my love? Where am I to go?"

The raging shouts of the mob came from the opposite bank. Their torches formed bright flames.

"Walks Through Mist, follow my voice."

His words continued upon the breeze, and she traveled through the forest. A thick mist surrounded her and swallowed her like a ship in a storm. The wind picked up, and she gripped the hound's collar. The crow floated on the air currents ahead of her, and together they sailed on the wind. In this place time had no meaning. All periods existed side by side with no division betwixt them, and she relived her life experiences. As she passed through her own lifetime, other centuries formed afore her eyes.

Men dressed in tailored coats, with tricorn hats and powdered wigs. She had seen such pictures in history books and presumed the men were from the eighteenth century. Cannon roared, and women wore hoop skirts. Men charged over a hill, firing muskets. The Civil War—she had no doubt, but on the other side of the mound cars honked. These vehicles were boxy, like an open carriage, and the horns sounded more like airy rattles.

The mist faded. "Follow the light," he whispered.

Up ahead, lights were everywhere. Confused, she was unable to determine which one to follow. She stepped out of the fog. The hound was no longer with her, and the crow and wind had vanished. The city bustled with people, and the lights blinded her.

Cars honked wildly. She moved into the street, and lights pursued her. Unlike afore, the car swerved to keep from striking her. Tires screeched. Like in slow motion, the car collided into another's side. Metal crashed. Glass shattered and rained upon her. She was a silent observer, watching on. Shouts and screams from other witnesses surrounded her and ran toward the cars to help. From inside one of the cars, a baby cried.

Phoebe inched toward the vehicle with the wailing child. In the faint light, she spotted black hair, thrashing arms, and kicking legs. She blinked back the image to Shae sitting across from her. Yet, she couldn't rid herself of the image of the baby. "I saw more," she said, closing her eyes. " 'Twas as if the centuries floated afore my eyes."

"Good. We'll focus on that next time. I think we're getting closer, Phoebe."

Unable to rid her mind of the accident, Phoebe reopened her eyes. "But there was something else."

Shae waited for her to explain.

"Instead of the car striking me, it crashed into another. I've ne'er seen it afore." The air crackled, and Phoebe broke into a cold sweat.

"Phoebe? What's wrong?"

The baby. *Heather!* The accident had been real. Phoebe stood. "I must go to Heather."

Shae gripped Phoebe's arm to keep her from running blindly out of the room. "I thought you said that Meg was watching her."

"She is." Heather's cries faded. She turned and Shae's face came into focus. Fear registered upon her friend's countenance.

"Phoebe, tell me what's happening."

" 'Twas like the time when Lee was shot—only now the feeling is gone. If she had been injured or . . . killed, I would know."

Shae handed her the phone. "Call Meg and make certain everything is all right."

Her hands shook, but Phoebe dialed the number to home. The answering machine picked up, and Lee's voice came across the line saying to leave a message. "Meg, if you're there, please call me and let me know everyone is well." She hung up and dialed Meg's cell number. This time, she received voicemail. Phoebe repeated her message. She hung up the phone. "I don't know where else to call. Meg doesn't have a land line."

"Are you certain there was an accident?"

"Nay, but something has happened. I felt it."

"Could Heather have been traveling in a car with Meg?"

"Mayhap."

Shae picked up the phone. "I'm calling Ed. He can tell us if there have been any accidents."

Confused by Shae's action, Phoebe said, "Detectives don't handle accident reports, 'less foul play is suspected."

"True, but they have access to the necessary computers. Ed . . ." Phoebe listened as Shae relayed her suspicion. "He's checking. What does Meg drive, Phoebe?"

"A tan Hyundai. I know not the make nor year. 'Tis not a new car."

Shae passed along the information. After what seemed like an eternity, she swallowed. "You're sure? Okay, thanks, Ed." She hung up the phone. "A black woman and two small children were taken to the hospital. One child was black, the other believed to be Hispanic."

Phoebe sank to the chair.

"I'll take you to the hospital." Shae helped Phoebe to her feet and guided her to the door.

'Twas so much like the night that Lee had been shot—only this time, Russ wasn't with them. Shae led her to the car and slammed the door behind her, then whisked them through the streets to the hospital. First Lee, and now Heather. She had to bite her lip to keep from screaming. *How much more could a body endure?* Of late she had been negligent in appeasing Oke's wrath. When she got home, she would be sure to present an offering of tobacco.

Outside the hospital, Shae braked to a halt. "You go ahead, while I park the car."

Numbly, Phoebe obeyed. The glass doors whooshed open. In the waiting room, the seats were filled with coughing and groaning people waiting to see a doctor. She approached the desk and inquired about Meg and the children.

"Are you related?" the desk receptionist asked.

"I'm Heather's momma. Meg is my friend, and Tiffany is her daughter." She showed her driver's license to the receptionist.

"I'll get someone to take you to your daughter."

Shae joined her. "Any word?"

"They said someone will take me to her."

A blonde-haired nurse in scrubs rounded the corridor and greeted them. "Mrs. Crowley, if the baby brought in is indeed your daughter, she's fine."

Phoebe gasped in relief. "And Meg and her daughter Tiffany?"

The nurse waved at her to slow down. "First, let's make certain the baby is your daughter. We've checked her for a concussion, and she's fine. Not a scratch or a bruise." She motioned for Phoebe to follow her down the corridor.

Thankfully, Shae accompanied her. After being hit by the car, Phoebe had decided she hated hospitals. When Lee had been shot, her feeling had only intensified. The halls seemed filled of naught more than pain and suffering. Now, her daughter was housed here?

They entered a room with a curtain round two cribs. The nurse escorted her to the one in the farthest corner.

Gripping the slats, Heather squealed with excitement and danced on her toes. Phoebe swept the baby into her arms and checked her condition. As the nurse had said, she was fine. "How are Meg and Tiffany?"

"The young girl is fine, but the woman is in surgery."

Phoebe had that sick feeling once more and hugged Heather tighter. "How bad is she?"

"We won't know until she's out of surgery. Does she have any next of kin that we can contact?"

"Nay, only her daughter Tiffany."

"I see. Anyway, if you like, you can wait with your daughter here until we know about your friend." She pointed to the chair aside the bed.

Phoebe thanked the nurse, and she left the room.

Shae squeezed Phoebe's arm. "I can wait with you if you like."

"That would be most welcome."

After a more complete inspection of Heather's body, Phoebe was convinced her daughter had suffered no physical harm. For the next few hours, she rocked, played, and nursed Heather. Round dinner time, Shae brought a tray. 'Twas nearly seven in the eve when the blonde-haired nurse returned.

"Mrs. Crowley, your friend is in the ICU. The doctor will speak to you and let you briefly see her if you like."

Shae watched Heather whilst Phoebe checked on Tiffany, then the nurse escorted her to the doctor's office.

"Mrs. Crowley, please have a seat," the doctor said. He motioned to a chair. "I understand that your friend's daughter is her only family."

She sat in the chair that he had indicated. "Aye."

"Your friend has three broken ribs and a lung contusion. We're giving her fluids, and if necessary, we'll use a ventilator to help her breathe. But, she's also suffered a concussion and is unconscious. We've run a CT scan, didn't find any serious brain injury, but will run an MRI to be on the safe side. Right now we remain hopeful that, with support and rest, she'll regain consciousness and be fine."

As a healer with some education in modern nursing, she comprehended what the doctor was saying. "May I see her?"

"Of course."

The doctor escorted her down the corridor. Most hospitals looked the same—dull and lifeless. They entered a room, and the blue curtains separating the beds seemed familiar. She had been wrong to think she could be a nurse in this century. She was a cunning woman, who personally cared for the sick and injured, working round the clock, if necessary. Although familiar with the extended hours dedicated nurses put in, a cunning woman often couldn't afford the luxury of a day off. Illnesses and accidents knew naught of holidays.

Tubes trailed from Meg's body, and she looked more like a broken doll. Bruises and bandages covered her countenance. Phoebe approached the bed. "Meg..."

Not a lash fluttered to signal that Meg had heard her voice, and Phoebe grasped her friend's hand. "Take as long as you need to heal. I shall tend to Tiffany." Unlike Lee after his gunshot wound, Meg showed no signs of awareness.

19

Wind Talker

A WEEK PASSED, THEN TWO. I TRIED to reach Phoebe through the dreaming without success. Unwilling to give up hope, I attempted again. As usual, the wind and Crow accompanied me, and a dragonfly flitted on the breeze beside us. When I emerged from the mist I entered a hospital room. An IV tube trailed from an unconscious woman's forearm, while the rhythm of a ventilator and beep of a heart monitor sounded. With her back facing me, another woman bent over the prone form on the bed. "Dammit, don't just lie there. Wake up!"

Her voice sounded familiar. "Meg?"

She turned toward me and blinked. "Lee? You can hear me?"

Fearing the person on the bed might be Phoebe, I stepped closer. It wasn't Phoebe, but—Meg. "I can hear you."

"Thank God." She covered her face and sank to her knees.

"Meg, what's happened?" I grasped her forearms and helped her regain her feet.

Her voice trembled as she spoke. "I was in a car accident. The girls were in the back seat. They're fine, but me . . . I keep hearing people say that I have a concussion and I'm in a coma." She lifted her arms and gazed at them as if they were alien body parts. "How can that be? I'm here, but yet . . ."

I thanked Ahone that Heather and Tiffany were fine and moved closer to the prostrate body on the bed. When I had served as a traffic cop, I had witnessed many such injuries firsthand. Some walked away. Others were left with severe disabilities, while an unfortunate few simply never woke up. "I'm sorry you went through that but, if you can, tell me what happened."

"Phoebe had an appointment with Shae. I had taken the girls to the park and was driving back to your house. I stopped at a red light when I saw Elenor's house in flames. Indians . . ." When I flinched, she fell silent.

"Go ahead, Meg. Tell me what you saw."

"They surrounded the house and were attacking. You and Charging Bear were there—on opposite sides. I wanted to tell Phoebe, but her phone went to voicemail. The light turned green. All I could think of was getting back and telling Phoebe. I drove into the intersection—the next thing I recall, I was standing over myself, like just now, unable to tell anyone what happened—until you came along." She placed a hand over her mouth and shook her head. "You're not really here, are you? I'm dead."

I glanced at the beeping heart monitor. "You're not dead, but I'm not really here either."

"The dreaming." She calmed slightly. "Lee, is there any way that you can get through to Phoebe and warn her about what I saw?"

"I've been trying. For some reason, I'm unable to reach her."

"She visits me every day. I try to warn her then, but for some reason, she doesn't hear me."

"She's probably preoccupied with everything that's happened. I'll continue to try and reach her. In the meantime, I can warn Elenor."

Meg's eyes widened. "But you and Charging Bear. What if the two of you end up on opposing sides?"

"We won't. We're brothers. I'll get word to Elenor." For nearly a month I had been a guest at Black Owl's hearth. While I rejoiced in getting to know my family, it was time for me to make the journey back to the homestead to make certain that all was well.

"Thank you." She gave me a sisterly hug. "And if you see Charging Bear, tell him . . . tell him—"

"I will." The wind picked up, warning me that my time in this realm would soon end. Meg's image faded, and I returned to my spot overlooking the river.

* * *

William chose to come with me, and Wildcat agreed to be our guide. I was thankful for my brother's help. Otherwise I would have stumbled aimlessly through the forest. At dawn, we said our good-byes. Black Owl saw us off, and we agreed to meet at Elenor's in the spring. With the onset of winter, the air was cold, and I was grateful for the warmth of the duck-down mantle the chief had presented to me for being Black Owl's long-lost son.

As we set out, I worried about my ability to contact Phoebe during our journey. If the trip was anything like my arrival to the Sekakawon town, I'd probably be too exhausted to even try to enter the dreaming during our few quiet moments. Wildcat set the pace and easily outdistanced William and me. Oftentimes, he needed to double back just to be certain nothing out of the ordinary had happened to us.

"You differ from the others, Wind Talker," William said, when Wildcat was far in front of us.

His words brought me out of my thoughts and momentarily distracted me from my encounter with Meg. "In what way?"

"For one, you speak English—quite fluently it seems—only it differs from mine."

I hadn't confided in William that I had spent most of my life in the twentieth century. "I was raised by a whi—colonials. I'm also married to one."

"Will I have the opportunity to meet her?"

I wished. "Not right away. It's difficult to explain." I debated whether to tell him the truth, but decided against it. Now was not the time. The others that I had revealed the truth to had been family or tribal members. So much remained unknown about William.

Like before, our trip went slowly. Once again, I placed my pack on Wildcat's back in order to slow him down, and when we met others on the trail, he was only too happy to stop for a chat and smoke. I attempted to express my urgency for haste, but Wildcat merely waved a hand that all was fine.

Before bedding down on the fourth night, Wildcat informed us that we should arrive at our destination the following day. Although

I had done my fair share of camping in my previous life as well as learning to sleep in some pretty strange places in my duties as a cop, I had not grown accustomed to sleeping on the cold, bare earth. I tossed and turned on the unforgiving hard ground until I finally gave up. I bundled my mantle around me. As I got to my feet, the winter wind cut through me. An owl's hoots traveled on the gusts, making the sound eerier than usual. Only then did it dawn on me: the wind *was* talking. I merely had to listen for the message.

I closed my eyes and envisioned the candle in my mind. Even the flame was governed by the wind—for if the blasts were too strong, the fire would be snuffed out. I settled back against a tree and for some reason, I thought of a wind chime, blowing gently in the breeze. Drafts. Squalls. Gales. Hurricanes. My head was overloading with information. All were forms of communication.

In the background, I heard a ferocious cawing—loud and fast. I covered my ears, but Crow's call only grew in intensity until the sound emanated overhead. I looked up, and Crow flapped his wings on the branch above me. "What's wrong?" I asked.

He took flight. At first I hesitated, but he circled back to me, cawing unmercifully. Never having seen the bird this agitated before, I had no doubt that I was meant to follow him. We traveled through the woodland until reaching the James River. The gentle roll of the land seemed familiar, but I couldn't quite place where I was. Upstream, I spotted smoke and ran toward it.

A familiar pitched-roof house came into view, engulfed in flames. Smoke billowed in the wind. The closer I got, the more difficult it became to breathe. Coughing and choking, I made my way through the black clouds. Near the door lay Christopher with an arrow in his back. I kneeled down and felt for a pulse. The boy was dead. Beside him lay Elenor with an arrow protruding from her breast.

I gasped for breath and struggled to my feet. Hoping that I might rescue someone inside, I kicked in the door. Smoke surged out, instantly blinding me. I tripped over something in the entryway and crashed to the floor. Glass shards that were scattered across the floorboards cut into my arms, but I reached out to the object.

The small arms were cold and lifeless, and the hair was long. A little girl. *Elsa.*

Was my whole family dead? Dizzy from the smoke, I struggled to my feet. In the parlor lay Henry, Bess, and the two-year-old Nicolas. Blood covered the top of Henry's head where his crown of hair had been cut away. The only person missing was Bess's son.

Throughout the years, I had viewed more murders than I cared to count, but nothing compared to the death of my own family—yet again. My legs weakened and I slumped to the floor. Ready to die with my family, I lay there, watching flames engulf the floor above. Coughing back the smoke, I sang my death song.

Wind Talker.

Phoebe's voice reminded me that if I chose death over life I would be shirking my responsibilities and abandoning her and Heather. With renewed determination, I crawled toward the door on my hands and knees. A blazing beam crashed to the floor next to me. Smoke nearly got the best of me, and I gasped for air. Near the door, someone tugged on my right arm, then my left. Gripped in an arm lock, I was unable to move.

"Wind Talker."

At the sound of my name, I blinked and Wildcat's face came into focus. Beside him stood William. I coughed, and a moment passed before I realized I was no longer in the burning house. "They're all dead."

Wildcat's brows wrinkled. "Who is dead?"

I cast my gaze around me. Dawn had arrived, and there was no smoke nor burning building. I had never left camp. Meg had somehow shared her vision with me. "I've had a vision that my people had murdered my English family."

"You were sent the vision for a reason," Wildcat said.

"Something that will come to pass?"

"I cannot say. Perhaps you've been given the opportunity to prevent unnecessary bloodshed."

All the more determined to reach Elenor and Henry's house, we set out. By midday, we reached the mass grave where my mother had been buried. I halted briefly to pay my respects. The bleached bones rekindled the death screams in my mind.

"What is it?" William asked.

"It's where I should have been buried," I replied.

I had to make certain everyone at the house was all right. I turned abruptly, and for once, I was able to keep pace with Wildcat. But I got that odd gnawing in my gut. I tried to dismiss the suspicion, attributing it to my earlier vision and passing the mass grave, but the forest had grown quiet. Too quiet—not even a bird sang.

At the same time that I reached for my Glock, Wildcat readied his bow. I motioned for William to remain behind us. His face paled, but being unarmed, he complied.

A flock of turkeys fluttered across the path. Breathing easier, I started to re-holster the Glock, but Wildcat waved at me to halt. A shot rang out, and Wildcat flew back. Before I could return fire, a gun butt connected with the side of my face. Blinding pain coursed throughout my head, and I reeled to the ground. Blood ran into my eyes.

A shadowy face loomed over me.

The fog nearly sucked me under. "William?" I managed to utter. "You speak English?"

The accent was definitely a colonial one. "I do." I struggled to sit up.

"Stay where you are, savage."

I wiped the blood from my eyes, and a bearded face shimmered in and out of focus. In his hands, he aimed a flintlock rifle at me. My own gun lay a few feet out of my fingers' reach.

"Don't e'en think about it." His booted foot kicked me in the groin.

Rage blinded me from feeling any pain, and I rushed at him. The flintlock discharged, but the ball struck the ground. My hands encircled his throat. The stench of his unwashed body only fueled my anger. He gasped, and the veins in his neck bulged. His hands clawed at mine, but my grip grew tighter. His lips turned blue.

"Let him go!" A red-haired colonial aimed my own gun to my temple.

Bloody bubbles appeared on the bearded man's mouth, but I loosened my grip. His own hands went to his throat as he leaped out of my reach.

"Poor bloody bastard," said the man holding my Glock. Menacing blue eyes stared at me, almost daring me to move. His fingers were poised near the trigger, and even though he would never have seen a Glock before, there was no doubt in my mind that he'd be able to carry out his intention. "On your knees."

I needed no encouragement. The pain that I had blocked from the blow to the balls doubled me over in agony.

Both men laughed. "He's not so mighty," said the red-haired man.

The bearded man rubbed his neck. "I'd like to teach him a lesson afore you shoot him." The other man waved him on, and he withdrew a knife. "My father was tortured to death by the likes of your kind. The women sawed away his fingers, then his hands, and threw them on the fire whilst he watched and screamed in agony. What do you have to say about it?"

"I wasn't there. I was raised by colonials."

"Then why were you traveling with other savages?"

I presumed Wildcat was lying somewhere either wounded or dead, and I had no idea what had happened to William. "I was paying my respects to my mother. She was murdered by colonials around thirty years ago. The warrior you gunned down is my half-brother." The pain in my groin eased somewhat, and I met the bearded man's gaze in challenge. If they were going to execute me, I would die like a warrior.

I spotted three figures behind the men in the distance, one carrying a flintlock. At first I thought they were joining the men in front of me, but one cried out, "You will release him!"

As they moved closer, I recognized Henry, James, and William. William retrieved the bearded man's flintlock from the ground.

"I said release him," Henry shouted once more. "Drop the pistol."

The Glock lowered slightly.

Henry placed the flintlock in the red-haired man's back. The Glock dropped to the ground, and I snatched it out of his reach. "Wildcat?"

"I couldn't find him," William said.

Unable to stand straight, I scrambled to my feet as best as I could. When I walked, I hobbled, but I returned to the spot where Wildcat had been shot. I followed the tracks. They led me to some scrub where I discovered his limp form beneath a tree. I bent down. His pulse was flighty, but he was alive.

"Wind Talker?" came Wildcat's voice.

I hushed him and inspected his wound. "Save your energy." Fresh blood oozed from his chest. Henry was beside me and handed me a cloth. I pressed the linen to Wildcat's wound to staunch the flow.

"Let's get him to the house," Henry said. "Elenor and Bess will be able to help."

I pulled Wildcat's left arm around my shoulder and helped him sit up. He wavered, but I held him steady. William got on his right side and together, we helped Wildcat stand. None too stable, he took a step, then another. Slowly, we moved forward. When we reached the area where we had met the colonials, there was no sign of them.

"They ran off," Henry said, as if reading my thoughts.

"As long as they don't return."

"If they do, James got their flintlocks."

I should have known that Henry would leave nothing to oversight, but my vision of the family's death remained strong in my mind. After we got Wildcat to safety, I would tell him about it. Although our progress was slow, the house came into view. Once inside, Elenor and Bess guided us to the other room, and we carefully placed Wildcat on the bed.

With shears, Elenor cut Wildcat's shirt away and inspected the wound. "The ball must be removed if he is to have any chance to live."

The thought of surgery without anesthesia nearly sickened me, and I questioned my fortitude more than Wildcat's. "If that's what must be done," I finally said. "Do you need my help?"

"Bess will assist me. Wait outside, and I'll let you know any news when I can."

Almost with relief, I turned away and staggered.

"I think you had best sit down, lad." Henry grasped my arm and led me to a chair.

"Thanks, Henry. I'm fine." Even William stood over me with an uneasy frown. "I'm just worried about Wildcat."

"Elenor and Bess will do their best to save his life."

"I know that."

A groan echoed from the other room. Anyone else would have screamed his fool head off, but Wildcat was a warrior and as such, he would do his utmost to not show pain. Resisting the urge to check on him, I waited. I'd only get in the way, I reasoned. Then, I heard a whisper, and another. Unable to make out their words, I presumed the women were discussing their course of action. While Elenor comprehended some Algonquian and Wildcat knew some English, they'd need a translator for any extensive conversations.

I stepped forward, but Henry drew me back. "They'll let you know if you're needed."

Or if Wildcat had died. Neither of us voiced the thought aloud, but he was right. Unused to being inactive, I paced. Even when Heather had been born I hadn't resorted to striding back and forth across the floor, but then I had remained involved by being at Phoebe's side and coaching her through the birth. Now, I felt totally helpless.

Suddenly the other room grew mighty quiet. I strained to hear any sounds, but there were none. No one came to the door, which led me to believe Wildcat must still be alive. I reseated myself and took a few deep breaths. Was this how Ed felt when I had been shot? I lowered my head to my hands. *Don't die, Wildcat.*

Time drifted. I had no idea how long I sat there, when a gentle hand went to my shoulder. "Lee?"

I looked up at Elenor, standing in front of me. Her usually neat hair strayed.

"Bess and I have removed the ball from Wildcat's chest. He lives, but I fear he has lost too much blood."

I swallowed. "So you're telling me . . . ?"

She squeezed my shoulder. "He will perish."

"Then he went through the pain of surgery for nothing?"

" 'Twas the only chance he had, but 'twasn't enough. I wish I could do more."

"May I see him?"

"Aye." Elenor turned and led the way to the other room.

Wildcat sprawled on the bed with his chest covered in a hemp cloth. Blood spattered the bandages. Thankfully, he was unconscious and suffered no pain. I, too, had lost a significant amount of blood after being shot, but I had received a transfusion. *Why not Wildcat?* "Elenor, you can give him my blood."

"Give your blood to Wildcat?"

"In the twenty-first century, we do it all the time. I'm O positive, and if I recall what I know about biology correctly that means I can donate to him, unless he's Rh negative. But if it's the only chance he has, it's the risk we must take."

Her eyes flickered. "I know not what you speak of. 'Tis something I've ne'er done. Where would I begin?"

"Your mother will know how. She took some nursing courses before Heather's birth."

"Then we must contact her."

"We?"

"Aye, I will need your guidance to reach Momma, but I need to speak to her in order to make sense of how I go about giving one's blood to another."

I worried about my recent lack of success in reaching Phoebe. Time was critical. I had to try. "We'll contact her right here. It's important that we remain near Wildcat."

Elenor nodded in agreement.

Phoebe. I attempted to clear my mind, but found it difficult with Elenor standing nearby. *Wildcat's life is at stake.* I pictured the candle in my mind's eye. *Absorb the flame.* Nothing. I tried again and closed my eyes. *Phoebe, I need to speak with you.* Still nothing. I reopened my eyes and shook my head.

"You're trying too hard," Elenor said.

"I've been unable to reach her lately."

"You shall be successful this time. Pray try again."

Her words gave me the confidence that I needed. I took a deep breath and formed the image of the candle in my head. Mist surrounded me, and Crow flew ahead of me on the wind. Once again, the dragonfly joined us. When the mist cleared, we entered a hospital room—the same one as before. Meg lay on the bed still unconscious, and another woman bent over her, talking to her gently—a red-haired woman. "Phoebe."

"Lee, I still can't get through to her."

The voice had come from behind me. I turned to Meg. She stared at Elenor, who looked about the room in wide-eye amazement. "Did you warn her?" Meg asked.

"Not yet. Meg, I'm here for another reason, and there's no time to explain right now. Phoebe—"

"I told you that I can't communicate with her."

How could I see Phoebe but be unable to speak with her? "I've got to get through somehow. Wildcat must have a blood transfusion or he'll die. Elenor needs to know how to go about it."

"Phoebe's never done a transfusion, but I have."

The dreaming had led me to Meg for a reason. I explained the situation.

"A transfusion might save his life," Meg agreed, "but what about typing?"

"I'm O positive," I said.

"Still a risk."

"A chance we must take."

"All right then." Meg looked toward Elenor. "Do you have anything to keep the blood from coagulating?" Elenor stared at her transfixed, and Meg tried again, "So that it won't clot?"

"Nay."

"I don't like the idea of someone who's inexperienced drawing from an artery." Meg shook her head. "I'm not certain . . . do you have syringes?"

"Aye."

"And needles?"

"Aye."

"But they won't be hypodermic needles. I don't think they were invented until the nineteenth century. Do you understand what I'm saying? The needle has to have a hollow point so the blood can be drawn into the syringe."

"Mayhap a quill will work?"

"Will that be strong enough to puncture the vein?"

"Nay, I use a fleam for bloodletting," Elenor replied.

Meg scrunched her face, and I wondered what I was getting myself in to. "Let me show you what you must do," she said to Elenor. Meg glanced at me, and I nodded for her to continue. She stretched my arm and shoved up the sleeve. "Are you familiar with this vein?" she asked, pointing to the crook of my arm.

"Aye."

"I hope you have help because you're going to need to be quick. Use your fleam on both men in this spot. If you have them side by side, that will help your speed. Insert the quill in the vein to keep it open, then place the syringe into the quill. Withdraw about 20cc's of blood—"

"How much is 20cc's?"

Meg let go of my arm. "Follow me." She led us to an empty operating room and went over to the open bins where the sterile syringes were kept. "Look carefully at the syringes, Elenor. Which size is closest to yours?"

Elenor studied the varying sizes. She picked up a package. "This size."

"Okay, fill the syringe. After you do that, you must immediately put another clean empty syringe to Lee's vein, and start again. At the same time, your helper will be injecting the filled syringe into Wildcat. You'll need about six syringes."

"I only have four."

"That'll make things tougher, but it still might be doable. After you use a syringe, you'll need someone else to flush it with saline—"

"Saline?" Elenor asked.

"Salt water should do, but boil the water first. Flush the syringe with the water before you use it again. You've got to keep the rotation going quickly, or the blood will clot on you. If Wildcat gets any tingling pains, back or head pain, difficulty breathing, or a weak or flighty pulse, stop immediately. The transfusion won't work, and there's no sense in risking Lee's life any further. The next thing you have to worry about is not to take too much blood from Lee. There's no easy way to measure, but I'm guessing you don't want to take anymore than, say—" She stopped a moment to calculate in her head. "—thirty-five syringe fills from him. That should be well below two pints, but I wouldn't want you to take any chances without exact measurements. Stop at any time, if he gets weak or faints on you."

"I can do that," she assured Meg.

I glanced at Meg. "It will be all right, Meg."

She nodded, but before either of us could say anything else, Elenor and I returned. Wildcat lay on the bed, and Elenor was already scurrying around the room, telling the household what tasks they would perform.

Wildcat's eyes had become glazed, but he still breathed. "Hold on, brother," I said. "We're going to help you."

A small smile appeared on his lips and his voice was barely a whisper when he spoke. "I don't fear death."

"I know you don't, but there's no reason to die if it's unnecessary." I went on to explain the procedure ahead.

"Lee," Elenor said, returning to my side. "I want you to lie down." She gestured to one of the children's cots near the bed.

I did as she instructed. The cot was small—definitely intended for someone shorter than I was. My feet hung over the edge, but momentary discomfort was a small price to pay if it could save Wildcat's life.

Before long, Elenor stood over me, and Bess was poised beside Wildcat. Both women held a small coiled-iron device with a pointed end that I recognized from pictures in books. They were tools used for bloodletting. The sight of it made me shiver.

"Are you ready to proceed?" she asked.

"I am."

She waved at Bess to begin, and both women set to work. The sharp end of the fleam pierced the crook of my arm. Strangely enough, in Elenor's expert hands, the puncture wound felt no worse than a needle prick. She placed a penetrating quill into my vein, then put a brass syringe inside the quill and drew some blood.

If I hadn't seen the entire operation take place with seventeenth-century instruments, I would have thought I was in a twenty-first-century doctor's office getting a blood test.

Elenor handed the syringe to Bess, and Henry gave her a clean one. Once again, she withdrew more blood. At first I kept track of the number of times she changed syringes, but after about five, I lost count. Another syringe went in and another. Every so often Elenor asked me how I was faring. Finally she stopped, placed a clean linen cloth on my arm, and bent it to staunch the blood flow. She handed me a flagon. "Drink."

Thankful the drink wasn't ale, I sipped some water. "I've always gotten a cookie when I've donated blood before." She frowned in confusion, and my stomach rumbled. I needed a sugar fix but what was available during the winter? At home Phoebe had fixed mince pies at Christmas. "Mince pie."

"Mince pie?"

Without being asked, Bess prepared a bowl and placed it in front of me with a spoon. I had never acquired the taste for the spicy, fruity mix, but I began to eat. "How's Wildcat?" I asked.

" 'Tis too early to tell," Elenor replied.

After I finished the mince pie, I attempted to sit up, but everything around me suddenly swayed. "Maybe that wasn't such a good idea."

Elenor and Henry grasped my arms to help steady me. "You must rest," she said.

Content to follow her orders, I laid back with their help. Except for being tired, I had previously never experienced any side effects from blood donation, but then Elenor had likely withdrawn more than I had ever given before. "Just let me know if there are any changes in Wildcat—good or bad."

"I shall," she promised.

More tired than I realized, I closed my eyes and envisioned the house in flames. Elenor had an arrow in her chest, and Henry had been scalped.

20

Phoebe

NEARLY TWO WEEKS HAD PASSED since the accident. Phoebe visited every day, whilst Shae minded the lasses. In the beginning, Meg's legs moved and her fists clenched. Occasionally, she muttered gibberish. After three days, her eyes were open more than afore. Phoebe spotted fear in them and spoke to her in a soothing voice. A week later, Meg ate solid food. She brought the spoon to her friend's mouth. Meg chewed and swallowed like she had recently learned the task. "Do you know where you are?" Phoebe asked.

"In a hospital."

'Twas a good sign 'til the next sentence was more gibberish. As the days progressed Meg seemed more and more aware, but on this day, for some peculiar reason, Phoebe sensed Lee's presence. The feeling faded as quickly as she had detected it. She gazed across a row of ten beds. Only a couple were empty. A doctor whispered to a nurse. Lee was nowhere in sight.

"Phoebe . . ."

She glanced at Meg and smiled. "You recognized me."

"He was here."

"Who was here?"

"Lee. He's been trying to contact you."

Phoebe grasped Meg's hands. "As I have him—and you."

Meg's countenance took on a look of despair. "And I you. Lee heard me."

"Through the dreaming?"

Meg nodded. "I think so. Phoebe..." The pupils in her eyes grew fixed.

"Stay with me, Meg." Her friend focused on her, and Phoebe continued, "What did he say?"

"I explained to Elenor how to do a blood transfusion."

Phoebe's breathing quickened. "Has he been injured?"

"No. He's the donor." Meg's eyes closed.

"Meg? Meg?" But she was once again unresponsive.

Over the next few days, Meg remained awake for longer periods 'til she was almost normal again. Her memory had languished. She recalled naught of the accident nor her encounter with Lee. She endured daily physical therapy, learning how to walk again, and by the end of the month, she came home. Like she had tended Lee after his gunshot wound, Phoebe cared for her friend. Betwixt seeing to the children and Meg's needs, she had little time to herself. When Lee had been injured, she had infused bangue, or what they called pot in this century, into butter. He had warned her that, in this time, the herb was illegal. She had difficulty comprehending why. It had far fewer side effects than the drugs prescribed by the doctors for pain. She wished she had some for Meg.

When Meg had difficulty sleeping at night, Phoebe gently massaged her 'til she drifted off. During the day, Meg attempted to distract herself by playing on the laptop computer, and gradually with each passing day, she grew stronger. In the meantime, the dreaming could bring Meg relief for 'twas the one place she could move about as afore her accident.

Phoebe followed the hound and Meg walked aside her. A dragonfly flitted betwixt them. The air was much too cold for the insect, and she realized that like her hound, the dragonfly was a spirit. Unable to fathom the meaning, she continued on, but she ne'er reached Lee. In failure, she blew out the candle. "Why can I not reach him? You spoke with him."

"I did?"

"When you were in a coma."

Meg shook her head. "I don't remember, but I don't think we should give up. Besides, I'd like to see Charging Bear."

"I know that you care for him," Phoebe said.

"You warned me, and it's stupid. Phoebe, I don't want to just participate in the dreaming. I want to go with you when you return to the seventeenth century."

She should have seen Meg's request coming. "And Tiffany?"

"I won't leave her behind, any more than you would Heather."

"Meg, Africans are treated little better than Indians during that time. Why would you risk your daughter in such a way?"

"For the same reason you're willing to risk Heather. She can't pass for white any more than Tiffany or me. Tiffany's never had a father. I know Charging Bear is a good one, and I don't just care for him. I love him."

Phoebe relighted the candle. "Then you must learn the dreaming on your own. Concentrate on the flame. My guardian spirit will help you, and in time you shall discover your own."

Meg giggled. "I never thought I'd be buying into this mumbo jumbo, but I've already seen too many things not to believe." She stared at the flame. After a few minutes, she blinked. "It's not happening."

"Try again. Absorb the flame. Let it become part of you. 'Twill happen, if you allow it."

Phoebe watched as Meg attempted to concentrate. When she had shown Lee the dreaming the first time, he had nearly given up, but he persevered.

In frustration, Meg blinked.

"Seek my guardian spirit. He will help guide you."

Meg glanced over at Phoebe. "I keep seeing a dragonfly."

Phoebe smiled. 'Twas the same spirit that had accompanied them on their last venture. "Your guardian beckons you."

"A bug?" Meg said with her voice laced in disappointment. "I was hoping for something cool, like a wolf."

"We don't choose the spirits. They choose us."

"But a bug?"

"Dragonflies are not mere *bugs*. They are creatures of the wind and water, capable of moving in almost any direction. Did you not ask for a change in your life? Allow your guardian to show you how that may come about."

"Well—"

"Meg, the dragonfly is a beautiful animal with wings that can be as colorful as a rainbow. Their speed is nearly unmatched by some of the swiftest birds."

"But what does it all mean?"

"Only you can determine the answer. You have been sent a gift. Embrace it and see where it leads you."

Meg cracked a grin. "I never quite thought of it like that. And they are pretty." With renewed intensity, she stared into the flame.

Phoebe watched and waited 'til she felt herself being drawn in with Meg. Following the course of the dragonfly, they walked aside each other. On Phoebe's other side was her spirit dog. On and on they walked. The mist faded, and when they emerged from the fog, Phoebe stood on the banks of the James.

"Where are we?" Meg asked.

Waves lapped against the shore, and the sun rose in the sky toward the east. "Near Henry and Elenor's house. 'Tis near dawn."

"Blossoms are on the trees, so I'm presuming it's spring. Aren't the birds usually singing by this time?"

"Aye." The sense of solitude was overwhelming. In the distance, Phoebe spotted smoke drifting in the air. At first, she thought it was from a chimney, but then, it intensified. "Noooo!" She calmed herself. 'Twas the dreaming. They were here to learn. "Let's proceed with caution."

As they made their way along the forest trail, fresh spring green leaves blew in the gentle breeze. Smoke assaulted Phoebe's nostrils. A fierce shout shattered the tranquility, followed by another. 'Twas the sound of warriors' cries. A gunshot rang out.

Phoebe and Meg crept toward the sound when a brown-skinned man in a breechclout, his face painted black, stepped in front of them. His countenance remained hidden in the shadows, but he aimed his bow.

"Don't shoot," Phoebe said in Algonquian, hoping she had kept her voice from trembling. Meg gripped her arm and hunched against her. Certainly her friend felt her arm shaking. She continued, "A warrior is shamed if he turns to killing women and children."

The bow lowered. "Your people have brought the shame to all of us."

His voice sounded familiar. "You are my people." Phoebe motioned in the direction of the house. "And they are my people. My daughter and her children live there. They have ne'er harmed any of our people."

"Do they not live on Paspahegh land?"

"Aye, and I was adopted by the Paspahegh, which makes my daughter Paspahegh. She lives on the land of her ancestors."

He stepped from the shadows to where his countenance came into full view. Phoebe gasped. "Lightning Storm."

Meg glanced from the warrior to Phoebe. "Your first husband?"

"Aye." Instead of elation, Phoebe felt fear. "Little Hummingbird goes by Elenor now. Our daughter will die unless we can find a way to save all of them."

Palms up, he held out his hands. "The blood of my shame stains them."

When he had participated in paramount chief Opechancanough's organized attacks, Lightning Storm had resorted to killing women and children. Phoebe gripped his hands. "You hid your torment in silence, my love."

He withdrew from her handhold. "Walks Through Mist, the *tassantassas* continue to take our land and force their ways upon us. The warriors here today face the same conditions as I did and will show the *tassantassas* their place. You are too late to save our daughter. She has forsaken our ways and will remain among her chosen people. Like before, those in the path of the coming storm will die. If she's among them, there is little hope for her survival."

His warning was clear. Elenor was in grave danger.

"What did he say?" Meg asked.

Almost forgetting that her friend stood aside them, Phoebe translated as best as she could.

"Walks Through Mist . . ." Lightning Storm placed his hand under her chin and raised it 'til their gazes met. "I'm aware you have taken another."

"His name is Wind Talker. You knew him as Lee. You showed him your life and death during the dreaming so that we might understand what happened."

He broke their contact and took a step back. "He was given an honorable name. I have no doubt he will prove worthy."

"Lightning Storm..." For so long, she had wanted to see him one more time. Now the moment had arrived, there was so much she wanted to say, but she had no idea where to begin. She opened her mouth only for naught to come out.

"Tell Elenor that I'm sorry I wasn't there to see her grow to womanhood," he said.

"I have been absent from much of her life as well. She understands that you died bravely, defending our people."

A small smile appeared on Lightning Storm's lips. "Dark Moon has grown into a fine warrior in the afterlife."

With this news, Phoebe was pleased. Their son had died from diphtheria—a white man's disease—whilst still a small lad. She couldn't bear losing another child. "What must I do to save Elenor?"

"Place your faith in your friend's vision. She and Wind Talker have seen what lies ahead." He turned and began following the forest path.

Phoebe took a step, then staggered. Lightning Storm vanished.

Meg clenched Phoebe's arm. "What did he say?"

"He says that you and Lee have had a vision."

Meg pointed to herself. "Me? A vision?"

"Aye, and we must discover what it was."

21

Wind Talker

WITHOUT THE BLOOD TRANSFUSION, Wildcat would have died, but he was slowly recuperating from his gunshot wound and regaining his strength. Elenor and Bess were amazed at his improbable recovery and concluded that my blood had some sort of miraculous healing qualities. I explained the transfusion had worked because I knew my blood type. After a while the cunning women seemed to grasp the concept and warned me that should the need arise again, they wouldn't hesitate to volunteer me as their blood donor.

Certain they were serious, I hoped no one else needed a transfusion in the near future, but the vision continued to plague me. The time had come. I had to warn Henry. Near dawn, I met him inside the barn as he and James tended to the livestock. He saw me as I approached and smiled. "How is Wildcat this morning?"

"With each day, he's getting stronger. Henry, I need to speak with you—in private."

He nodded and gave James instructions for the horses, then joined me outside. "You're leaving."

"It's nothing like that, and I don't know how to tell you this, except straight out. I've had a vision."

"A vision?" he asked.

"It's similar to the dreaming, but I didn't go through the steps to enter the dreaming. I just saw it. I know you may have difficulty believing—"

"Nay, you know I have seen much since coming to Virginia that questions what I was taught as a lad. What sort of vision?"

"It's about my people, killing your family, including you."

He wobbled on his feet. "Elenor, Christopher…"

"All of them. The only one I didn't see was James."

Henry paled. "Do such *visions* normally come to pass?"

"I don't know. Wildcat told me that sometimes they're warnings to prevent such disasters. And you know I'll do whatever I can to keep it from happening, but I have no idea as to when it might take place. If I could reach Phoebe, she might be able to search the records for this century. Even then, the records are sparse for this time period."

"What should I do?"

"Be on your guard. That's all I ask."

"Aye, I shall, and I'll make certain the family takes proper precautions."

During the winter, Charging Bear visited twice, bringing pelts and deer meat in exchange for English goods. Although the colony was more sustainable than when it had first been settled, it remained considerably dependent on England. The spring ships had yet to arrive at port, giving Henry little to trade.

More to the point, Charging Bear's manner troubled me. I couldn't quite put my finger on what was wrong. After dealing with Henry, we passed a pipe around, and he asked about Meg and Phoebe. "I haven't been able to reach Phoebe, and Meg… she's been in an accident," I said. I described what I knew as best as I could, yet Charging Bear asked no questions. He was clearly distracted. It was almost like the vitality had been sucked right out of him. "How's Strong Bow?" I asked, changing the subject.

"He's in good health," he replied.

I had been a cop for far too long. Something was definitely wrong. Finally, I pulled him aside when the others were nowhere around. "What's wrong, Charging Bear? You're my brother. Tell me what troubles you."

He shook his head. "I don't know the details."

"Details? What details?"

"Come spring, there will be an attack on the colony. I don't know when and won't be allowed to trade again before then."

Attack? Paramount chief Opechancanough had attacked the colonists in 1622. Phoebe's first husband, Lightning Storm, had been involved. Had there been another? If only I could recall my history, but an organized attack could be the source of my visions. I squeezed Charging Bear's arm. "You may have saved Walks Through Mist's family."

"I wish I could say more, but the *weroance* plan in secrecy until shortly before it is time to make their move."

The fact that he had managed to gain some knowledge of the leaders' plans was useful. The vision Meg and I had seemed a possible reality. I had to keep trying to reach Phoebe. She might be able to provide me with more information.

When I entered the dreaming, Crow led the way, but the wind was absent. Foreboding filled me, yet when the mist vanished, I entered my own dining room. Phoebe, Meg, and Tiffany sat around a table with kiddie party favors. I waved, but no one returned it, nor did they look in my direction.

Phoebe rose and blew out a candle on a cake in the shape of cartoon-looking yellow duck, labeled with a one. From the high chair, Heather squealed in delight. I was missing my daughter's first birthday. Although my job had kept me away from the house for many hours at a time, I had never expected to be the sort of dad who missed milestones. My heart ached.

"Phoebe." But she didn't look in my direction. "Meg, I've reached you before." Nothing. I could see and hear them, but for whatever reason, I was invisible.

Like any kid's party, there was cake and ice cream. Afterward, Heather charged around the room while holding onto Phoebe's fingers for support. It wouldn't be long before she'd take the first step under her own power. And Meg seemed to be recovering slowly from the accident. She resorted to the use of a cane in getting around.

The idyllic scene lulled me into believing that I really was present. That if only I wished hard enough, I could stay and forget about the reason why I had come. I could call Ed and have my old job back. After spending most of the winter huddled around a fire, even Shae's comment about central heating haunted me. I had spent more nights than I cared to think about shivering in cold cars during stake outs; I thought how nice it would be to not have to worry about a fire going out in order to keep warm.

Oh what the hell. I *was* with my family—even if only in spirit. Tiffany blew bubbles, and Heather crawled after them. One popped on the floor near my foot before Heather could reach it. I knelt down. "Heather..." She looked up as if she had heard me, and I repeated her name. "If only you could talk, you could give your mother a message. I miss you—all of you."

Phoebe stepped beside our daughter and I straightened. For a moment, she seemed to gaze in my direction. Crow cawed a warning.

"Lee?" She smiled. "I knew you wouldn't miss Heather's birthday."

I had finally broken through whatever barrier had kept us apart. But the breeze came between us. Before the wind could separate us, I drew her into my arms, kissed, and hugged her. If only I held onto her tight enough... the gusts grew stronger, and my arms were empty. I sat near the James River in the same place as I had when first entering the dreaming. I clenched my hands and struggled to keep from screaming. I didn't know how long I had sat in the same spot, unmoving, when the spring air ruffled my hair. I cast my gaze to the tranquil waves and blinked. A small boat sailed toward Henry's dock. Uncertain whether I was visible to the crew, I ducked behind a clump of trees and watched as a couple of men secured the mooring.

Before I could alert Henry to the crew's presence, he appeared on the dock, grinning from ear to ear. The kids scampered after him, screaming with excitement and jumping up and down. No one needed to tell me who the men were. Henry's son and Elenor's husband had returned.

I sought out Wildcat and William and waited until the initial welcomes and hugs were over. Finally, the group turned in our direction. Elenor held Christopher's arm in a stranglehold grip. Around five foot ten with light brown hair and blue eyes, he reached out to shake my hand. Maybe due to the fact that he had a mixed heritage wife, he showed no hesitation greeting me. His grasp was strong and confident, but before my eyes his face shattered like glass.

Blinking back the vision, I withdrew my hand, and Christopher went on to meet Wildcat and William. My hand shook, and I waited a moment to catch my breath.

"What's wrong, brother?" Wildcat asked.

"Another vision." But he kept his place and didn't inquire further. I collected myself before following everyone else inside. As usual, the women outdid themselves and cooked a feast to welcome Christopher and David home.

Over the meal, Christopher told us about the war in England. Their ship and cargo had been seized, which was why it had taken them two years to return to Virginia.

My history of seventeenth-century England was even worse than my history of Virginia. When I thought of a civil war, I thought of the American one. I really had no idea what the English one was about, but I picked up on the fact that it affected the ships to and from England. Surprisingly, Virginia had remained neutral and benefited through trade with the Dutch, New England, and the West Indies.

By the time we retreated outside to pass the pipe and share more stories, Christopher and Elenor had withdrawn from the group. I hoped that Phoebe and I would be able to share a similar reunion soon, but reality hit me. Troubled by my visions and where they could be leading, I worried this reunion celebration might be cut short.

22

Phoebe

Even though lee's appearance had been fleeting, at least Phoebe had relished a moment in his arms. But like always, he had vanished too soon. Throughout the day, she maintained a cheerful countenance—for Heather's sake. 'Twas her first birthday, and Phoebe wouldn't mark the occasion with a sullen face. Whilst the lasses played, Meg attempted to reassure her, but her friend had her own worries. Her memory continued to lapse, and she had frequent headaches. Though she grew stronger, she had resorted to the use of a cane due to an unsteady gait from her head injury. The dreaming was a release from Meg's ailments, but the time had come to focus on her vision.

After the lasses went to bed, Phoebe went into the kitchen and collected the candle. In the parlor, they sat across from each other. She lit the candle. "Now concentrate."

Instead of seeing the hound, Phoebe spied a dragonfly flitting upon the wind.

"I see it," Meg said.

"Follow it. Your spirit has shown us that you shall lead."

"Am I ready?"

"Your guardian spirit must think so."

The blue-green insect's iridescent wings beat a steady rhythm and led them straight into the mist. Aside Meg, Phoebe called for Carol, a woman they had known when they lived in transitional housing.

Meg begged for Carol to come out of her room, and then Lee appeared aside them. Phoebe resisted the temptation to go to him. This was the dreaming. He motioned for them to stand away from the door. "Carol, I'm Detective Crowley with the county police. Are you all right?"

Behind the door, Carol choked a sob but said, "Yes."

"Open the door and let me see that you're all right." When no response returned, Lee tensed. "Carol..."

The door slowly opened, and a man with tattoos stepped out. Lee asked Carol, "Do you want to press charges?"

She shook her head and cried into a tissue.

Whilst Lee escorted the man out of the house, Phoebe and Meg went to Carol and asked her if she was all right.

The scene shifted and the dragonfly hovered. Meg smoked a glass tube. "Phoebe, I don't wish to relive this."

" 'Tis all right, Meg. Your guardian won't ask you 'til you're ready."

The dragonfly switched direction, and they continued through the mist. When they emerged from the fog, smoke rose from a chimney. They crept closer, and the brick house was engulfed in flames. "I've been here before," Meg said, as if half remembering.

The sight of flames from Elenor and Henry's house tore through Phoebe's heart. *'Twasn't real*. She took a deep breath and moved forward. They were here to discover answers. An arrow sailed past her shoulder. Near the door, a boy screamed and fell. *Christopher*. She charged to his side and bent down. No pulse.

"Phoebe..." Meg pointed.

Two feet away lay Elenor with an arrow protruding from her breast. "Elenor..." She took the broken body of her daughter into her arms and cried on Elenor's shoulder. "Elenor, 'tis my fault. I have failed you."

"Phoebe!" Meg shook her. "We're here to learn—to try and prevent this." She pulled Phoebe away from the lifeless corpse.

"Elenor..." In silent grief, Phoebe reached out, turned away, and stepped inside the house. Elsa lay inside the door. Nicolas and Bess were in the parlor. Blood covered the walls and furniture. It pooled across the floor. Phoebe and Meg followed the trail. A warrior stood over Henry. He held Henry's scalp lock in one hand. In the other, his knife cut around it. Henry screamed. The skin loosened, and the warrior jerked at Henry's hair, lifting the scalp from his head.

Without seeing Phoebe and Meg, the warrior tucked the bloody scalp into his belt and slipped out the back door. Henry slumped to the floor.

"Henry..." Phoebe bent down to him. His breathing was shallow, but he was alive. Meg placed a cloth to his head to stifle the blood flow.

"Phoebe..." He gripped her arm. "You came."

" 'Tis Meg and Lee's vision."

"Aye, he... he told me." He coughed up blood, and Phoebe examined him for another wound. "Phoebe..." His voice was so soft that Phoebe leaned closer to hear him better. "I ne'er meant to hurt you."

"Oh Henry, you didn't. Now, don't do anything foolish." She found the source of his bleeding. He had taken at least two knife wounds—one in the stomach and another in the chest. "Henry, I ne'er told you, but I did love you." She continued, whispering words of comfort.

"Phoebe..." Henry's eyes rolled up into his head, and his body writhed in fits. His shaking stopped, and he gasped for breath. "Phoebe..." His eyes flickered closed, then opened again in death. Elenor, Henry, her grandchildren, and her beloved servant... she couldn't think straight.

The smoke from the fire thickened around them, and Meg bent aside her. "There's more."

"More?" How could her body take any more? Yet, she sensed a presence, then heard a death song near the door where Elsa lay. "Wind Talker."

Meg and Phoebe groped their way through the smoke. Sputtering and coughing, Phoebe couldn't locate him. His song came from nowhere and everywhere at the same time. She had no guidance. 'Twas like the time that he had been lost in the woods as a lad. She stretched her arms afore her and fumbled. "Wind Talker, where are you?" She repeated his name, and his voice went silent.

A warrior emerged from the smoke. He wore black war paint on his face and chest and carried a bow and arrow.

Meg gasped. "Charging Bear?"

"Go back. You mustn't be here now."

"Charging Bear," Phoebe said.

He glanced in Phoebe's direction, and his gaze hardened. "Especially you, or you will die with your family."

"Is there any way we can change what is to come?" Phoebe asked.

"I don't know. There will be an attack. Of that I am certain. Whether you can save your family remains to be seen. On that day the *tassantassas* will be my enemy."

"Then you and Wind Talker . . . ?"

"The choice is his."

"You're brothers—not enemies."

"The choice is his," Charging Bear repeated.

"Charging Bear," Meg said. "This is how I envisioned you just before my accident. It scared me."

His countenance softened slightly. "My heart sings when you're near, but I must focus on the days ahead." He looked to Phoebe. "Walks Through Mist, tell her of our ways, so that she may understand."

"How can I? For *I* do not understand. Do not shame yourself as Lightning Storm did. He ne'er forgave himself for fighting the cowardly way of the *tassantassas*." With her words, Charging Bear vanished. Phoebe blinked, and they were once again in the living room.

"I remember now," Meg said. "That's what I saw before the accident. Charging Bear and Lee were enemies. I was so afraid from the vision that I didn't see the other car coming at me. It caused the accident."

Phoebe went round the table and hugged Meg. "There may not be much time, but we'll try to contact Lee to warn him and the family."

Meg withdrew from her grip but remained tense. "I already have."

"You have?"

"In the hospital. When I was in a coma. He heard me, and I told him about my vision."

Phoebe hugged her friend once more. "Then you may have saved them."

Meg grasped her cane and stood. "There might be more."

"More?"

"I can't believe that we were given the visions without a good reason. Maybe, just maybe, we can discover a date." Meg shuffled over to the desk, sat in the chair, and began tapping away on the computer.

Phoebe followed Meg and peered over her shoulder. Of all of the twenty-first-century devices, computers confused her the most. The keyboard was in disarray, and she wondered how anyone found the correct letters. Tab key, shift key, enter—she was unable to recall what function the differing keys performed, but Meg's fingers sailed across the keyboard in ways that Phoebe could only dream of.

"I think I found it!" Meg said. "In 1644 there was an Anglo-Powhatan War. Like the attack in 1622, many colonists were killed, but because there were more colonists in Virginia, the attack had less impact. It took place on April 18, 1644."

Such an attack would explain Lightning Storm's warning, as well as Charging Bear's appearance. " 'Twas spring when we caught glimpses during the dreaming. We need to find a way to warn them."

Meg gripped Phoebe's hand. "We both got through to Lee before. We can do it again."

"Aye. We shall try again."

23

Wind Talker

I LAY IN A DREAM STATE and imagined Phoebe calling my name. "Walks Through Mist," I whispered. More than anything, I wanted to draw her into my arms.

"Wind Talker," she repeated.

Her voice sounded urgent, and I sat up. "Phoebe?"

"The attack will come on April 18th."

The date—what was the date? In my muddled state, I couldn't think clearly. Spring had arrived, but I had lost track of the days. I suspected April had arrived because the trees were almost fully in leaf. "I don't know what the date is."

"Henry will have an almanac."

"Good. I'll ask him. Elenor's husband and Henry's son have returned."

"Then you're not here to aid in their return?"

I had never believed I could be helpful in that regard. "No. I'm convinced I'm here to help your family in the upcoming attack." Though she remained silent, I spotted fear in her eyes. Paspahegh women voiced their worries between themselves, so as not to distract the men from taking dangerous but necessary actions. "It's no different than when I was a cop," I said. "I have a job to do. I'm convinced this is why I was sent here." Her brow furrowed. "You know I'll do whatever I can to see that everyone is safe, including myself."

"Aye. I know." She wrapped her arms around my neck and gave me a kiss. "I love you."

"And I you." The breeze was at my back. I woke fully and she was gone. Wildcat slept several feet away from me on the barn floor, and William lay a few feet away yet again. I lowered my head, contemplating whether Phoebe had ever really been here.

April 18th kept going through my head. I blinked back the remaining traces of sleep. Phoebe had been here. That was the date of the attack. I stood. The pale light in the sky indicated that dawn was near.

Wildcat rose. "What's wrong, brother?"

"I think the attack may be near." I sprinted toward the house. Bess greeted me at the door as the family was stirring to life for the new day. She motioned for me to step inside. "I need to speak with Henry," I said. "It's a matter of urgency."

In the hall, Henry overheard me and moved toward me.

"What's the date?" I asked.

"Date?"

"I'm guessing that it's April."

"Aye." He showed me the way to his desk where he kept his almanac. " 'Tis the sixteenth."

A new urgency hit me. "In two days' time, the vision I told you about will become reality. Is that enough time for you to seek refuge in Jamestown?"

Henry swallowed. "What about you and Wildcat? You won't be welcome."

"Never mind us. Wildcat needs more time before he can travel, but if the rest of you are gone, the war parties shouldn't bother us. We speak their language. Do you have enough time to get to Jamestown?"

"Aye, but the shallop won't hold everyone."

My heart sank. "Then there is no choice—take the women and children."

Still in their night clothes, Christopher and Elenor joined us. I explained the situation as best as I could. "I'll stay," Christopher said.

Henry shook his head. "Nay, I shall stay behind. The shallop needs young men to guide the women and children to safety. I'm no longer young, and I can stay to protect the farm."

I gripped Henry's shoulder. "You're aware of my vision. You'll die if you stay."

"But the others will live."

"I'll do my best—"

"Aye, I know."

William stepped beside me. "I shall stay amongst those who have provided me sanctuary." I opened my mouth to argue, but before I could respond, he continued, "If I go to Jamestown I'll be recognized and returned to Master Pierce. My indenture will be extended. I'll take my chances here. I'd rather die amongst friends than return to that gluttonous bastard who by law owns me."

Until that moment, I hadn't fully realized the level of William's loyalty. The time had come to share the truth of who I was. I motioned for Christopher to move closer in order to tell both at the same time. They listened carefully as I relayed how I had arrived in the seventeenth century. When I finished, William cracked a wide grin. "You don't believe me," I said.

"On the contrary. For some reason you didn't fit in with the Indians you travel with. Though you speak their language, 'tis not the same. Nor is your English like mine."

I held out my hand, and William interlocked his index finger with mine. Turning from William, I glanced in Christopher's direction. He nodded that he accepted my story. I looked to Elenor and understood why. She had already shared my time travels with him. "Now let's get the women and children to safety," I said.

Within a couple of hours, the shallop was loaded with a few supplies. Elenor hugged me goodbye. "Thank you," she said. She turned to Henry and squeezed him even tighter. "Poppa, pray stay safe."

Christopher, David, and James helped the women and children into the boat. Elenor wiped her face in a fruitless attempt to hide her tears. Bess hugged her before turning her attention to settle the children down. Squiggling and squirming in their seats, they viewed the trip as nothing more than a great adventure. The men gave the shallop a shove away from the bank before climbing in themselves.

They grasped their paddles. Christopher glanced over his shoulder and sent a silent goodbye.

The rest of us stood on the bank, watching until the shallop faded from our sight.

"What do we do now?" Henry asked.

"Prepare and wait."

Throughout the day and into the next, we gathered the firearms and ammunition together. I had three bullets left in the magazine of my Glock. After that, I would need to resort to Christopher's musket. Wildcat was more comfortable using a bow, but we hoped our presence could divert the warriors elsewhere.

Near the end of the day, I made my way to the mass grave. At the sight of the bones, my throat constricted. How I wished I could give them a proper burial. If I had a forensic anthropologist's help, I could separate the bones into individuals. Perhaps I might even find my mother. "I may be joining you soon," I said aloud.

Then Black Owl would be the only Paspahegh left alive.

Ironic that I had survived the Paspahegh massacre only to be slain by my brothers.

"Speak to them."

The voice sounded like it had come from behind me. I glanced in that direction and found no one standing there. Had it been real?

"Speak to them, Crow in the Woods." The feminine voice whispered to me on the breeze.

A crow flew to a nearby tree limb and perched. The bird was a sign, and I finally comprehended what the spirit had been trying to tell me all along. "Mother, I hear you. I'm Wind Talker now. Who should I speak to?"

"The warriors—in your native tongue."

That had been my plan before I had known that Henry and William would remain behind. Both knew some Algonquian—not fluently—but enough to get their basic ideas across. "Thank you, Mother. I will do as you ask."

Night had fallen when I returned to the homestead. Tomorrow, we would be facing the warriors. If Wildcat and I had been among our own people we would have gone through a purification ceremony performed by the *kwiocosuk* to prepare for the upcoming attack. Yet I was relieved. With the women and children safely away,

I took comfort in the fact that my vision had warned me in time to possibly change the outcome.

In silence, the four of us passed the pipe around. On this night, we would partner in turns, keeping watch while the other two slept. As usual, I thought of Phoebe. I would not attempt to contact her until the assault was over. My resolve of what I must do in the next day might weaken if I tried.

"I want to thank you," William said, breaking the silence, "all of you. I have ne'er known people who care about my well-being afore. If it should come to . . ." He choked slightly, and I translated what he had said to Wildcat.

"It will be an honor to die with you," Wildcat replied.

I was uncertain whether William truly comprehended the honor Wildcat had given him. "But I'm not like you," he responded. "I'm . . . I'm afeared to die."

Unlike the colonists, the Algonquian-speaking tribes were unafraid of facing death. "William, I am too. Over the years, I've simply learned how not to show it."

A small smile appeared on William's face, and Wildcat nodded in understanding. "I shall take the first watch," William said.

"I shall be your . . ." Wildcat said in English. He stopped to think over his next word. ". . . partner."

William's smile widened to a grin, and Henry and I agreed to their offer. I got to my feet, but Henry remained deep in thought. "We should get some rest, Henry. Our watch will be here all too soon."

"You're right." He stood across from me. "I can't help thinking if your vision will come true on the morrow."

"We've already altered part of it. We can change the rest."

"Aye. I can ne'er thank you enough for allowing me the time to save Elenor, my son, and the children."

"You already have. Now let's get some sleep." We went inside. Henry took the larger bed, while I lay on one of the children's cots, but it wasn't the tiny bed that kept me from sleeping. Thinking of the day before me, I tossed and turned. Would the warriors come in the morning? The element of surprise had been their greatest weapon. Now, with Phoebe's warning, the advantage was ours for the taking as long as we used it wisely.

Barely had I dozed off, when Wildcat called me. From the other bed, Henry rubbed sleep from his eyes. We moved to the front of the house and waited. Even nights spent on stakeouts could not have prepared me for the endless waiting.

Suddenly I grew homesick for the twenty-first century. Maybe I could return to the future and my family after the attack. How would I explain my absence to Ed and get my job back? I entertained thoughts of telling him the truth. After all that had happened, he would likely believe me. If not, Phoebe could find a way to verify what I said. But did I really want to return to my old job? In this century I had given up caffeine and alcohol. The only thing missing—I ached to hold, really hold, Phoebe and Heather.

"They could be out there already—poised for the attack."

Henry's comment brought me back to reality. "They could indeed," I agreed.

With only a single candle to see by, we waited. After about an hour, I heard the soft tread of footsteps behind me. I raised my Glock and went to investigate.

In the dim, flickering light, I caught William standing over the pisspot and lowered my weapon. "Trepidation," he said.

"We call it nerves where I come from." I returned to my post beside Henry. "After Phoebe and I were married, we visited England. It took us about seven hours to fly there from Virginia."

"Seven hours? Fly?"

"By airplane. It's sort of ship that sails through the sky."

His eyes widened. "Did they take you captive on this ship?"

I laughed slightly. "No, they're a little more enlightened in the twenty-first century, but many people treated me as a bit of a novelty. Most thought Indians had died out or been killed off."

"Do they die out?"

"Not by a long shot, but most were forced from their homes."

"Like now? And that is why they're retaliating."

I nodded. "When this is over, Henry, I'd like to hear more about your sailing adventures."

"I will share them," he promised, "if you tell me more of this ship that sails through the sky."

"That's a deal." We fell into another silence, and as the hours wore on, my eyelids grew heavy. What I wouldn't give for a strong dose of caffeine. So much for being proud of having given it up.

As if detecting my weariness, Henry spoke about his captaining a boat that had crossed the ocean. His story almost made me feel the rocking motion of the ship, the wind ruffling through my hair, and breathing in the salt air. His descriptions made me realize how difficult life must have been surrounded by ocean water for months on end, before finally the welcome relief of seeing land when he seriously thought that he might not ever see it again.

Henry finished his tale and said, "You vowed to tell me about the ship that sails through the sky."

"I said when this is over."

"Wind Talker . . . Lee, if anything should happen—"

"Don't say it."

"You know it needs to be said. In your vision, several of us died. The others are safely away. Only I remain. She has already given me her goodbyes, and I merely want your assurance that you will care for her in the way she deserves."

"You know I will, but that won't be necessary."

"Spare me. From your tales, I trust you comprehend the meaning of danger. I'm certain you also understand when one has a feeling of his own demise."

All too well. "Henry—"

"There is naught more to be said."

"But there is," I insisted. "I despised you when I first met you through the dreaming. You saw my people as savages, and Phoebe—she was forced to marry you."

In spite of the dim light, I saw him swallow. "I knew little about Indians upon my arrival, except for what had been told to me. I thought I was saving Phoebe from damnation. I could ne'er have conceived that 'twas the other way round. I trust you know that now."

"I do, but I believe you already know that as well."

"Aye," he said with a slight laugh. "Who would have e'er believed that the two of us could be more alike than either might have reckoned? Now, pray tell me about the ship that sails through the air."

All too happy to relay the story he longed to hear, I told him about airplanes. Toward morning, the eerie cry of a screech owl called from outside, and I became instantly alert. "Get the others, Henry. They're here."

The acrid scent of smoke assaulted my nostrils. Smoke drifted from the barn. *Face them.* Henry returned with Wildcat and William. "I'm going out there," I said.

"They will test you . . ."

Wildcat left the rest of his sentence unsaid. If I failed, I would certainly die a lingering death. I quickly shoved that thought from my head. "If at all possible, I would like to prevent bloodshed on both sides."

"Agreed."

Glancing at each of them in turn, I handed my Glock to Wildcat. "Don't fire on them unless I fail." I took a deep breath and stepped outside. "I'm unarmed," I shouted in Algonquian and held my hands out in plain sight. An arrow sailed my direction and hit the ground beside my foot. Unable to spot my assailant, I remained standing with my arms stretched out. "I'm unarmed," I repeated.

From inside the barn came the frightened nickers of the horses and their stamping of restless hooves. The milk cow bellowed her fear as the smoke and flames spread. Two more arrows shot toward me, striking the ground around me. Unable to keep from moving, I struggled to maintain my stance. Loud unearthly sounding whoops surrounded me. Painted warriors carrying bows and arrows, clubs, and flintlocks rushed toward me. My breath quickened, but I held my ground.

The first warrior to reach me struck me on the left side with a club. I fell to the ground with staggering force. A crushing pain spread through my chest. Another warrior seized a clump of my hair, poising a knife to scalp me. I struggled for breath and stared at my attacker. "I'm Wind Talker . . . son of Black Owl and Snow Bird . . . brother to Charging Bear, Wildcat . . . and New Moon. I am Paspahegh."

The warrior released his grip but kept his knife within striking distance. He spat on the ground. "Do you dare lie to us on sacred Paspahegh land?"

"Black Owl and I are still alive," I said, choosing my words carefully, "as well as my wife's daughter."

"How do we know that you speak the truth?"

I started by telling him about the assault on the Paspahegh and my mother's death, which annihilated most of the tribe. "Upon learning of the attack, Black Owl fought bravely against the colonists at Jamestown. Afterward, he sought refuge with the Sekakawon."

The man's gaze softened, but he seemed unconvinced. A mass of warriors gathered around me. All had their bodies and faces blackened, some with geometric designs. A few had white paint mixed with the black. With some difficulty, I rose to my feet. My side hurt like hell. Each breath was like a knife stabbing into me, but I couldn't show any signs of weakness in front of these men.

A ghostly-looking warrior with his face and body painted completely in an ash white stepped in front of me. "You describe the attack on the Paspahegh with great accuracy. Yet if you were but two winters at the time, how do you recall the minute details?"

"Wind Talker speaks the truth." Out of the corner of my eye, I saw Charging Bear step forward and join me. Like most of the other warriors, he wore black war paint on his face and chest. "My brother is Paspahegh, and I am Charging Bear. I have been adopted by the Appamattuck."

The ash white warrior nodded and motioned to the men around him. "We are the last Quiyoughcohannock. I have heard of Wind Talker. The elders say you have traveled through time and back again."

Meg's vision had shown Charging Bear as an ally, not an enemy. Feeling more confident with his voice added to mine, I said, "I have."

"Tell us."

I thought of Henry's wish to know about airplanes and described them. I continued with cars, TVs, computers, and high-rises. The men's aggressive stance changed to fascination. "May we rescue the animals from the barn now?" I asked.

They said yes.

I placed a hand to my aching chest and waved with my free one for the others inside the house to join me. Soon Wildcat was by my side. He handed my Glock to me, and we headed in the direction of the barn. "You did well, brother."

When I opened the barn door, smoke poured out, instantly blinding me. I raised my arm to protect my face and stepped inside. Ghostly figures were beside me, and I could no longer identify who any of them were. Staggering through the smoke, I sputtered and gagged. Finally, I reached one of the horses.

The mare danced nervously and landed a shod hoof directly on my foot. I muttered a stream of curses in both Algonquian and English but managed to loosen the taut rope. She was free, and I led her toward the door.

Another horse had broken free and raced half-crazed past us. The cow bawled behind me. I handed the mare's line to someone else and returned for her. With a nervous mooing, the cow snorted. I barely had the line free when intense heat engulfed me. A blazing beam struck me squarely in the back. Gasping for breath, I dropped to my hands and knees.

My vision. Circumstances had changed, but it was coming to pass nonetheless. Refusing to surrender, I wouldn't give up. *I couldn't.* I struggled to my feet.

Someone gripped my left arm and tugged. Charging Bear led me to the door. Outside in the cool morning, I could breathe again.

Behind me, a scream pierced the air. *Henry!* I moved toward his panic-stricken shrieks, but many hands held me firmly in place. As the wails from inside the barn gradually died down, I smelled a musky odor. I had been a cop long enough to recognize the scent of roasting human flesh.

As the wind fanned the flames, I could hear a voice speaking in it.

'Twas my time, Wind Talker. There was naught you could have done to change what was meant to be, but you have saved the others. Tell them not to grieve for me.

Embers danced and swirled. I sang Henry's death song. Charging Bear, Wildcat, and the ashen-painted warrior joined me.

* * *

How many times had I personally delivered the news to families that a loved one had died? I couldn't begin to count the number. Each time I somehow had managed to maintain a stoic face, while inside I cried my tears. Upon hearing the news, some people would cry hysterically, others would go on a screaming rampage, and some simply fainted.

On a few occasions, I had been pummeled for being the evil messenger. I overlooked the attacks. The individuals were grief-stricken, and I didn't need to add to their misery by charging them with an assault. Sometimes, I had to stay with a family for hours, repeating what had happened until the news sank in or making certain they were all right.

During my years as a cop, I had been trained to shoot guns, pursue suspects, and arrest and interrogate bad guys, but the toughest part of the job was delivering that god-awful news. The toll of the task on my soul was more than most people could ever imagine. When my duty was complete, I shed my tears over a six-pack in order to fall into a drunken stupor.

Except for a few ales I had shared with Henry, alcohol was generally no longer accessible. More importantly, I no longer needed to resort to its use and worried that I might fall short, for I had never faced bearing such news to my own family.

I entered the dreaming and, thankfully, the wind carried me where I was meant to be. I stood over Phoebe asleep in the bed that we had once shared. Enough light filtered from the hall that I could see her hair curled against the pillow. She looked so peaceful that I resisted touching her.

She had a right to know, and no matter how much it pained me, I had to inform her about the events that had transpired. Events? *Henry was dead.* The news had to come from me for it would be wrong if she heard it from anyone else. I bent down and whispered her name.

With a smile, she stretched but did not waken.

"Phoebe," I said a little louder.

She woke with a start, but upon seeing that it was me, she relaxed and hugged me. She switched on a light and returned to my arms. "You're safe," she said.

I momentarily closed my eyes, calling on my inner strength, then withdrew from her embrace. "Elenor, Bess, and the children are fine. They sought refuge in Jamestown before the attack." A smile of relief crossed her face, and I gripped her hands. "Phoebe, the shallop couldn't carry everyone."

She swallowed. "What are you saying?"

Again my training had taught me that the details surrounding Henry's death were unnecessary—for the time being. "Henry didn't make it."

She shed no tears, nor did she scream or hit me. She simply stared at me as if she were suddenly stricken numb.

In similar circumstances, I had followed a loved one's death announcement with something lame like "I'm very sorry for your loss." For some reason, no words of comfort were forthcoming. Instead, I was pissed. *Henry, you bastard! Why did you risk your life for a fucking cow? The cow survived, you fool.* Not wishing to intensify Phoebe's sorrow, I refrained from speaking my mind and silently cursed Henry one more time.

'Twas my time, Wind Talker. There was naught...

I struggled to keep from covering my ears to drown out Henry's last words.

"E'ery time he sailed for England," came Phoebe's soft voice, blocking out the sound of Henry's in my head, "I wondered if I would see him again. On his last voyage, I waited three long years, but he survived the smallpox in order to return to me. He ne'er asked anything from me. He gave me all that he had."

As she poured out her heart, I listened and wondered how I might feel if Shae had died. She leaned her head on my shoulder and sobbed. I brushed back her tears, mixing my own with hers in my grief for Henry.

24

Phoebe

PHOEBE HADN'T VISITED THE AREA where Lee had struck the deer since Ed had driven her to the spot after his disappearance. She gripped Heather's hand. Had half a year passed? She had lost count of the months. First, Lee, now Henry. The ache would likely ne'er fade. A long time had passed since she had prayed to Henry's god, but she knelt and bowed her head, asking Him to accept Henry in heaven.

When Phoebe looked up, Heather pointed to the James River and squealed. A heron fished along an inlet.

"Rest in peace, Henry."

No sign existed that Henry or Lee had ever been to this place. *Four hundred years*. And now that Lee had saved the rest of her family, his mission was complete, yet they remained separated. Visiting the site hadn't relieved her melancholy. She gathered Heather in her arms and returned to the car, where Meg and Tiffany waited. "Find any answers?" Meg asked.

"Nay, only more questions." Phoebe got in the car and nursed Heather. Tiffany romped under Meg's watchful eye whilst she finished nursing. Afterward, she and Meg buckled the lasses into their seats. Meg got in on the passenger side, and Phoebe drove along the winding route that Lee had taken on that fateful night. She neared a gas station and supermarket. A voice inside her head shouted for her to stop. She parked the car.

"What's wrong?" Meg asked.

Years afore, Lee had brought her here. " 'Tis the place where Lee had been found wandering as a toddler after the attack on the Paspahegh town." Her breath quickened. Could the portal betwixt centuries remain?

She placed Heather in her backpack and got out of the car. Meg gathered up her cane. She and Tiffany joined them.

"He said that when he was a lad, trees and hiking trails existed instead of this." She gestured to the strip mall and wandered past the stores. Aside the grocery store was a restaurant, a card shop, and a book store. 'Twas naught here. She sighed.

"I know you had been hoping for some sort of sign," Meg sympathized. "It'll be dark soon."

Phoebe looked to the sky. The sun was on the horizon. Less than an hour of daylight remained. Most of the day had passed without her realizing. "Let's pick up something for the lasses to eat from the store, then we shall venture home."

After feeding the lasses, Phoebe's cell phone rang. She answered, and Shae's voice came across the line. *"Phoebe, are you all right?"*

"Aye, I'm with Meg and the lasses. Is something wrong?"

"For some reason, I had a strange feeling."

"What sort of feeling?"

"I don't know. Never mind. As long as you're all right."

"Meg and I were visiting the places where I had felt Lee's presence, but we're heading home now." After a round of goodbyes, she started the trip home. Along the way, she stopped at a grassy knoll to watch the sunset. A mist formed over the water, and thunder and lightning raged. Instead of seeking shelter, she watched as the storm got closer to the bank.

"We really should be getting back," Meg said.

In awe, Phoebe remained in place. The wind kicked up. Branches with rustling leaves creaked. Heather clung to her and cried.

Whispering words of comfort, Phoebe turned toward the car. Only she discovered she was lost. "Nay, it can't be." Her heart pounded. 'Twas like the night she had arrived in the twenty-first century, except that she hadn't heard Lee's voice. "Wind Talker, where are you, my love? I can't find my way."

The wind grew stronger. She almost expected to hear shouts from a mob and the flames of their torches behind her. A thick mist surrounded her. "Wind Talker, where are you?"

"Phoebe! Phoebe! Where are you?"

She attempted to locate Meg, calling for her from somewhere nearby. But the wind—nearly a torrent—pushed her deeper and deeper into the mist. She kept a tight grip on Heather, but could barely remain standing. She stumbled over a tree root and crashed to the ground.

Heather cried harder and faster.

To calm her daughter, Phoebe began singing a lullaby in Algonquian. Long ago, she had sung it to Elenor, but Henry had forbade it because she hadn't known the English words. The song had vanished from her memory 'til now.

The white hound appeared afore her, and she regained her feet. The hound and the wind would lead her to him.

"Phoebe! Noooo!"

" 'Tis time, Meg." Phoebe slung Heather over her hip and latched on the dog's collar with her left hand. The crow floated on the air currents afore her. No longer afraid, she moved with the hound as he traced a familiar circle.

From far above, she peered at the ground below. Cars looked to be the size of ants, and high-rise buildings seemed more like a mushroom patch. 'Twas her first sight of London, and her return to the land of her kinsmen. How they would have marveled at the changes from the rocking and swaying of wooden ships to the flight of an airplane.

The scene shifted. Bright lights filled the night sky, and cars raced to and fro. The sidewalks were crowded with people. 'Twas when she had arrived in the twenty-first century. But the scene shifted yet again. People wore bell-bottom jeans. Some wore headbands. Women had their hair parted down the middle, and men had long hair and unkempt beards. Their shirts were made in tie-dye patterns, and they carried signs of protest. They shouted in unison, "Peace now!"

As she passed the psychedelic-clad demonstration, Phoebe's heart quickened. She was traveling through time, but where was

Lee? "Wind Talker, pray hear my voice."

A black carriage trimmed in red and drawn by two white horses trotted past her. A heavily corseted woman sat next to a man attired in a black frock coat. Up front sat a coachman in a box, guiding the horses.

Phoebe continued on. Buildings on the waterfront burned, and men in redcoats ran betwixt them. The centuries floated by faster than her mind could comprehend, but the hound kept walking forward. She spied a light and at last, she heard a voice. 'Twasn't Wind Talker, but... "Henry."

He stood afore her. "Phoebe, I'm at peace. I have rejoined my Mary and only wish to say goodbye."

"But Henry—"

" 'Tis the way it's meant to be. But Phoebe, danger lies ahead."

"Danger?"

"Aye, you will once again face what was. I fear I cannot aid you this time. I shall add my voice to yours to reach Wind Talker. Goodbye." With his farewell, he vanished.

The hound guided her forward, and the wind was at her back. On and on 'til her legs grew weary. Her body ached from carrying Heather. The mist grew thinner. She emerged from the fog, and the dog vanished, but a dragonfly hovered nearby.

The bearded faces of colonial men stared at her.

Wind Talker.

25

Wind Talker

A SHARP WIND MOANED THROUGH the trees. In the gust, someone called my name. I raised my bowed head and glanced around. "Phoebe?" Her voice sounded like it had come from nearby. I moved away from the empty hole in the ground.

William gripped my arm. "You mustn't leave yet. We require your aid to lower Henry."

I blinked. A mound of dirt and the wooden casket lay beside the six-foot hole. From accidents to murders, I had viewed enough burned corpses to know what to expect. Inside the barn rubble, Henry's charred body had been found in the typical posture of flexed elbows and knees with clenched fists. Someone new to crime investigation often mistook the pose to mean the victim had been attempting to fight off an attacker. In reality, the heat from the fire contracted the muscles. But this time was different. I had known Henry and called him a friend.

I had no idea what was customary for the seventeenth century, but I needed to keep active to bury my sorrow. With Charging Bear, Wildcat, and William's help, we had constructed a pine casket. Thankfully, Henry's body was safely hidden away before Elenor returned from Jamestown. Aware that she regarded Henry as her father, I recommended she not view the blackened mass. Fortunately, she accepted my advice, and I along with the rest of the men set about to digging a grave.

Using hemp ropes, we lowered Henry into the sandy earth. Until a pastor could travel the distance to the plantation and offer his blessings, we made do with Elenor saying a prayer. Tears streaked her cheeks, and after a round of amens, we began to shovel dirt to cover the casket. When the job was complete, we returned to the house where Elenor served dry cornbread and wine. I gathered she was mimicking some sort of tradition from England and improvising with what was available in Virginia.

When the gathering came to an end, I turned to leave. Elenor called after me. "You're welcome to stay. Poppa would have wanted it that way."

"Thanks, I'll stay until Black Owl arrives, but afterward, I'll either be traveling with Charging Bear to the Appamattuck or returning to the Sekakawon with Black Owl and Wildcat."

"I understand." She placed her hands to her face and sobbed into them.

Like so many other times when comforting grief-stricken individuals, I drew her into my arms. But she wasn't just any grief-stricken individual. She was Phoebe's daughter—my stepdaughter. I *should have* gone after Henry. But I recalled the hands holding me back. They had saved me from making a foolish mistake and causing my own death. "I'm sorry I couldn't save him."

With a tear-streaked face, Elenor looked up. Her face was etched in sorrow, but she stepped back and wiped the tears from her cheeks. " 'Tis not your fault."

I wished I could forgive myself so easily. I guess it was the nature of having been a cop. Any scene resulting in a death, the "should haves" and "what ifs" plagued my mind. After thanking her once more for her hospitality, I traveled to the mass grave. When I reached the site, a crow flew to a nearby branch. At first I thought the black bird was real, but when he began to speak, I knew he was a spirit.

She calls for you on the wind. Why do you not listen?

"Who calls for me?"

Walks Through Mist.

I *had* heard Phoebe's voice earlier. "What does she want?"

I do not know. Listen to the wind, and she will tell you. Crow flew away.

I concentrated. As time went on, I needed less immersion to enter the misty world of the dreaming, but it didn't always take me where I wanted to go. I stumbled blindly, calling Phoebe's name. Time and time again, but no response returned. I stepped into the house we once shared, but the murkiness refused to lift. The house was empty.

The fog engulfed me, and the scene vanished from my view. When I emerged from the haze, I entered an office—the office where I had once worked as a detective. I had been sent to my old haunt for a reason.

Ed sat behind a desk. When he looked up, his jaw nearly dropped. "Lee, I almost didn't recognize you. You look . . . you look like an . . ."

"I think the word you're looking for is Indian."

A wide grin spread across his face. "I didn't want to cause offense."

"None taken."

He jumped up and gave me a brotherly punch on the arm. "Lee! I didn't think I'd ever see you again."

"Ed," I said, returning a thump to his back, "I need your help."

His shaggy brows creased together in confusion. "What can I do for you?"

"I can't find Phoebe."

"Phoebe? I haven't talked to her in months."

"Can you check the reports to see if anything has happened? I couldn't find her at home."

"She may be out."

"The house was empty. I'm worried that something has happened to Phoebe and Heather."

"All right, but I'm going to call her first." He picked up the phone and dialed. "Her cell phone goes to voicemail." He dialed again. "No answer at home."

"Try Meg and Shae." I gave him Meg's number.

He shook his head and said, "Voicemail." Once more, he dialed a number. "Shae, this is Ed—"

I grasped the phone from Ed's hand. "Shae, have you talked to Phoebe recently?"

Shae's voice came across the line. *"Lee?"*

"I didn't mean to be abrupt, but I'm worried about Phoebe. Have you talked to her recently?"

"As a matter of fact, I have—a couple of hours ago."

"Do you know where she was?"

"She said she was visiting the places where she had felt your presence."

My concern for what might have happened heightened. "Did she say anything else that would give any clues as to where she was?"

"No."

Promising that I would find a way to let Shae know what had happened, I thanked her and hung up. "Shae talked to her a couple of hours ago," I said to Ed. "She said Phoebe was visiting the places where she had felt my presence."

"I'll look into it for you, partner. Let me make a few calls and check the reports."

I glanced around the office while Ed made his calls. With a bit of nostalgia, I leafed through some of the files. Nothing had changed—murder, rape, and arson. I no longer cared to return to the daily grind.

"Lee?"

I gave Ed my full attention.

"A Ford Fiesta registered in yours and Phoebe's names, was found about an hour ago on Route 5 about fifteen miles west of Jamestown. There was no sign of an accident, no sign of a struggle, and no hospital reports that anyone was admitted fitting her description. Like you, she just seems to have vanished."

A moment passed before I absorbed all that he had said. *Like me*—she had vanished. Her voice *had* come from nearby. And Heather? I hoped she was with Phoebe.

"Lee?"

"I think I know what's happened."

"Care to enlighten me?"

"Like me, she's traveled to our real home. I'm sure you've already guessed that we're not from this time."

Not from this time. He mouthed the words but nodded. "I didn't want to believe, but it was the only thing that made sense. You wouldn't have left the way you did otherwise. And the skeleton—was that really you?"

I had almost forgotten about the skeleton, but that wasn't my primary concern now. "I need to find Phoebe."

As we said goodbye, Ed gave me a parting handshake. Another true friend I would never see again.

26

Phoebe

THE THREE BEARDED MEN CARRIED muskets. In her T-shirt and jeans, Phoebe realized she must have looked out of place. "I've lost my way," she said. "Could you guide me to the Wynne plantation?"

A grimy man with unwashed hair and a missing front tooth snorted a laugh. "What would Captain Wynne want with the likes of ye?" He eyed her garb. "Is that what the savages are wearing now?" He turned his attention to Heather. "Aye, looks to be a savage."

She *had* reached the seventeenth century. She clutched Heather to her breast. "My daughter is not a savage."

All of their gazes focused on Phoebe, and the man with the missing tooth said, "Rumor has it that the first Mistress Wynne ran off to the Indians years ago aft she was discovered to be a witch." His firm hand latched onto her arm. "You wouldn't happen to be the first mistress, now would ye?"

She sized up the man, who stood half a foot taller. With all of her strength, she could break his grip, but carrying Heather, she would ne'er be capable of outdistancing him.

"Don't e'en think about it. Wouldn't want the babe getting hurt, now would ye?"

"Come along peaceably," a blond-haired man, standing behind the lead man, said, "and we'll let ye keep the babe. E'en if ye're not the one in question, a woman hasn't got any business out here alone."

"We could tie ye, if ye don't want to accompany us peaceably," the man who gripped her threatened.

"I shall come peaceably," she replied in defeat.

They walked through the forest for a short distance 'til arriving at the banks of the James River where a small boat was tied. The man with the missing tooth motioned for her to get in. She waded through the water and climbed into the boat. With Heather seated on her lap, the men shoved the boat from the bank and joined her.

Back and forth, the boat swayed as they sailed downriver. The constant motion made Phoebe ill to her stomach. Thankfully, Heather showed no signs of sickness. Her daughter gripped her, whilst contentedly sucking her thumb. Phoebe focused on the scenery, hoping the diversion would relieve her ailment. Betwixt the oak and hickory forests were houses and plantations lined with tobacco fields. The trees were in full leaf. 'Twas spring, of that she was certain.

Her stomach settled. Mayhap she could jump from the boat and swim from the men's clutches. Nay, she couldn't risk such a maneuver with Heather in her arms.

Unlike the previous time that paramount chief Opechancanough had led a mass attack against the colonists, plantations had not been abandoned, and she spotted farmers in their fields planting and weeding crops. She longed for the sight of dugouts, where she could seek safety, but there were none. Lee and his father were the only Paspahegh that remained. Why could he not hear her now? *Wind Talker.*

Like afore, no response returned.

By late afternoon, the boat set into port at James Towne. Large sailing ships and pinnaces were moored to the docks. Workers rolled barrels unloading goods from one of the larger ships. The men showed her to the thoroughfare that was lined with houses. In the distance, she spotted a few houses made of brick. James Towne had grown since her leaving.

The men escorted her to a building on the main street. "We caught us a witch," the blond-haired man said upon entering.

Behind the desk sat none other than the bearded, greasy-haired gaoler who had made advances upon her person when she had been tried as a witch. He stood. "Indeed. I have ne'er seen anyone dressed quite like ye." His gaze wandered the length of her body and took on a predatory look. A grin slowly spread across his countenance. "Phoebe Wynne, I thought ye had vanished for good. Allow me to reintroduce myself. Richard Waters. Aft we get ye settled, I'll fetch the sheriff to charge ye formally."

The thought of his unwanted touches drove terror in her heart. Like her momma when facing the Paspahegh for the first time, she had to remain strong for Heather's sake.

He moved closer. "How long has it been? No one here forgets the witch trial. 'Twas 1630. That makes it—" He counted on his fingers. "—nearly fourteen years, yet ye don't look a day older. How do ye explain such an anomaly, Mistress Wynne?"

To answer him would only fuel his presumptions. Instead she remained silent.

He took another step toward her. "What have we here?"

As he inspected Heather, Phoebe held her closer.

" 'Tis not Captain Wynne's daughter, but another savage child," he said. He motioned to the other men. "Take her. Mistress Hopkins will see to the babe. She's been wantin' one for some years now, without much luck. I reckon she won't mind given the babe is part savage, and if the magistrates see fit, they may e'en allow her to keep her."

When the men reached for Heather, Phoebe pulled away. "Nay, you mustn't. She's my daughter."

"Rest assured, Mistress Wynne. The babe will be appropriately cared for."

"You're not taking my daughter!"

The man with the missing front tooth gripped Heather's hand. Phoebe struggled to maintain her hold, whilst Heather screamed. She lost her grip. He had Heather. Her fist flew, striking him square in the face. Another man caught her arm and yanked it behind her back. The third man joined him. She fought them with all of her fury and stamped the man's foot.

Free at last, she rushed toward Heather's wails. The men caught her by the waist and dragged her down, shoving her face to the dirt. A knee pressed into her back, and her arms were twisted behind her.

Heather's cries faded, and Phoebe lost her will to fight.

The men jerked her to her feet but retained a firm grip on her arms. Waters grinned at her.

She strained to break free, but the men maintained their hold.

"Let's take her to the back," said Waters.

They brought her to a windowless room and shackled her arms and legs. Like years afore, she was chained to the walls. A rat scurried across the floor. The men left, slamming the heavy wooden door behind them.

Phoebe lowered her head and cried.

The bed of straw neath Phoebe had grown moldy from her own waste. In the darkness she had no idea whether hours or days had passed. Her stomach rumbled in fits of hunger, and her breasts were swollen and tender, needing to nurse. Even when Waters brought in food, she refused to eat, and the rats feasted.

She thought of the time afore. In the end, she had been found innocent of witchcraft, but she had been publicly flogged for fornication and consorting with the Indians. The judges would likely be less forgiving on witchcraft charges in a second trial. Condemned and alone, she sent a silent prayer to Ahone. Naught remained for her, but to die.

Would Heather and Lee ever forgive her? *Take action.* But how? She had tried to contact Lee, but the mist ne'er captured her. Henry had assured her that he would attempt to reach him, but his voice had also gone silent. 'Twas like she had been abandoned. Determined not to yield to fear, she concentrated on the hound who would guide her through the mist. In her mind's eye she saw a candle.

Absorb the flame.

"Aye, that's her."

Phoebe hadn't heard anyone enter the cell and lifted her head to the matron who had overseen her body search those many years ago. Her hair had gone gray, and age spots and wrinkles riddled her countenance. "Pray let me see my daughter," Phoebe pleaded.

"Nay, the only thing you'll see aside the inside of this cell is death. You haven't aged. Only a pact with the devil could accomplish that." She motioned to Waters. "The sooner we get it o'er with, the sooner we can hang her."

He unlocked the shackles about her wrists. Phoebe rubbed them to restore some feeling, and he bent over to remove the chains from her legs, touching her thigh in doing so. She punched him in the ribs, and he seized her arms, yanking her to her feet. "Strike me again, and you'll receive in kind. E'eryone knows yer a whore who fornicates with savages. Yer babe is proof enough, and no one would question a few bruises on yer body. Now, get moving."

Phoebe wobbled from being cramped in the same position for days on end, but she managed to stand under her own power.

Waters fixed shackles about her wrists and ankles that allowed her to walk, and they led her from the cell to the outdoors. Suddenly blinded, she squinted against the light, but recalling her previous treatment by the gaoler, when she stumbled she kept moving. The matron's presence suggested that she was to be stripped and examined for devil markings. Like the time afore, they led her to a wood-frame house. Seven women awaited her with glares. One gasped. "She doesn't look a day older than the time afore."

"Aye," the lead matron responded. "That alone proves she's a witch." She turned to Phoebe. "As you may recall, we have been assembled to examine you."

Waters removed Phoebe's chains and stepped outside.

When the door closed behind him, the matron continued, "Now disrobe."

Aware of the threats the elder woman would resort to if she refused, Phoebe removed her T-shirt. Having ne'er taken up the twenty-first-century practice of wearing a bra, she was naked to the waist. When she unzipped her jeans, one woman stared at her aghast, whilst another narrowed her eyes in suspicion.

"What is that device?" the lead matron asked.

" 'Tis a zipper," Phoebe responded. She lowered her jeans and handed them to the matron.

The matron struggled with the zipper.

"Like this." Phoebe grasped the jeans and showed her how to the work the zipper.

The matron raised her hands as if she were suddenly scalded. " 'Tis a devil's device." She snatched the jeans away from Phoebe and searched the pockets. She withdrew a wallet. A credit card, some change, and a driver's license tumbled out. The matron picked up the driver's license and glanced at Phoebe. "Looks like a painting of you, but 'tis not." She bent the plastic 'til it cracked. "More devil devices."

Another matron studied a quarter. "United States of America." She flipped the quarter over. "In God we trust. 1983." She handed the quarter to the lead matron for examination.

"Devil's currency with God's name used in blasphemy." She motioned to Phoebe. "Finish disrobing."

Obeying the matron's command, Phoebe lowered her lacy red panties.

The matron picked up the garments as if they were tainted and inspected them. "What sort of devil's garments are these? Under-drawers of a harlot. And why would a woman wear trousers, 'less she has privates like a man? 'Tis apparent you don't." She passed the clothing around for the other women to inspect and motioned for Phoebe to take the chair that looked like a birthing stool.

Again, Phoebe complied. As hands sifted through her hair, she thought of Lee. Why could she not reach him? Fingers poked and prodded her ears and nostrils. One woman lifted her arm, looking for extra teats, then the other. Another examined the webbing be-twixt her fingers, squeezing 'til it pinched. She refused to cry out.

When the probing hands reached her breasts and privates, Phoebe closed her eyes. Though she had known what to expect, she struggled to remain brave as the women spread her legs. Hands probed her to make certain she possessed no male organs. On and on, they explored and poked 'til her entire body had been thoroughly searched.

The numerous hands withdrew from her body, and the matron said, "You may stand."

Refusing to submit to their insult, Phoebe got to her feet and stood straight with her shoulders back.

"The time afore, you admitted to being left-handed. Is that true?" the matron asked.

"Aye."

"And the devil markings upon your bosom and arms were designed by the Indians?"

Like the Arrohateck, who had designed her tattoos, Phoebe had always regarded them as artistically beautiful. "They are not devil markings."

"Let it be noted, Phoebe Wynne denies naught. You may dress."

Numb and beaten from everything she had endured, Phoebe reached for her clothes. Like the previous time, Waters returned whilst she was still naked. With a distinct bulge under his breeches, he leered at her.

Phoebe quickly dressed, and he shackled her wrists and ankles.

Once outside, Waters tugged so hard on the chains that she barely remained on her feet. She faltered, and he yanked harder. "I told ye afore that I'll have ye, witch."

"Ne'er."

Inside the gaol, Waters shackled her to the wall. "When ye were here afore, I meant it when I said I can help ye."

"I shall die first."

He smiled a wicked grin. "Naught has changed, has it now? Mistress Wynne, the judges will sentence ye to death this time. I can take ye to a place of safety and say that ye escaped."

"I shall take my chances afore the judges."

"Have it yer way." He left the cell, banging the door behind him.

Once again, she sat alone in the dark. She mustn't give in to her fear and attempted to concentrate on contacting Lee.

"Phoebe . . ."

"Henry?" She didn't see him, but it had definitely been his voice. "Henry you helped me the time afore."

"I shall do all that I can so Wind Talker hears your voice."

27

Wind Talker

Unable to locate Phoebe, I entered the dreaming at every opportunity. She was nearby. That much I was certain. But where? I went to the mass grave, where I felt a stronger connection to my being—my soul—if you will. "Phoebe, I heard you before. Why can't I now?"

The mist captured me, and I grew hopeful. Crow flew ahead of me, and the wind was present. The signs were right for my success. I entered the house that had once been mine and became confused. Why was I here if Phoebe was in the seventeenth century?

Unlike the time before, the fog lifted. Hoping against all hope that Phoebe hadn't become lost in the past, I wandered the rooms and called for her. A dreamcatcher with white, red, yellow, and black beads hung over the fireplace in the living room. When I had lived in my apartment, Phoebe had found the same dreamcatcher hanging on a sliding door. She had informed me that the colored beads represented the four winds—the sacred circle. Time was definitely a part of the circle.

"Lee?"

At first, I thought it had been Phoebe, but I turned to Shae. Her brows were creased, and she had a worried frown. She had been looking for Phoebe too.

"Have you found Phoebe?" she asked.

"No. I've been looking, but I can't seem to find her."

"Has she traveled to the seventeenth century?"

"I think so, but I can't verify it."

"Let me know when you find her."

I assured her that I would, and the mist vanished. Once again, I stood beside the mass grave. A blue-green dragonfly hovered like a helicopter. The insect darted in my direction but halted before reaching me. Wings vibrated against the air, and its compound eyes wrapped around the top of its head, giving it a wide field of vision. Undoubtedly, it could see almost everywhere at once. The view must have been incredible.

"Wind Talker." I turned to my sister's husband, Swift Deer. He was out of breath as if he had been traveling at an incredible pace for some distance. "A woman and her child—the woman seems to have suffered a shock. Your father has remained with her."

A woman and child—I hoped against hope that they had located Phoebe and Heather. Without taking time for proper greetings for my brother's return, I accompanied him through the forest. Shock could have been caused by time travel. Swift Deer lived up to his name and moved like a fleet-footed quadruped. I, on the other hand, couldn't keep up. Adrenaline alone pushed me forward. After a couple of miles, I had to catch my breath. "How much farther?" I gasped.

"Not very."

Sheer willpower got me running again. Swift Deer's not very far turned out to be at least another two miles. I nearly collapsed, but I finally spotted Black Owl, whispering words of comfort in Algonquian. At first, I couldn't see any woman or child. I moved closer. A woman huddled in the brush, clutching a squalling child to her breast.

My heart sank. It wasn't Phoebe or Heather, but— "Meg?"

"Don't come any closer," she cried.

I inched closer and knelt. "Meg, it's me, Lee."

"I told you to not come any closer!" She closed her eyes, shutting off her tears.

"No one is going to hurt you, Meg. Or Tiffany. We're here to help."

She reopened her eyes and stared, not really seeing me.

"It's me," I repeated. "Lee."

Tiffany leaped at me, nearly bowling me over, and wrapped her arms around my neck. "Lee!"

Still uncertain, Meg glanced at Black Owl and Swift Deer, then reached out a trembling hand. "Lee?"

I nodded. "This is my father, Black Owl, and my sister's husband, Swift Deer."

"Oh God, Lee. They took Phoebe and Heather." She clutched my woolen shirt as if suddenly afraid to let go. The words poured out of her mouth, and I had difficulty making out exactly what had happened. "I saw hippies and carriages. It's like we were caught in some sort of wave. I kept calling to Phoebe, but I couldn't reach her. Then, when the mist cleared, she was surrounded by three guys." She cried into my shirt. "They looked horrid. I didn't know what to do. They didn't see me, and I couldn't move."

I patted her back, reassuring her. The men had taken Phoebe and Heather to somewhere unknown. Imagining every gruesome scenario from all of the cases I had ever worked on, I resisted the temptation of leaving Meg and Tiffany with my family to search for Phoebe. Meg was my main lead. I had to see to her and her daughter first. Her condition would only improve back at the homestead.

With Tiffany still clinging to me like she was holding on for dear life, I struggled to my feet. After doing so, I helped Meg to hers.

"Is there anything we can do?" Black Owl asked.

"If you can go ahead to the homestead and have Christopher or James bring one of the horses, we could make better time."

"I'll do it," Swift Deer said.

Any other time, I would have been amazed. He'd already run around eight miles and was ready to go another four, but he charged off without looking back. I encouraged Tiffany to walk under her own power, so that I could help Meg, but the girl remained stuck to me like glue. "She's missed you," Meg said, almost apologetically. "She's never had a father."

An awkward silence descended between us. I gathered that she hadn't meant to reveal the sentiment. I needn't have worried about Meg, who was still a bit gimpy from her car accident, because Black Owl came to her aid, even though I hadn't had a chance to translate the conversation.

"Lee, I'm sorry I failed Phoebe."

"You didn't fail her. If you had taken action, you would have most likely put yourself and Tiffany in danger. You'll be able to help us after we get you back to the homestead and checked out by Elenor and Bess."

"Then you think they'll be okay?"

More than anything I wanted to respond in the affirmative, but the bloody images of murdered women and children filled my head. "I hope so," I finally responded.

Meg halted in her tracks with tears filling her eyes. "It's my fault. It's all my fault."

"No, Meg. It's not your fault. The truth is, I don't know what's happened to Phoebe and Heather. You were the last person to see them, so I need to get you to safety, where you can help us. I will do everything in my power to bring them back safe and sound. Do you understand? In the meantime, I have to believe they will be fine and I won't rest until I know the truth. I have an excellent network, like my father here, who will help me, but we need your help too."

With renewed determination, she began walking again. I attempted to explain to Black Owl what had transpired. He nodded that he understood. After nearly a mile, Meg needed rest. Black Owl pointed to a spot under a shady oak, and Tiffany finally let go her stranglehold grip of me and scrambled to her mother.

Meg looked up. "Thank you," she whispered. "Both of you." She broke down crying on her daughter's shoulder.

Tiffany touched Meg's face. "Don't cry, Mommy."

Meg brushed back her tears. "I feel like such a fool. I had asked Phoebe to come with her when she returned and now that I'm here . . ."

How could I have forgotten? My worry about my own family must have clouded my thoughts. "Charging Bear is at the homestead."

"He is?" she asked, wiping away her remaining tears.

"I know he'd like to meet you for real." I offered my hand, and she rose to her feet once more.

Black Owl glanced at me, wondering what I had said to restore Meg's energy. When I told him, he gave a knowing smile. After we walked a few hundred feet, a chestnut horse trotted toward us with

Christopher and Swift Deer on the gelding's back. The horse came to a halt beside us, and the men dismounted. Without wasting time, I boosted Meg onto his back.

"I don't know anything about horses."

"You don't need to," I reassured her. "Christopher will lead, and we'll make it back to the homestead faster." I placed Tiffany on the saddle in front of her mother. Unlike the saddles I had seen growing up, this one had no horn and was flatter than an English riding saddle.

Having recovered somewhat from the ordeal, the girl clasped the gelding's mane and giggled about the prospect of horseback riding. As soon as they were settled, Christopher led the chestnut in the direction of the homestead. Meg gripped the saddle tightly and gulped for air.

"Relax, Meg," I said. "You're not going to fall."

"Lee, thank you."

Afraid that she might burst into tears once more, I nodded, but this time her eyes stayed dry. Even though our gait was faster and steadier than before, the pace seemed like a crawl. Every minute that passed meant more time had elapsed since Phoebe's arrival. Was each step taking me farther from her? We reached a stream and waded across. We continued on.

Midday arrived by the time we reached the mass grave. There was no time to stop and mourn. We pressed on. Finally, the house came into view, and Christopher brought the horse to a halt out front. I helped Tiffany from the saddle, then turned to Meg. By the time her feet touched the ground, Charging Bear stood beside us. "Meg?"

She nodded. "It's me, Charging Bear."

He drew her into his arms. "And this must be Tiffany."

"We need to get them into the house and make certain they're all right," I said. "Meg may be able to help us find Phoebe and Heather."

Sensing my urgency, Charging Bear helped Meg to the house. By the time we reached the door, Bess appeared in the frame. "Bess," Meg said, "Phoebe's told me much about you."

Bess waved the way inside, and we helped Meg and Tiffany to one of the beds. Elenor greeted us. In spite of her grief, the cunning woman took over, and she began checking Meg and Tiffany for injuries. "If the rest of you would wait in the other room . . ."

I escorted Charging Bear to the other room, and this time, he was the one pacing, waiting for word. "I can't believe that she's actually here. How did it happen?"

There were still missing details, but I explained the circumstances to him as best as I could, then I looked to Black Owl and Swift Deer and thanked them. "We were glad to help, my son," Black Owl said. "I know you're still worried about your wife and daughter."

Just having my family near comforted me. "I can't even begin to imagine what you went through when you lost my mother and thought I was gone too."

Black Owl placed a hand on my shoulder. "For a long while afterward, I let anger rule, but how is taking one innocent life for another justifiable? When I rid myself of vengeance, I went to live with the Sekakawon." He lowered his arm. "I found love again and eventually, the son that I thought had died returned to me."

His message was clear. No matter what happened, I had to retain my composure enough to think rationally. "I trust if I falter in the days ahead, you will lend me guidance."

"I would be honored."

Elenor returned. "Beyond a few cuts and bruises, Meg and her daughter appear to have sustained no injuries. They're weary from all they have endured and need rest."

I had no doubt Elenor was aware that her mother's life could be at stake. With difficulty, I bowed to her wisdom. "How long before I can speak to her?"

"Soon. Then she will tell you what she knows."

Those of us waiting inside the door went outside. Because the earlier events had been jumbled and hurried, we made the official round of introductions for those who hadn't met before. The distraction helped me concentrate on something besides Phoebe and Heather. Even then, my thoughts wandered. The longer I sat there, the more restless I became. Finally, the door to the house opened.

Supported by a wooden cane with silver flowers etched into an enamel head, Meg shuffled toward us. Bess lent her support. Charging Bear and I moved to meet her. "Let's try to find Phoebe and Heather," she said.

Over the next couple of days, we scoured woods. We showed Meg where she had been found. Excellent trackers, Charging Bear and Swift Deer backtracked several miles of forest where Meg and Tiffany had wandered. When Meg claimed nothing looked familiar, I wished I had Shae's assistance. With the use of hypnosis, she might have been able to unlock Meg's memory and find the location where Phoebe had been taken captive.

Then, the trail vanished a short distance from the James River. Meg clenched her hands together. "I don't know. I do remember seeing the river, but..."

Remain calm. I took a deep breath. "Take your time." A gentle breeze stroked my face, and I envisioned the mist. "This is it. It's where the time portal brought you through."

"That's right. Three men surrounded her. I was too afraid to move. They must not have seen Tiffany or me. They focused on Phoebe and called Heather a savage. They threatened Phoebe, telling her to not try and make a run for it, then took them to the river."

Charging Bear quickly translated for Swift Deer, and they began searching for signs that Phoebe had been nearby. We followed a trail to the river. Near the bank, Swift Deer pointed to the ground. "Three men and one woman."

"They boarded a boat here," Charging Bear added, showing where the vegetation was flattened where a boat had rested.

I stared downriver. "Jamestown?" I asked.

Christopher nodded. "Or a nearby plantation. 'Tis too late to continue the search today. We'll begin anew on the morrow. We shall return to the homestead and collect a shallop."

I gazed at the sinking sun in the sky. Another day lost—but he was right. "We can bed down here tonight." After a meal of corn pone that Elenor had packed for us, we settled in. I tossed and turned on the hard ground. At least, with the onset of spring, the earth wasn't as cold as it had been during the winter. All the same I wrapped my mantle snugly around me.

Even though exhaustion overwhelmed me, I struggled to reach Phoebe through the dreaming. The previous night, I had focused on the flame and drifted off to sleep. On this night, as darkness fell, an owl hooted. I longed for the day spirit of the crow. He would guide me, but as I envisioned the candle in my mind, the wind rattled tree branches. The mist captured me.

A tunnel loomed before me with a weak light in the distance. A shadow appeared, and I moved toward it. As I got closer, I could see the shadow was a man. He wore breeches, a slash-sleeved doublet, and a plumed hat. A sword was on his left hip and a pistol on his right.

I blinked. *Henry?* He appeared youthful. The same as when I had first viewed the dreaming through his eyes.

"She seeks you, Wind Talker."

"Phoebe? Do you know where she is? I've been looking for her."

"She's in jail. She's to be tried as a witch." He delivered his message and vanished.

Not again. I closed my eyes and recalled what she had endured the first time—a strip search and being chained to a wall in a cell crawling with rats. Did they execute witches in Virginia? I had to find a way to help her escape. And what of Heather? Henry hadn't mentioned her.

28

Phoebe

FOR THE SECOND TIME IN HER LIFE, Phoebe was led into the courtroom. Unlike the time afore, Henry was absent. A row of justices attired in black sat behind a long table. In the middle sat the presiding judge, the same one who had ruled on her case afore. Though wrinkles in his countenance were deeper than she recalled, he retained an air of distinction.

"Phoebe Wynne," came the magistrate's voice, "once again a jury of women hath searched your person and found webbed skin betwixt your fingers and toes. Do you deny their assessment?"

"Nay," she replied with her voice barely above a whisper.

"And how do you stand afore us today untouched by the passage of fourteen years?"

Time travel would definitely be considered an act of the devil. Her hands and legs trembled. "I don't know."

The justices studied her skeptically, and a man in the courtroom stood and pointed. "Witch!"

A loud murmur filled the room, and the magistrate banged his gavel. "I decree order!" The buzzing voices halted, and he continued, "Mistress Wynne, are we to believe the passage of time has remained still for you without your making a pact with the devil? After all, you bear his marks."

"I have made no pact with the devil."

Another round of voices mumbled throughout the courtroom. Once again, the magistrate banged the gavel, and the room quieted.

"Let it be recorded on the twenty-eighth day of April in the year of our Lord 1644 that, by your own admission, you bear the marks of the devil, yet deny making any pacts with Satan. Once again, you stand afore the court accused with a sundry of acts of witchcraft and fornication. How do you plead?"

"I am innocent."

A gasp echoed throughout the courtroom.

"Mistress Wynne, the last time you were seen, you had been found guilty of fornication and consorting with the Indians. You escaped the gaol aft receiving twenty stripes, but afore you could be returned to England to complete your sentence. E'en aft marrying a law-abiding citizen of the Crown, one who was murdered by said savages, you continued to consort with them. You hath returned to James Towne with a child begotten by an Indian, not your lawful husband. Do you deny this?"

The vision of Heather being wrenched from her arms engulfed her, and she barely kept the tears at bay. "Captain Wynne thought I had died, and he remarried. In turn, I married a Paspahegh warrior."

The magistrate sighed. "If such a union was not made in a Christian ceremony, then no marriage exists in the eyes of God. Once again, you hath admitted to fornication. As to the charges of witchcraft, I shall call witnesses, who knew you from the time afore, but e'en I can see you are unchanged by fourteen years. And your garments, did you receive them from the Indians?"

"Nay, I found them when I was without."

"You stole them?"

Stealing was regarded as a lesser offense than witchcraft. "Aye."

"Bring forth the witnesses."

Witnesses stepped forward agreeing that Phoebe had not aged. Some mentioned that she had practiced herbs, and that livestock had fallen ill, even though she had ne'er treated anyone in James Towne. The judges debated amongst themselves and afore long arrived at a decision.

The magistrate pounded the gavel. "Phoebe Wynne, for the second time in this courtroom you hath freely admitted to fornicating with an Indian. You are found guilty on that charge. Howe'er, we find the more serious charge of witchcraft is in question. A trial by water shall be held. Sentencing shall be given aft the results of said trial are reached."

The gavel pounded once more.

Afore the trial by water, Phoebe had been given a shift and a simple woolen dress. The gaoler brought her to the bank of the river, where a crowd had gathered to watch. The same jury of women who had strip searched her waited along the edge.

"Disrobe to your shift," the matron ordered.

Phoebe swallowed but lifted her dress over her head and dropped it to the ground. Only her shift covered her body.

"The shoes and stockings as well."

Phoebe obeyed, and the women searched her to make certain she possessed naught to aid in an escape. She was escorted to a rowboat where four men waited.

The matron gestured to the boat. "Get in."

After Phoebe stepped inside, two women tied her right thumb to her left big toe, and her left thumb to the big toe of her right foot. Whilst the men rowed, the crowd gawked and pointed fingers. The boat halted in the center of the river, and the men heaved, tossing Phoebe overboard. The crowd cheered.

Phoebe held her breath and entered the cold water with a huge splash. Her arms and legs attempted to move in all directions, but due to the ropes, she was unable to rise to the surface and swim. She sank. Panic set in. She struggled, but the bonds refused to release their grip. She screamed, but the sound was lost amongst mute bubbles. Down she continued, and her limbs grew weary from attempting to paddle. Her lungs ached—and she surrendered.

A calm washed over Phoebe. Shafts of sunlight wavered in the water. The reflection of the white hound stood near the surface. If only she could reach him, he would lead the way to refuge. Aside the hound stood a crow. Lee *had* heard her call. She imagined the crow lifting her upward.

Once they were airborne, time had little meaning. Was she dead? She spotted the hound on the ground, racing toward a copse of trees. Unconcerned, she preferred rising into the sky with the crow. Against the gentle wind she flew. The breeze lifted her further, and she gasped and sputtered.

Water surrounded her. The ropes no longer bound her, and rough hands pulled her from the watery grave. Phoebe lay on the bank, coughing up water.

The magistrate loomed over her. "Phoebe Wynne, you hath floated. As a result, you hath failed the water test. You are found guilty of being a witch. As punishment, you shall be put to death by hanging."

Totally dazed from the ordeal, Phoebe failed to absorb the magistrate's words. "*Kesutanowas Wesin*," she responded.

29

Wind Talker

A TEARING AND BURNING SENSATION spread through my chest, and my arms attempted to climb an invisible ladder. *Wind Talker.* "They're torturing her."

William placed a hand on my shoulder to calm me. "We'll be there soon."

He was right, and I couldn't allow anger to guide me. Others would pay the price if my actions weren't calm and reasoned. With all of my experience I knew that—rationally—but this time Phoebe and Heather were involved. I must finish preparing for what was to come before going to them.

After we returned to the homestead, Black Owl instructed us on how to build a small dome-shaped structure from willow saplings near a shallow stream running through the settlement. We covered the frame with woven mats like those used for building Appamattuck houses. Sweat houses existed in both of the towns I had visited, but they contrasted from the Lakota pictures I had seen growing up of larger lodges and animal hide coverings. And unlike the Lakota, the Appamattuck and Sekakawon entered their sweat houses naked.

Black Owl had prepared the pit in the sweat house. Besides me, William and Christopher had never participated in a sweat before. William had surprised me with his ambition to accompany us because even when we bathed in a stream, he never removed his undergarments, and now when he stripped off his shirt, I understood his reason why. Like Phoebe, he bore the scars of the whip. Unlike Phoebe, the scars on William's back crisscrossed in raised pink welts.

"Now you know why I longed to escape," he said.

"I never doubted your reason," I replied. "Why would you risk being caught again to help me?"

"You . . ." He looked from me to the other men. "All of you have shown me acceptance and the true meaning of loyalty."

All of us nodded that we understood, and Black Owl signaled that he was ready. After stripping, I ducked my head and followed Charging Bear into the dark interior of the sweat house. With the structure too low to the ground to walk in, I crawled in on my hands and knees. I moved in a clockwise direction. Once inside, I sat cross-legged, hunching my shoulders forward to keep from hitting my head. The six of us formed a circle.

One by one, Black Owl scooped up four glowing red rocks with forked green sticks and brought them to the pit in the center. He placed beaten oak bark over the stones to keep them burning, then draped a mat over the door, effectively sealing us in complete darkness from the outside world.

Already time had slowed. Black Owl tossed sweet-smelling herbs on the rocks. Flames sparked and swirled. I had no idea of the meaning, but I was caught in the starlike glow. He offered a prayer to Ahone before pouring water onto the hot stones. The stones hissed and steam burst into the air, filling the hut. With the heat encompassing me, I breathed deeply.

On a couple of occasions I had gone to a sauna, but the sweat house was different. The sauna was a relaxing experience—a great way to break the tension after a particularly hectic day—but here, it was almost as if the steam unified those of us inside. Under the dome, the warmth nourished me, and it seemed divine. The only comparison I could envision was what it must be like in utero. And now, I awaited rebirth.

As the heat intensified, every pore in my skin opened and sweat dripped from my body. Now and then, Black Owl sprinkled my face with water. He then turned to Charging Bear on my left and did the same. Soon after, Black Owl began singing. Charging Bear,

Wildcat, and Swift Deer joined him. From some unknown depth, I knew the words, the melody, and rhythm. The meaning became crystal clear, and I sang what was in my heart. More to my surprise, a rich tenor voice rose above my own to my right. William sang along with the rest of us. Together, we were one being, sharing a single heartbeat.

Time after time, Black Owl splashed more cold water onto the rocks, pouring more steam around us. The heat grew unbearable, and I began to have difficulty breathing. Christopher was the first to break, gasping for air. Those of us new to the experience had reached our limits.

Recognizing the signs, Black Owl removed the mat from the door, and a cooling breeze swept in. Once again, the wind had rescued me, and I thought I finally understood its message. I could barely crawl my way toward the door, but Black Owl urged us on. Once outside, I struggled to my feet. Along with the others, I rushed in a staggering gait toward the stream and plunged in.

My skin tingled, and my short, shallow breaths changed to gasps, taking in lungfuls of air. Invigorated by the sensations, I was now ready to face my task ahead of me—to rescue Phoebe and Heather.

Fortunately for me, most seventeenth century clothing was baggy, and I borrowed some of Henry's old things. I put on a linen shirt but had to pass on the doublet. The fit was tighter and trimmer than the shirt and Henry had been a few sizes smaller than me. After I had covered the shirt with a brown woolen coat, I struggled into a pair of gray button breeches. If they hadn't been loose-fitting on the original wearer, I would have never fit. Even then, their snugness reminded me of the commercials I had seen of young women squirming into a tight pair of jeans. Then came "the hose," as William called them. Socks, in other words, made of scratchy wool. Henry's shoes were too small, but Christopher loaned me a pair. For some reason, they looked unusual. I held them up to the light. The left and right shoe were cut exactly the same. Even so, I managed to wiggle my feet into them. The unforgiving leather pinched, and I realized how accustomed I had grown to moccasins.

To look the part of a colonist, I topped the getup off with gloves and a broad-brimmed felt hat, hoping that I could conceal the fact that I was an Indian. *Think undercover.* I looked into Elenor's mirror. Undercover, indeed. I reminded myself of one of the three musketeers and doubted that if anyone got a close look at me, I'd be able to fool them. Unlike most of the colonists I had very little facial hair, and I certainly wasn't young enough to pass for a pubescent teenager.

Christopher stared at me as if he had read my thoughts. "William and I can go alone," he suggested. "Both of us know some of the townspeople who can aid us if necessary."

"It'll be dark most of the time we're there, and you know I can't stay behind."

He nodded, and we hugged Elenor, Bess, and Meg goodbye. Black Owl and my brothers met us outside. "Take care, my son."

"I will." No more words were necessary. We intertwined our index fingers. I turned to my brothers and did the same.

Along with William, I climbed aboard a workboat that resembled a twenty-first-century rowboat. Christopher shoved the boat away from the dock and guided it downriver toward Jamestown. Growing accustomed to the river as the fastest mode of transportation, I rowed and looked out to the river banks. Plantations passed. White and black workers hoed side by side in the tobacco, hemp, and cornfields. I sighed. All of the land had once belonged to the Paspahegh.

A man looked up from his weeding in the field and waved. "It seems strange," I said, returning the wave. "They're not trying to shoot me."

"Your disguise," William replied with a noticeable swallow, "effectively hides who you really are."

"You mean a former police detective from the twenty-first century?"

His tension eased and he snorted a laugh. "Aye." Once more, he glanced at the workers in the fields and a haunted fear registered in his eyes. " 'Tis the labor I used to perform."

"You shouldn't have come—either of you."

"You wouldn't succeed without our aid," Christopher said.

True, Christopher knew Jamestown, but William.... Fear wasn't the only thing I saw in his eyes, but something more. I had witnessed it often enough in suspects—ready to flee. Confused by what might lie behind his motives, I rowed harder.

"We are within schedule," Christopher reminded me.

William didn't matter, I repeated to myself. I calmed down and matched my rowing rhythm to Christopher's. If William fled, so be it. If he truly took flight along our journey and made a life for himself elsewhere, then I'd be the first to wish him well. I only hoped he would have the guts to be honest with us if he had made such a decision.

I concentrated on rowing and my task ahead. After several hours, Jamestown Island neared. No Colonial Parkway or bridge led to it like in the twenty-first century. Other boats were on the river, and up ahead near the port, sizable sailing ships that Henry had called pinnaces were anchored. The ships reminded me of the replicas moored at one of the living history parks. But these ships weren't replicas. They had actually sailed on the ocean from England to Virginia.

Instead of heading directly to the port along the river where the ships were docked, Christopher turned into the bay. The current was less swift, which made our rowing much easier, then he pointed to his left. " 'Tis shallow with mud flats o'er there."

Even with my inexperience, I was aware that such an area must be avoided. I counted my blessings that such a knowledgeable seaman had accompanied me. We bypassed more sandy shoals. The bay narrowed, and we turned onto the Back River. Behind Jamestown we traveled less than a mile before Christopher slowed and rowed toward shore. Along with the others, I got out and sloshed through the water to help bring the boat onto the bank. With Christopher's help, I gathered ferns and branches to conceal the boat, while William stood and watched.

As the sun began slipping beyond the horizon, we traveled through the cypress and pine forest. Instead of trees, I envisioned an asphalt parking lot and cement sidewalks leading to a visitors' center. Even as a kid I had been haunted by my trips to Jamestown. My adoptive parents had always pointed to the Indian exhibits in hope of giving me a sense of heritage, but the connection was far stronger than anyone could have imagined at the time. After Phoebe's arrival in the twenty-first century, I had shown her the mostly underwater remains of the fort she had escaped from to join the Paspahegh. At least on that visit, I comprehended why the island plagued me. Black Owl had likely hunted and fished on the island before the colonists had arrived.

Beyond the site of the visitors' center was the footbridge crossing the marsh. Only now, no footbridge existed, and we slogged through the reeds. Fortunately, the water levels were low, but the ooze sucked at my feet. A beaver gnawed on a tree, and a doe watched us as we trudged through the swamp.

We finally reached dry land, and a double-pitched wood house came into view. Christopher gave the building a wide berth. " 'Tis the governor's house."

Neither William nor I needed any prodding to make haste around the structure. A rutted lane passed by a brick house with lattice windows.

"Back Street," Christopher informed us. " 'Tis not much farther."

After we passed a plain wattle and daub house with shutters instead of glass windows, a church tower loomed in the fading light. Darkness was my friend, but unlike the twenty-first century, that also meant absolutely no light after twilight unless the moon happened to be out. People wandered along the riverfront, and a pair of oxen drew a cart. Loose pigs rooted in the soil while goats grazed. Christopher headed for another wattle and daub building on the main lane and led the way inside.

Behind the desk sat a bearded man with disheveled hair and the musky odor of an unwashed body. Recognizing the bastard jailer from the dreaming as the one who had sexually harassed Phoebe, I clenched my fists and took a deep breath to keep from beating his face to a bloody pulp.

"What can I do for ye?" he asked.

"We've come for Mistress Wynne," Christopher replied.

He stood. "Have ye now?"

Any semblance of restraint faded. I drew my Glock. Three rounds remained in the magazine, and I would make them count. "You will take us to her. Now. Make any noise and you're dead. Understood?"

He glanced from the Glock to Christopher, who had drawn his pistol, and nodded. When he opened the heavy wooden door leading to the next room, the hinges creaked. The stench nearly assaulted my nostrils. Phoebe had been forced to live in her own waste, and I gagged.

William raised a lantern, and I cried in anguish. Phoebe huddled in the corner with her wrists and ankles shackled. "Give me the key," I demanded. The jailer's hand shook but he obeyed. With the keys in my hand, I let Christopher guard the jailer and unlocked the cell door. As I stepped inside, rats scuttled from a bowl of food on the floor that looked more like hog slop. I bent down. "Phoebe?"

Sunken eyes looked in my direction. She stared at me as if not really seeing me, then blinked. "Lee?"

I unshackled her wrists. She rubbed them to regain circulation as I unlocked the irons around her ankles. Chains clanked to the dirt floor, and she gripped my shirt, trembling with fear. Without thinking, I took her into my arms and held her. "Where's Heather?"

She clung to me and sobbed on my shoulder. "They took her."

I glared at the jailer. "Where is she?" When he answered me with a defiant smirk, I hurled toward him and clenched his grimy collar in my hands. "I asked you a question. Where's my daughter?"

His fist connected with my face, knocking my hat to the floor. "So yer the savage."

I tightened my grip on his collar. "If that's what you think of me, then I had better live up to my name."

"Lee!" Christopher grasped my arm. "You don't want to be like him."

I tossed the jailer into the cell that had once housed Phoebe and locked the chains on his wrists with his hands behind his back. "I'll ask you once more: where's my daughter?" Met with silence, I raised a fist, ready to beat the answer from him.

"Mistress Hopkins," Phoebe whispered. "They sent her to Mistress Hopkins."

I stuffed a clump of straw into his mouth to keep him from crying for help. "They'll find him in the morning." After locking the cell door behind me, I helped Phoebe toward the door. Her legs were stiff from having been chained in the cell, but she managed to keep a respectable pace. Once outside, I asked, "Where does Mistress Hopkins live?"

"We haven't the time tonight," Christopher replied.

Impatient to rescue my daughter, I continued, "Then when?"

"Elenor and I shall collect her, but when the time is right. By birth Heather is Elenor's sister. We will make a claim to return her to her rightful family."

Unable to believe his suggestion, I clenched my hands, then Phoebe's gentle hand touched my arm. "He speaks the truth."

Almost as if Black Owl stood over me, reminding me of my pact, I relaxed my stance. "You're sure?"

"Aye, Elenor will help."

"As long as you're certain."

"If you were to react in a rash manner, I might lose both of you."

Her words reminded me of my duty. As much as I hated the idea of leaving our daughter temporarily behind, I needed to focus my immediate concern on getting Phoebe to safety.

Christopher waved at us to be moving. Helping Phoebe, I retraced my steps. Away from the main buildings, only faint light penetrated the darkness. We reached Back Street and something didn't feel quite right. I halted.

"What's wrong?" Christopher asked.

Human shadows moved along the main street, but I couldn't make out any of the individuals. "William's missing."

"William?" He glanced around.

To call out for William would have drawn too much attention. "I saw it in his eyes when we traveled here. I thought he might run."

"Would he turn us in to the authorities?"

While I didn't know everything about William, I never had a gut feeling of corruption or anything sinister. "No, I believe he's just run off."

"Then we shall make haste. Mayhap he'll catch up with us later."

"Perhaps," I agreed. But I had the distinct feeling we might not see him again.

30

Phoebe

COMFORTED BY LEE'S SOLID GRIP on her hand, Phoebe stepped forward. Under cover of darkness they passed the remaining houses and went into the swamp. They traveled silently with the water barely making a ripple. A dog barked in the distance, and she feared the hounds would be sent after them. Mud seeped round her feet, slowing her down. She slipped, fanned her free arm to remain upright, but lost her balance and fell into the mire.

Lee lifted her from the muck. For so long, she had wanted to see and touch him again. He hesitated a moment as if sensing her thoughts, then hurried her to get moving again. Wet all over, she shivered. His arm went round her, lending her some warmth, 'til they arrived at the river.

Nestled in amongst the trees rested a boat. Christopher and Lee removed the ferns and branches that would have concealed it from roving eyes during daylight. Lee helped her in. After the men climbed in, they cast off. Phoebe rowed alongside them. Soon, they left the Back River and turned into the bay.

Christopher was familiar with the way as much as any of the Paspahegh she had known as a lass. Once on the James River, the current intensified. Not only was the river stronger, but they rowed against the flow. Thankful there was a half-moon to lend some light to see by, she continued to row. Christopher hugged the bank as closely as possible without running aground.

Years had passed since she had last rowed a boat. She gasped slightly. 'Twas when Henry had saved her from gaol after being tried as a witch the first time. *Henry*. Now was not the time to grieve. So much history kept repeating. Still, if Heather wasn't missing, she would rejoice at having been reunited with Lee. She silenced her worries by concentrating on the task at hand. Soon, her arms ached. By early morn, they arrived at the homestead.

Elenor and Bess greeted her with hugs and tears. They made their way to the house, and Meg stood in the doorframe. She blinked in disbelief. "Meg?"

"Phoebe. Thank God you're safe." They embraced.

Phoebe stepped back. "How did you come to be here?"

"Apparently Tiffany and I got caught in your wave." Meg glanced around. "Where's Heather?"

Afore she could respond, Lee interrupted, "I hate to spoil the reunion, but we can't stay here. Not until the danger has passed. This is the first place they'll look for you."

Phoebe stepped back from Meg and gave a weak nod. He was right, but when did the running end? With a flurry of activity, the men started preparations whilst Elenor pulled her inside. "Momma, I'll make certain you have supplies for your journey. We'll send a messenger when they've stopped looking for you."

Yet again she was faced with leaving her family behind—not one but two daughters. "I can't go through with it."

Elenor grasped Phoebe's hands into her own. "You must. Lee and Charging Bear will keep you safe."

"The last time I left, I failed to return 'til my daughter was grown. I missed most of your childhood, Elenor."

"Had you refused to leave the time afore, you would have ne'er returned to me alive. I want the chance to know my momma and sister."

Meg stepped closer. "Phoebe, please—we've come too far to give up now. And I'd like to come with you."

Their arguments swayed her. "I shall heed your warnings, but nay, Meg. 'Tis too dangerous now. When we've reached safety, Charging Bear will collect you."

With a frown, Meg agreed. Whilst Elenor set about to gathering food supplies, Phoebe took a few moments to cleanse herself from the washbasin. No matter how hard she scrubbed she was unable to rid herself of the grime and stink of the gaol. Proper bathing must wait 'til later. As swiftly as she had arrived, she was leaving. She hugged Elenor, Bess, and Meg goodbye. Outside, the men gave each other parting handshakes. Lee had changed from his colonial attire to a woolen shirt, deer-hide breechclout, and leggings. He moved toward her. "We're ready to go. Charging Bear is taking us to the Appamattuck. They're the closest refuge."

After final farewells, they followed the trail to the riverbank. A dugout was hidden amongst the shrubs. The men shoved the dugout away from the bank, and once again, Phoebe rowed. Each stroke carried her further from her daughter. Lee sent her reassuring glances, but she spotted vexation in his eyes. He had been amongst his people long enough that he no longer felt the need to make idle chatter. When they were alone, she would relay the details of her ordeal. 'Til then, she remained silent and concentrated on the task at hand.

At midday, they came ashore and shared the rations Elenor had provided for them. Sparing little time to rest, they rowed upriver again. After another mile, Charging Bear pointed across the river at a colonial shallop. In an attempt to avoid danger, they guided the dugout toward shore and hid amongst an overhanging branch. The boat sailed past, and they resumed their journey.

By nightfall, Phoebe was exhausted—both mentally and physically. After eating some dried pork and cornbread, she fell asleep in a wasted heap. In the middle of the night she roused slightly, stretched, and snuggled into the arms that held her. The sound of Lee's heartbeat next to her brought solace, and she nestled closer.

Without saying a word he traced his fingertips across her lips, but his touch vanished as quickly as it had appeared. The tension in his muscles warned her that he was restraining his true feelings. Whether his reason was due to all that had happened or the fact that Charging Bear slept a few feet away, Phoebe was uncertain. In the twenty-first century she had learned a sense of privacy. Afore that time, she had almost ne'er been alone. As a child, she recalled the grunts and groans of her momma and adopted father coupling. From the beginning, she had been taught 'twas impolite to watch. Lee, on the other hand, had always known seclusion—'til the past few months. But right now she needed him. She trembled with fear and clung to him.

He clenched her tighter.

Overwhelmed by the passage of events, she sought his mouth and kissed him. No longer holding back, he reciprocated with a kiss full on her mouth. She reached a hand under his shirt and explored the length of his body. As she had guessed, he was ready for her.

He lifted her skirt, parted her drawers, and caressed the spot betwixt her legs sending a wave of pleasure coursing through her body. In the darkness, his presence seemed like naught more than a figment of the dreaming again. Yet his warmth radiating against her, reminded her it was reality. After so much sorrow, their bodies pressed together. She spread her legs wider for him, and he penetrated her. Meanwhile, she rejoiced in his presence. He plunged inside her harder and faster, and she bit her lip to keep from crying out. With a shudder, she peaked. She could no longer hold back. She cried silent tears.

Lee held her and whispered comforting words in a mixture of English and Algonquian in her ear. With his words, she realized how much he had blended the cultures—past, present, Paspahegh, and colonial. They were home, and together. Stronger united, they would overcome the shadows hanging over them.

She brushed away her tears. Her body molded to his in the comfort of his arms and she finally slept. When she opened her eyes, the sun had risen and a robin trilled from a nearby tree. But Lee was gone. The skeleton that had been uncovered those many months ago entered her thoughts. Suddenly wide awake and frantic, she sat up, looking in every direction. "Lee!"

"Relax, I'm here."

He bent down to her, and she touched his countenance to make certain he was real. "When I thought you were gone, I envisioned the skeleton."

He reassured her that he was fine. "We're not anywhere near the area we found the skeleton, and we'll be safely with the Appamattuck by nightfall."

His words brought relief, but the feeling had been incredibly strong. Lee distracted her by handing her some of Elenor's cornbread. Charging Bear stood off to the side to avoid intruding, but her brother's eyes reflected concern. She nibbled on the cornbread and stood. "I'm fine now."

Lee frowned. They still hadn't found Heather. As if reading her thoughts, he said, "We'll get her back."

"Aye," Phoebe agreed. 'Til then, she would remain in sorrow.

Charging Bear finally spoke up. "We should be making haste."

All in agreement, they made their way to the river bank. Once again, Phoebe paddled the dugout upriver. In shallow areas, they disembarked and tied lines to the boat, leading it through the water. As the day passed, Phoebe looked forward to the opportunity to finally rest. Afore they crossed the James River to the Appomattox River, a colonial shallop appeared on the opposite side.

Charging Bear hugged the dugout near the bank. Instead of passing, the men in the shallop rowed toward them.

"It might be best if we observe from a greater distance," Lee suggested.

Charging Bear agreed. They brought the dugout onto the bank and watched the boat. The shallop continued in their direction.

"They've seen us," Lee said. "I count five."

Charging Bear gathered his bow and arrows from the dugout. "Follow me."

Lee grasped Phoebe's elbow and led her further from the bank. 'Twasn't long afore men's voices trailed after them. If it hadn't been for Lee's grip, she would have bolted. They quickened their pace through the tangled woods. The voices faded. The colonists likely continued on their trail, but Phoebe breathed a momentary sigh of relief. After a couple of miles, she grew footsore and weary. Her brother pressed on and only halted after another mile had passed. "You watch over Walks Through Mist," Charging Bear said to Lee, "and I'll double back."

"Be careful," Lee said.

With a nod, Charging Bear retraced his steps in the direction they had come. Dizzy from the rapid hike, Phoebe sat neath an oak tree. Lee moved in aside her and held her hand. "This isn't exactly the reunion I had envisioned," he said.

"Aye. I had hoped—"

"I know. It will all work out."

Now that she could see him in the light of day, Phoebe studied his countenance. The day afore had passed in a blur, and she couldn't let their moment alone vanish without treasuring it. In the months of their separation, his black hair had grown to nearly shoulder length, and his dark brown eyes held a sadness. She reached out and stroked the side of his face. "For better or worse, we are home, Wind Talker."

"Indeed, we are. How are you holding up? I have a hard enough time keeping up with Charging Bear. I can't imagine after what you've been through . . ."

The need to talk overpowered her. She told him about her venture through the vortex. She spoke of the gaol, the body searches, the ducking, but she left out the harassment from the gaoler.

Lee quickly picked up on the omission. "If I did anything to hurt you further . . ."

"Nay, you would ne'er hurt me, and you can set your mind to rest. He did not ravish me."

"I had to refrain from beating him to a bloody pulp," he admitted, breathing out in relief.

Afore Phoebe could respond, Charging Bear returned at a full sprint. "They're half a mile behind."

Lee got to his feet. "Damn."

Charging Bear led the way through the forest, guiding them along barely discernible trails, whilst Lee brought up the rear. Phoebe struggled to keep pace with her brother and stumbled over a tree root. Lee caught her in his arms, but Charging Bear barely broke stride. As the day wore on, the sun sank in the sky. In spite of the fading daylight, Charging Bear pressed on. Barely able to see the path ahead of her, Phoebe gripped his shirt. 'Twas well into the night afore they stopped. Thankful for a chance to rest, she sank to the ground and drifted into a fitful sleep.

A gentle shake on her shoulder woke her. "We need to be moving," Lee said in a low voice.

She rubbed the sleep from her eyes. Torches alighted the path in the distance. 'Twas like the time she had escaped gaol afore, only this time she wasn't alone. She scrambled to her feet and held Lee's hand as they pushed deeper into the forest. The advantage was

31

Wind Talker

A T THE SOUND OF THE bloodhounds my skin crawled. How many times had I called out the dogs at a crime scene when a responding officer hadn't done so himself? Now, right along with Phoebe, I was among the hunted—and could no longer rely on Charging Bear's superior knowledge of the forest to get us home free. Keeping us safe required all of my experience. "Quick," I said, "we need to move as fast as we can—downwind. Anything we do will only slow the dogs, but if we can tire or confuse the handlers, they might call off the dogs."

Following my instructions, Charging Bear remained in the lead. After half a mile a fallen tree blocked the trail. Instead of going around, we climbed over. Another mile passed, and we came to a stream. "Cross at an angle," I said.

Charging Bear did as I instructed. We slogged across the water and followed its course for another mile before crossing again. Over several miles, we crisscrossed the stream three more times. The hounds' barks faded. Even so, we couldn't let our guard down. We had only temporarily outdistanced them and continued on. Phoebe's hands were clammy and cold. I rubbed them with my own to help her warm up, but her gait was getting slower and slower. "We've got to keep going, Phoebe."

"Aye, I'm doing my best."

"I know." For a moment, I thought about facing the colonists myself. I had three shots left in my Glock. If I—*foolish thinking*. Exhaustion must have been hitting me too. By confronting the men who wanted to hang Phoebe, I would make it easier for them to succeed.

"We will be entering Monacan hunting ground soon," Charging Bear said.

"Enemies on both sides—that could get interesting," I responded.

"We're not near their towns. Unless we encounter them whilst hunting, we should be able to avoid them."

Thank goodness for small favors, but I also remembered how often we had come across travelers on my other journeys. Somehow since none of us spoke the language, I didn't think sharing the latest gossip and available foodstuff, or passing a pipe would hold a determined Monacan warrior off, any more than the colonists who were doggedly tracking us. Still we continued on. "Have you traveled into Monacan territory before?" I asked.

"Once or twice," Charging Bear answered.

So we really were on our own. Deeper and deeper into Monacan territory we traveled. Several crows cawed making a loud racket. The black birds dive-bombed a hawk that had intruded in their air space. The scene reminded me of the time I went across campus to speak to the forensic anthropologist, who had shown me the reconstructed skull that resembled me. How many months ago? This time, I understood the sign. The official boundaries were many years in the future, but I was beginning to comprehend the fluidity of time. We had crossed into the county where I had served as a cop.

Not wanting to upset Phoebe further, I maintained silence. As it was, I supported more and more of her weight the farther we walked. "Charging Bear, Phoebe needs rest." He agreed, and I helped her find a suitable place to sit on the ground.

"I shall double back and see if our pursuers are nearby," Charging Bear said.

Once again, I warned him to be careful, and he assured me that he would. I sat next to Phoebe and held her. She rested her head on my shoulder and fell asleep. I truly had no idea how much longer I could remain awake without dozing myself. I longed for a strong dose of caffeine. All of the stakeouts, physical training, and overly long night hours—nothing could have prepared me for the past few days. I closed my eyes until a voice called out. Waking with a start, I drew my Glock and stood.

"Relax, brother," Charging Bear said. " 'Tis me."

I breathed out in relief and holstered the gun. "What did you find out?"

"They follow us but are a good distance behind. I believe they've halted their search for the day."

Only with his words did I realize most of the day had passed. The sun was low on the horizon. Phoebe joined me and hooked her arm through mine. "Then we should make use of what daylight we have left to put more distance between us," I said.

"Agreed. Afterward, we shall rest."

I looked at Phoebe, and she nodded that she was ready to continue. "I'll carry you if necessary, but we will get you to safety."

She covered her mouth, hiding a yawn, and shoved her disheveled red hair away from her face. "I shall manage."

Her words bravely said one thing, but her struggle to keep up said another. The farther we traveled, the more she leaned on me. By nightfall, she could barely put one foot in front of the other. As on the previous night, Charging Bear and I exchanged watches while Phoebe slept. In the morning, thunderclouds greeted us. As much as I hated walking through a storm, the turn of weather was a blessing. Rain would slow the tracking dogs, and their handlers were more likely to make mistakes.

Instead of seeking refuge, we struggled to remain on the trail as rain pelted us. The wind gusted, and in my mind I heard its voice saying, "This way." But was it leading me to my death?

The rain turned into a torrential downpour. No longer left with a choice, Charging Bear found us refuge in a hollow. We covered ourselves with branches and leaves to wait out the storm. In my arms, Phoebe trembled. I held her tighter and soon she slept in my arms again. "Charging Bear, if anything should happen, will you see that my family is taken care of?"

"Aye. That is the way it's done here."

At least that much was a comfort. "Thank you, brother."

After about an hour, the lashing rain changed to a drizzle. As we returned to the trail, I spotted a crow in a nearby tree. When the bird cawed, I realized it wasn't a spirit but a real bird. We continued on, and a flock gathered, almost as if waving me on.

By midday the sun had come out, and we rested in its growing warmth. Even though we had skimped, the last of Elenor's rations were consumed. I gave Phoebe my last bite of cornbread when I heard a rustle of leaves. Charging Bear nodded that he had heard it too, and we reached for our weapons. From the trail where we had already traveled appeared two Native men. I blinked in disbelief and lowered my Glock. They weren't Monacan warriors but Black Owl and Swift Deer. "How did you find us?" I asked, holstering my piece.

"We followed the hounds," Black Owl replied, "until the *tassan-tassas* could go no further."

Swift Deer laughed. "They became mired in the mud. We've come to take you home."

No words could have brought me greater pleasure. Even Phoebe had renewed energy, and in case the colonists decided to take up the chase again, we began the return journey along a different trail. About an hour later, Phoebe could barely walk and we rested.

After another hour, she stood. "I'm ready to continue now."

The others got to their feet, and we returned to the trail.

With each step, I knew in my heart that we got closer to where the skeleton had been found. Then, I heard the bloodhounds. They were hot on our trail. "We need to split up," I said. "They're after Phoebe. I'll stay with her. We can meet..." I was slow to think—exhaustion had hit me.

"One of us must stay with you," Charging Bear said. "You don't know the land."

"I know it better than you may realize, but I agree—"

Baying hounds in the distance cut off my words. Charging Bear made arrangements with Black Owl as to where we would meet at dusk. Without bothering to say farewells, we separated and set off again. Each step brought me closer to that deadly spot. The dogs would finally catch up with us there. "We need to change direction."

Without asking why, Charging Bear obliged. Shifting course became a tactic. We did so repeatedly, hoping that we might confuse the handlers and elude the dogs. Before long, I realized we were on the very path I had been avoiding. We went up a hill to a copse of trees. At the top, I envisioned the house where the landowners would uncover a skeleton, forcing them to call in the police. I tried to lead Phoebe away from the spot, but she stumbled and would have fallen if I hadn't caught her. She attempted to take another step but crumpled in my arms. I could no longer evade my fate. The ground was easily defensible. I looked at Charging Bear. "Go on without us."

"We will stand our ground here—together," he replied.

"Nay," Phoebe said, "I cannot have you do this because of me."

While Charging Bear notched his bow with an arrow, I took out my Glock. Before I went down, I would make my remaining rounds count. "Walks Through Mist, you knew from the beginning this is our way. Now seek shelter."

When tears filled her eyes, I nearly apologized for being harsh, but she scrambled on her hands and knees to the undergrowth behind a tree. My gaze met hers, and I knew that she understood. The barking dogs grew closer. Charging Bear and I sought cover for ourselves. Several crows gathered in the branches above us. Five colonists, following two bloodhounds on long lines, appeared on the ground below. The crows screamed and swooped over the men's heads, dive-bombing them like they had the hawk. The commotion created a distraction.

At the same time that I fired, Charging Bear loosed an arrow. Two men sank. One fired a flintlock in our direction, missing us entirely. Another raised his rifle. At the same time I fired, Charging Bear shot off another arrow. The man fell. The two that remained standing ran away. Something didn't feel right. Instead of celebrating our victory, I motioned to Phoebe to remain where she was.

The surrounding area had grown quiet. Not even a bird sang. I had that uneasy feeling in my gut that we weren't alone. I traded a glance with Charging Bear. No words were necessary. A seasoned warrior, he felt it too. I surveyed the ground below and the woods behind us. The only sound was my own uneven breathing and pounding heart.

I checked to my right, then my left. Behind us, the woods could easily provide cover for a number of men. If there had been more than five of them, the others could have circled around. A branch snapped. *Definitely behind us.* Gunfire. I wheeled around and fired my last bullet. A scream rose from the forest, then I felt the pressure of a sharp blade against my throat.

Our gazes locked. Only hatred existed in his blue eyes. The knife nicked my neck, but before he cut my throat, he screamed and sank to his knees. A tomahawk protruded from his back. *Black Owl.* That's when I knew the secret the skeleton held. *"Nows!"* I cried in warning.

Too late. Black Owl pitched forward.

I wasn't fast enough. My father hit the ground before I could catch him. More screams surrounded me, then stillness descended on the forest once more. Phoebe was soon beside me checking Black Owl to see where he had been hit. His back was covered in blood, and she pressed a cloth to it. The bleeding slowed.

Charging Bear and Swift Deer stood beside us. "The remaining *tassantassas* are dead or have run off," Swift Deer reported.

Black Owl spoke, but his voice was so soft I couldn't make out his words. I leaned closer to hear him better. "This time . . . I was where . . . I was needed."

Phoebe looked over at me. "I can remove the ball. My momma taught me how."

I had hope. She could operate. I would be the blood donor like in Wildcat's case. "What tools do you need?" I asked.

"A fine knife."

Before I could get up, Black Owl grasped my wrist and gasped for breath. "No, Wind Talker. Both of us . . . know . . ."

As a cop, I had seen many families take heroic measures only to put their loved ones through needless suffering. I swore to myself that if such a situation ever occurred in my own family I would be stronger. Black Owl had made his wishes known. I intertwined my index finger with his, letting him know that I would honor his request.

A slight smile appeared on his lips. "I shall tell your mother . . ." He coughed up blood.

Phoebe held him and whispered words of comfort until his coughing spasm halted. Sadness lingered in her eyes, but she was doing the job she had trained a lifetime for. How foolish I had been to think she could have been a twenty-first-century nurse. I touched her arm. "I'll see him through to the afterlife," I said.

"Both of us shall."

We positioned ourselves on each side of Black Owl. His eyes rolled up in his head, and his muscles quivered. *A death spasm.* Bleeding from the wound increased, and Phoebe pressed the already saturated cloth to it. When the spasm halted, a euphoric grin crossed Black Owl's face. "Your mother . . . she calls to me."

His muscles quivered as another spasm captured him. I stayed by his side, waiting for him to be taken. But I had witnessed death far too many times. It was rarely that simple. While his body writhed, I spoke to him about growing up in the twentieth century, my life as a cop, and finally when Phoebe had joined me. Every so often the spasms let him rest, and he would tell me of his life with my mother. "Once on . . . a hunting trip . . . I broke my leg. The *kwiocosuk* and . . . your mother made me whole again . . ."

Finally, his muscles relaxed, and the wind blew gently at my back. For the first time, I could hear its words clearly. Like time, death was merely another dimension. "Let the wind carry you, *Nows.*"

Black Owl's breaths grew short, and his pulse fluttered to a halt. His eyes opened in the sightlessness of death.

We had journeyed too far to return Black Owl's body to his native land, so we buried him in the spot where his skeleton would be unearthed approximately 370 years later—for a renovation project. I took comfort that my future self would contact the Virgina Council on Indians to make certain that he would receive a proper reburial. My only regret was that I had never discovered which tribe had taken him, or where they had made his final resting place.

As was tradition, Phoebe smudged her face to look black and wailed. My brothers sang. Numbness spread throughout me, but a crow cawed and I looked to the sky. Two more flew over the grave.

They perched in the trees near us, calling the entire time. Soon, a dozen or more flew toward us. Was I dreaming? I pointed to the flock, and the others admitted to seeing the birds.

The group perched in the branches. They cawed for a while, then one flew in front of the others, like it had taken center stage, and gave a shrill call. The others grew silent, and the lead bird made sounds as if giving a speech. The pattern continued until another crow flew forward. Four more birds took their turns. When they finished, all but one flew off. The remaining crow cawed constantly. Instead of the usual high-spirited ringing caws, these sounds were raspy and descended in pitch. Finally the last bird flew away.

Uncertain what I had witnessed, I inquired to the others.

"Isn't the crow your guardian?" Charging Bear asked. "They joined you in your moment of need."

A funeral? I had once read about "crow funerals," but at the time, I had believed it was nothing more than a myth. The birds had come to pay their respects and eulogize Black Owl. I faced the east and held my hands out with my palms facing up. I had much to learn, but I was thankful. Black Owl's sacrifice would not be in vain. For the first time in my life I said a real prayer—a silent one to Ahone.

When I finished, I placed my arm over Phoebe's shoulder. "Let's find Heather."

32

Phoebe

FOR TWO DAYS, PHOEBE traveled with the others across land, then along the river in a dugout. At the town of the Appamattuck, she and Swift Deer were greeted as guests. The last time she had visited an Indian town Henry had taken her to the Arrohateck when the smallpox had broken out. Not 'til she had studied nursing in the twenty-first century had she learned the native people had no natural immunities to English diseases, which was why they suffered more losses than the colonists. During the pestilence, her momma and stepfather had died, but others had survived due to her treatment.

Now, she mindlessly went through a long line of people, each and every one of whom was introduced by the *weroance,* including her nephew Strong Bow. If it hadn't been for the crisis with Heather's absence, she would have rejoiced at being surrounded by her people once again. After a round of speeches of welcome, they feasted on venison and rabbit.

Afterward, the men smoked pipes, and the women chatted amongst themselves. Phoebe told them about her recent adventure and missing daughter. The women sympathized with her loss. She managed to keep a brave countenance, but inside she wept. When the dancing began, she watched from the sidelines, not wishing to participate.

So numb and exhausted, all she wanted to do was sleep and begin her quest anew for Heather. The dancers moved in rhythmic steps to the tempo of the drum round the fire. Lee joined her. "I know the last thing you're in the mood for is a party."

"I cannot rest 'til she's found."

"I know, and as soon as you've recovered your strength, we'll set out for Elenor's house." He held out a hand and showed her to a guest house. Weary to the bones, she climbed onto the sleeping platform. Lee moved in aside her. Comforted by his arms round her, she fell into a deep sleep for the first time in weeks.

As Phoebe entered the dreaming, the mist grew thinner. *He* whispered in her ear to follow the light. Up ahead, she spied what looked like thousands of torches. She emerged from the fog. Lights upon lights, swarming with people surrounded her. And the clattering noise. She covered her ears and stepped into the road to escape the racket.

More lights chased after her, blinding her. She froze. The earth trembled, and she went flying. *Soon, my beloved, I will join you.*

But she was no longer afraid and ready to relive what had come next.

When she awoke from the accident, men and women in blue garments clustered round her. Some wore white coats, but the light . . . unlike dim candles, the light blinded her. *Demons.* Fearing that she had been cast into the bowels of hell, she fought against the garbed people. One masked woman put a slender tool against her arm, and she felt a pin prick. After a few minutes, she grew dazed and slept.

"Ma'am."

At the sound of a man's voice, she fought through the layers of fog, and her eyelashes fluttered open. Aside the man in a white coat, stood another man—a tall one with black hair and brown skin. Though he dressed strangely and had short hair, for some reason his presence brought comfort. *"Netab?"* she asked. Friend?

He pointed to himself, then opened his hands to her. "I'm Detective Crowley." He gestured to her. "And you are?"

He looked so familiar. Soothed by his presence, she grasped his hand. *"Netab."*

"Whatever she's saying," the man in the white coat said, "she's comfortable with you. She hasn't exhibited that kind of feeling toward the rest of us." The two men relayed an exchange of words, but they spoke too fast. She had difficulty understanding their words. 'Twas English—of that she was certain, but it differed from the way she spoke. She tilted her head, attempting to single out their words and make sense of them.

"I'm Detective Crowley," the tall man said one more time. "You are?"

His countenance was uncanny. "I'm Walks Through Mist," she replied in Algonquian. "Walks Through Mist. Surely you've heard of me?"

"I'm sorry, ma'am. I don't understand."

She leaned forward and traced a line with her fingertip across his prominent cheekbone. His features reminded her of someone. *"Netab,"* she repeated.

A woman in blue garments joined the tall man and handed him a book. He opened it and began turning the pages. "Point to where you're from," he said.

Henry had shown her maps, but she had ne'er seen one in a book afore. Amazed by their bright colors and the feel of the paper, she ran her hands along the pages as the man flipped them. She had him halt at one page.

"The West Indies?" he asked.

"Tongoa," she said. Let me see. She grasped the book from his hands. Frustrated that she seemed unable to communicate in English, she turned the pages on her own 'til England was afore her. She jabbed a finger to the page.

"England?"

She looked into his dark brown eyes and nodded. Satisfied that her message had been received, she blinked back the residual effects of the dreaming. She sat near the fire in the guest house. Why had she envisioned their first meeting as adults?

Lee stared at her momentarily. His appearance had changed to shoulder-length hair, and he wore a woolen shirt, instead of a suit. "You asked if I was a friend. At the time the language sounded familiar, but I couldn't place it."

"You reminded me of Black Owl. That's why you looked so familiar."

His countenance etched in sorrow. "I had such a short time to get to know him. What if we end up like our parents?"

"We can't know what the morrow will bring, but we have Elenor's help. 'Tis time that we return."

Phoebe swayed in a rocking motion as the dugout headed down-river to Elenor's. Charging Bear and Swift Deer had joined Lee and her on the trip. Like the times afore, she rowed alongside the men. More than once, they had to halt their journey to elude English boats or nearby plantations. The settlements dotted the landscape and extended far beyond what was once Paspahegh land. How vast the colony had grown since her arrival in 1609.

Charging Bear brought the dugout to a halt a few miles from Elenor's plantation, and they set out on foot. As the one most familiar with the land, her brother led the way, but even she felt the familiarity of the trail from the time she had lived there. Thankfully, she had cast off her English garments and traveled in the comfort of doeskin and moccasins.

Alongside the river, they made their way through the forest trail. By the time they reached the pitched-roof house, the sun had sunk in the west. Smoke drifted from the chimney, but no candles were lit yet. Phoebe shivered. On another occasion, the guards had waited for her, ready to take her back to James Towne and try her as a witch. If they were present again, there would be no trial.

As if reading her thoughts, Lee gripped her arm. "You wait here."

"But—"

"Phoebe, please, you know we can do our jobs better if you remain here until we're certain the coast is clear."

She blinked. "Coast is clear?"

He gave her a slight smile. "Never mind. Let us find out what awaits us. I'll call you if there's nothing to worry about."

She vowed that she would remain where she was. The men readied their weapons and set out. Lee no longer had a gun, but he carried a knife. They crept forward and crouched neath the windows. After a quick check, they approached the door. Her heart thumped a frantic rhythm as they went inside. No sounds. Minutes passed. She stepped forward, but halted, recalling her vow to wait.

Finally, the door opened. Lee waved at Phoebe to join him. Afore reaching it, he reappeared outside the door with a squirming child in his arms. At first she thought it was Tiffany, but—she blinked. Tears of joy entered her eyes, and she ran toward them. "Heather!"

Heather squealed. As soon as she had her daughter in her arms, she checked to make certain she hadn't been harmed, but 'twas growing difficult in the fading daylight.

"She's fine, Phoebe," Lee said. "Elenor, Bess, and Meg have already checked her."

Elenor joined them. Satisfied that Heather was fine, Phoebe hugged her other daughter. "I can ne'er thank you enough."

" 'Twasn't me, Momma. I had naught to do with bringing her here."

In confusion, she looked up at Lee. "Then how?"

"You can thank William and his friend Chloe."

"William and Chloe?"

Lee looked over his shoulder. "William, your presence and your friend's have been requested."

A shy lad with shoulder-length brown hair stepped outside and joined them. She vaguely recalled seeing him with Lee and Christopher when they had broken her out of the James Towne gaol. After that, he had vanished. The lass had dirty blonde hair peeking out from her linen cap, and her skirt was rumpled.

"Phoebe," Lee said, "I'd like for you to meet William Carter and Chloe. My wife Phoebe. When I thought William had run off, he had gone back to rescue Heather. When he originally came to James Towne, he sailed with a future servant to Mistress Hopkins's neighbor."

She planted a kiss on William's peach-fuzz cheek. "I'm fore'er in your debt." Fighting the tears, she grasped Chloe's hands. "Thank you."

Embarrassed from the attention, William shuffled a foot in the dirt. " 'Tis my repayment. I was naught but a runaway, but these kind people didn't turn me in. Instead, they made me part of their family. Your daughter is the sister I ne'er had, and now Chloe has joined me."

"Momma," Elenor said, "shall we go inside to greet e'eryone?"

Phoebe brushed aside her tears and nodded. Lee's arm went about her waist. Inside the door more hugs and kisses were exchanged with Meg, Bess, Tiffany, and Phoebe's grandchildren. For the first time in as long as she could recall, her melancholy faded. Surrounded by family, she joined everyone in the parlor. They sat in chairs and chatted, whilst Heather clung to Phoebe's bosom.

Sadness filled the room when Lee relayed Black Owl's death to Wildcat. "He died bravely," Lee said, "saving my life."

Wildcat's eyes were downcast, but he nodded. "I would have expected nothing less from our father. After all, you saved my life."

Phoebe gripped Lee's hand. In the coming days, they would face many difficulties. Lee, Wildcat, and Swift Deer would need time to grieve, but they were amongst family and friends. She most of all could put months of separation behind her. They were a family again.

33

Wind Talker

Aᶠᵗᵉʳ ᵒᵘʳ ʳᵉᵘⁿⁱᵒⁿ ᵃᵗ Eˡᵉⁿᵒʳ's, I traveled to the mass grave to say goodbye to my family. Instead of death screams running through my head, there was silence. The quiet didn't fool me. Their souls weren't at rest, and I vowed that someday I would return and give my tribe a proper burial. Only then would they truly be able to journey into the afterlife in peace. As I turned away from the grave site, a gentle spring breeze blew. If I listened carefully, I *could* hear the wind talking. I walked along the path to the homestead when Phoebe appeared on the path before me. "Where's Heather?" I asked.

"She's with Meg and Elenor. Lee, there is one thing that we must do afore we set out."

"And that is?"

"I vowed to Shae that I would let her know what had happened."

Shae. In all of the recent turmoil, I had forgotten that I had made the same promise. "I did too."

She grasped my hands. "Then, pray join me."

"You know I will."

We located a secluded spot in the woods away from the burial site. With Phoebe beside me, I found it easy to enter the dreaming. Crow guided me, and when we emerged from the mist, Phoebe and I stood outside Shae's office. "You should be the one to speak to her," Phoebe said.

With a nod, I opened the door and stepped inside.

"Lee?" Shae stood by the desk.

I approached her. "Phoebe and Heather have joined me in the seventeenth century."

"I see. So this is a final goodbye."

"I suspect so."

"And the skeleton?"

"It wasn't me." She released a noticeable breath. "It was my father, and with the help of my family, I buried him. I barely had the chance to get to know him."

"That must have been difficult for you. I'm sorry for your loss."

"I appreciate the condolences, but I've got the rest of my family to help me through it."

"I'll miss you and Phoebe."

This time I was not tempted to spar with her to lighten the mood. "I'll miss you too." As I gazed upon her face, I realized I would most likely never see her again. "Thank you—for everything."

She forced a smile. "You're welcome."

An awkward silence descended between us. "I should be going," I said.

As I turned, Shae called after me. "Lee! You were my first love too."

Recalling the night she had asked me for a divorce, I faced her once more. "You were right. We were mismatched."

"At the time, I could have never known the real reason why."

"Neither of us could have." Crow cawed, signaling our time had come to an end. "I have to leave now."

Shae came around the desk and gave me a quick kiss on the cheek. "Bye, Lee."

"Bye, Shae." As I walked toward the door, I couldn't look back. That chapter of my life had ended. If I gazed over my shoulder for one last look, I would be afraid to let go. Outside the door, I met Phoebe. I held her hand, and the mist captured us.

Out of the fog came a woman with her black hair tied back in a single long braid. Beside her stood a warrior with an uncanny resemblance to me. My parents looked the same as they had when I was two. There was so much I wanted to say to both of them, but no words came out. With a knowing smile, Black Owl glanced at Snow Bird, and they vanished. I found myself sitting in the woods next to Phoebe. On the wind, voices whispered through the trees. I could hear them loud and clear. They were my family—and ancestors—for I was on former Paspahegh land. I looked to Phoebe. "I can hear them."

"Aye, you have become part of them."

"Our decision to return to the Appamattuck and Sekakawon is the correct one. I must learn all that I can."

She smiled at my words.

"When the time is right, I'll become a liaison between the tribes and colonists. I have no idea if the future can be changed, but I must try to save my people."

Phoebe reached a hand to my face. "I'm pleased."

At that moment, I knew my parents were proud of my decision. At long last I had reclaimed my heritage, for I am Paspahegh, the last of my tribe.

Author's Note

As in the first book of The Dreaming series, *Walks Through Mist*, the dreaming is not meant to represent the belief system of the Virginia Algonquian-speaking people, who were composed of approximately thirty tribes commonly referred to as the Powhatan. Lee was taught the world of the dreaming by Phoebe, an English cunning woman. The cunning folk were the healers of society, using herbs and magic during the seventeenth century, and often had familiar or guardian spirits. At the same time, I firmly believe that the spirituality of the Native people would have equipped them to understand the concept of the dreaming and to most likely embrace it.

Compared to earlier seventeenth-century archives, records for Virginia in the 1640s are sparse. As a result, I took some liberties and interpreted the available records as best as I could. Paramount chief Opechancanough organized an attack on the colonists on April 18, 1644, twenty-two years after the first raid. As in the 1622 attack, approximately four hundred colonists were killed. However, unlike in the previous attack, the slain were a significantly smaller segment of the population.

Even fewer records survive about the Virginia Indians than those of the colonists. As in my research for *Walks Through Mist*, I have read as much as possible on the tribal people from period-biased sources, plus archaeological and contemporary sources, to try to recreate some semblance of their daily lives. Even so, gaping holes exist. The scenes depicted are entirely my own interpretations. For many scenes, I have also drawn from texts about similar tribes.

The first known successful blood transfusions took place during the seventeenth century. As might be guessed in light of the prevailing knowledge of the time period, there were many disasters along with the successes. Scientists of the time went so far as transfusing animal blood to humans. After a number of deaths resulting from such experimentation, the French and English parliaments, as well as the Vatican, banned transfusions. Their experiments gave me information on the techniques of the time period and allowed me to pose the "what if" for a successful transfusion with the help of twenty-first-century knowledge.

On more than one occasion, I have portrayed scalping. In *Walks Through Mist*, only the English were shown as scalpers. Many myths surround the act of scalping. Some argue the colonists brought scalping from Europe and introduced it to the indigenous populations. While it is true that some Europeans in the past had taken scalps, in 1607 at Jamestown, the English were more in the habit of beheading. Several written records exist that suggest some of the Powhatan people did indeed scalp at the time of settlement. However, those records by themselves are inconclusive as to who actually started scalping first.

Archaeological evidence indicates that some indigenous people did scalp in the pre-contact era. Also, the major European languages did not have a term for the action until colonists arrived on North America's shores. When the Europeans first arrived in the sixteenth century, they noted that certain tribes scalped enemy warriors. What's often overlooked in the literature is that not all tribes scalped. In fact, some authorities claim that the majority of tribes did *not* scalp.

Although the historical record seems to verify that Europeans did not originate the act of scalping, they quickly discovered it was much easier than beheading. For tribes that participated in scalping, the general idea behind the act was that a scalp lock symbolized a warrior's life force. Generally a scalp lock was regarded as more than a trophy of war. Not only did an enemy's scalp prove that a warrior was brave in taking casualties, but it was part of the soul or life force. To lose one's scalp to an enemy meant that one became spiritually dead, even if not biologically. Furthermore, scalping did not appear to be very common until metal knives and firearms were introduced. English settlers adopted scalping as a retaliatory measure and began paying bounties for scalps.

In *Walks Through Mist* I had chosen a crow to guide Lee because in many Native American cultures, the bird is a shape shifter. I do not know if such a belief is held among the Algonquian-speaking people, but it fit my plot purpose. Shape shifters are regarded as masters of illusion, beings that can transform themselves and travel through many realms, including between the physical and spiritual worlds. Crows have been known to protect humans who feed them by dive-bombing a nearby threat in the same manner as crows will harass hawks. They have also been observed holding rather complex "funerals." After getting to know my own local crow population, I have discovered the intelligence of this bird. Because it is Lee's guardian spirit, I felt it would behave in the protective and respectful manner that I have portrayed.

Acknowledgments

A special thank you goes to my editors, K.A. Corlett, Sarah Grey, and Catherine Karp, and my cover designer, Roberta Marley. And of course, I wish to thank my family: my son, Bryan, and especially my husband, Pat; both are now hopeful that my retreat through the centuries has stabilized, and that I may eventually rejoin the twenty-first century.